# TRIANGLE CLASSICS
### ILLUMINATING THE GAY AND LESBIAN EXPERIENCE

Oranges Are Not the Only Fruit
by Jeanette Winterson

Orlando
by Virginia Woolf

The Picture of Dorian Gray
by Oscar Wilde

The Price of Salt
by Patricia Highsmith

Rubyfruit Jungle
by Rita Mae Brown

A Single Man
by Christopher Isherwood

The Sophie Horowitz Story/Girls, Visions and Everything/
After Dolores
by Sarah Schulman

Surpassing the Love of Men
by Lillian Faderman

The Well of Loneliness
by Radclyffe Hall

What Is Found There/An Atlas of the Difficult World/
The Fact of a Doorframe
by Adrienne Rich

Zami/Sister Outsider/Undersong
by Audre Lorde

# BERTRAM COPE'S YEAR

# BERTRAM COPE'S YEAR

## HENRY BLAKE FULLER

Introduction by
Edmund Wilson

Afterword by
Andrew Solomon

QUALITY PAPERBACK BOOK CLUB
NEW YORK

# Contents

# Introduction

## Henry Blake Fuller
## The Art of Making It Flat

### BY EDMUND WILSON

T HE NINETIES and the early 1900s, when looked at from the later decades, are likely to seem a dim period in American literature. The quality and the content of the fiction were mainly determined by the magazines that aimed to please a feminine public. There were writers of great reputation whom no one except the literary historian would think of looking into today. But there did exist also—outsold and out-publicized—a kind of underground of real social critics and conscientious artists who were hardly recognized or who were recognized only when one of them struck off some book that was daring or arresting enough to call special attention to its author. Harold Frederic's *The Damnation of Theron Ware*, which dealt in a disturbing way with the contemporary problems of the clergy, was a book that was much read both in England and here; Stephen Crane's *The Red Badge of Courage* was so intensely conceived and written that, though pooh-poohed by academics like Barrett Wendell, it could not be disregarded, and Crane himself became a public legend, although every effort was made to see that this legend was a disreputable one; George W. Cable, in the eighties, had had his success with a serious novel, *The Grandissimes*, but his treatment of situations created in the South by the mixture of white and black blood and his pamphleteering books on the Negro question became so repugnant to his editors and so outrageous to his Southern neighbors that he was forced to fall back on sentimental romance and exploitation of the then marketable "local color"; Kate Chopin, who wrote also of Louisiana, was also acceptable as a local-colorist, but she so scandalized the public in 1899 by her treatment of adultery in *The Awakening* that she is said to have been discouraged from writing any more novels; and, in spite of the championship of Howells, the New Englander John DeForest, in his Balzacian effort to cover his own era as well as parts of the historical past—the Revolution and the Salem witches, the Civil War and the corruption of the Grant administration—in an objective and realistic way, was never accepted at all.

It has been only in quite recent years that this area has been gradually excavated. The first collection of Crane, who died in 1900, was brought out in 1925, in a very limited edition. DeForest's *Miss Ravenel's Conversion*, his most notable Civil War novel, was reprinted only in 1939, *The Grandissimes* only in 1957. *The Damnation of Theron Ware* has suddenly been resuscitated in no less than three recent reprintings, and Frederic's stories of the Civil War have now for the first time been collected in one volume. The latest of these writers to be discovered and the one who has in general had least justice done him is Henry B. Fuller, but now at last *With the Procession*, one of the best of his novels, has been reprinted, and this provides an occasion to give some account of Fuller, a unique and distinguished writer who does not deserve to be dumped in the drawer devoted to regional novelists for a chapter in an academic literary history.

Henry Blake Fuller was born in Chicago (January 9, 1857), but his family on both sides had been New Englanders. His grandfather was a cousin of Margaret Fuller. This grandfather, following a frequent progression, had moved first to western New York, then to the Middle West. He was one of those Americans of the period who combined making money in business with a sense of public responsibility. He had been a dry-goods merchant in Albion, New York, a county judge in Michigan, and in still-pioneering Chicago a railroad man and the entrepreneur of the laying of forty miles of water pipes.

Henry was an only son. At school he was a brilliant student. He did not go to college but had all the New England will to self-improvement. He learned languages and studied music, composed, wrote poetry, kept a diary, and made lists of necessary reading. He led a protected and isolated life, saw little of other young people. Out of school, he worked at first in his father's bank, but when Henry was twenty-two, Judge Fuller died, and he probably left his grandson some money, for Henry sailed for Europe that summer. He traveled in Europe a year, and thereafter, through the eighties and nineties, continued every few years to return for six months or so.

The first result of these visits, published in 1890, under a pseudonym and at Fuller's own expense, was a short novel, *The Chevalier of Pensieri-Vani*. This book, which was called in its time a little classic and a minor masterpiece, became the object of a kind of cult, of which I believe the last representative was the late Carl Van Vechten. It is an account of the travels in Italy of a cultivated Italian gentleman and is something of an actual travel book in the taste of the then frequent articles in the more serious magazines, with their drawings of Old Chester and Picturesque Tuscany, intended especially for ladies who were obliged to stay at home or who saved up to and looked forward to eventual trips. But it is also something other than this. It is diversified by little adventures and flavored with demure humor. *The Chevalier*—which soon went into a better edition, published under Fuller's own name—was the first of a series of novels all preserving the same tone and dealing with the same group of characters. The names of these characters alone will convey Fuller's playful humor: besides the Cavaliere himself, there are his friend the

French Seigneur of Hors-Concours; the Swiss Chatelaine of La Trinité and her companion Miss Aurelia West of Ohio, who later marries a Lyon manufacturer and becomes Mme. la Comtesse Aurélie de Feuillevolante; the Duke of Avon and Severn; Baron Zeitgeist and the Freiherr von Kaltenau; the Prorege of Arcopia and the Marquis of Tempo-Rubato; and Mr. Occident, also from Ohio. The second of these books, *The Chatelaine of La Trinité*, appeared in 1892, but Fuller did not follow these up till *The Last Refuge*, of 1900, and did not conclude the series till 1929, when, just before the end of his life, he published *Gardens of This World*. These books belong to a school that is nowadays of little interest. The then fashionable stories of Americans encountering sophisticated Europeans, usually embellished by titles, have today become rather embarrassing. They are one of the symptoms of the longing to get away from the ugly and crass society that flourished after the Civil War. Americans then had a mania for looking up their family trees and trying to establish connections with some noble house in England or elsewhere. Henry James had his Passionate Pilgrim, Mark Twain his American Claimant. At its gaudiest, this dream produced Graustark, the imaginary Balkan kingdom of glamour, dashing deeds, and gallant romance which was created by George Barr McCutcheon, originally a farm boy from Indiana.

A more alembicated product was the late fiction of Henry Harland, a coy kind of fairy tales—marvels of American snobbery and syrupy *fin-de-siècle* fine writing—which, so popular in the early 1900s, are ridiculous, though still readable, today. The enchanting young hero and heroine, conversing in well-bred banter, are either royal or of very high rank, which, in their willingness to fall in love with commoners, they implausibly manage to conceal till they are headed for the final embrace. Harland's *The Cardinal's Snuffbox*, once thought so utterly delightful and the author's greatest success, is actually so absurd that when the editor of *Punch*, Owen Seaman, attempted to parody it in his book *Borrowed Plumes*, he could only fall short of the original. Edgar Saltus, the New York "society" novelist, is also in this tradition, but a man of real worldly experience, he is genuinely amusing and witty, and he cultivated a certain perversity which prevented him from becoming saccharine as it prevented him from being popular. The European novels of Fuller belong to this tradition, too, but though they are not so wicked as Saltus's, they are very much more intelligent and much better written than Harland's. And Fuller, who so loved his noble connoisseurs, with their self-assured Old World savoir-faire, is nevertheless drolly ironic about those Americans themselves who admired and exaggerated these qualities. The happiest episode in the series seems to me the account of the efforts of Miss West of Ohio to induce the Chatelaine of La Trinité to live up to her ancestry and social position, which she has always taken for granted and to which she has not given much thought, and to arrange matches for her with suitable men, none of whom are much interested in her. The Chatelaine herself loses interest in the operation and retires to a house of retreat in Lausanne. In *Gardens of This World,* which is supposed to take place after the First World War, these characters, now grown old, are still wandering around Europe, still in search of charming quiet spots, but they everywhere encounter Americans—a millionaire who wants to buy up ruins and works of art and transport them to the United States, but also two adventurous and energetic boys who are interested in flying and one of whom (he is half French, the son of Feuillevolante) eventually goes into his father's business.

For, in spite of Fuller's regret at the decline of Europe and his harsh or sad criticisms of his own country, there was a strong strain of patriotism in him, even a feeling of loyalty to Chicago. In the intervals between his trips abroad, he had always had to return to his native city, where, after his father's death in 1885, he took over the responsibilities of the family's business affairs. In those of his books that take place in Europe, one is impressed by the thoroughness and exactitude of his knowledge of history, geography, literature, art, and architecture. He was equally well informed about Chicago. He seems always to have been up-to-date on the streets, the population, the buildings, on new developments and organizations. The objection sometimes made to Henry James that he knew nothing about American business is not at all in order in the case of the part-time expatriate Fuller. He knew everything about the interests which he had to administer—industry, real estate, finance, and the legal procedures entailed by these. In connection with the family properties, he collected rents and checked on the buildings; he could even himself mend the plumbing and complained that this took up too much of his time. And he now began to write about Chicago. The results of this were rather surprising. The precision and elegance of Fuller's style—so unusual in the United States of the nineties—really make a better showing here, because they lend a distinction to often crude material, than they do in the European books, where they still leave a little arid, a little bleak with accurate fact, material which the author has labored to render graceful and alluring and foreign. In his travels, he is not very far from the tinted impressionism of Henry James, which seems to emanate from his mind like a vapor.

Fuller now writes two novels—*The Cliff-Dwellers* (1893) and *With the Procession* (1895)—about the life of the new, energetic city. The first of these dramatizes the organism of an eighteen-story office building, the Clifton—the man who built it and the people who work in it; the second the fortunes of a family of more or less simple Western origins (the father is a well-to-do wholesale grocer) who, as the city grows and prospers, are unable to adjust themselves to its more and more accelerated progress and, borne along by the money-driven tide which is symbolized in the first pages by the traffic of a Chicago street, become bewildered and broken in their efforts to keep up "with the procession." The general situation is embodied in the figure of the rich Mrs. Granger Bates, compelled by reason of her money to try to live up to a high position and to occupy a grand mansion, but reduced by her homely tastes to reconstituting a kind of inner sanctuary in the image of the snug and vulgar home of her youth. The author has summed up in these novels both his intimate observation of Chicago and his half-alien criticism of it. There is the overpowering faith of the Chicagoans in the future of their new city:

"Individually, we may be of a rather humble grade of atoms," he makes one of the men in *The Cliff-Dwellers* say, "but we are crystallizing into a compound that is going to exercise a tremendous force.... You may have seen the boiling of the kettle, but you have hardly seen the force that feeds the flame. The big buildings are all well enough, and the big crowds in the streets, and the reports of the banks and railways and the Board of Trade. But there is something, now, beyond and behind all that. ... Does it seem unreasonable that the State which produced the two greatest figures of the greatest epoch in our history, and which has done most within the last ten years to check alien excesses and un-American ideas, should also be the State to give the country the final blend of the American character and its ultimate metropolis?" "His wife sat beside him silent, but with her hand on his," adds Fuller, "and when he answered, she pressed it meaningly; for to the Chicagoan—even the middle-aged female Chicagoan—the name of the town, in its formal, ceremonial use, has a power that no other word in the language quite possesses. It is a shibboleth, as regards its pronunciation; it is a trumpet call, as regards its effect. It has all the electrifying and unifying power of a college yell." And there is the social insecurity of Chicagoans: "Commercially, we feel our own footing; socially, we are rather abashed by the pretensions that any new arrival chooses to make. We are a little afraid of him, and, to tell the truth, we are a little afraid of each other." Fuller is able, from his knowledge of Europe, to understand the beginnings of gangsterism, which, with the increase of immigrant workers, is already manifesting itself as an unruly and dangerous element: "The populations of Italy and Poland and Hungary," says one of the characters in *With the Procession*, "what view now do *they* take of the government— their government, all government? Isn't it an implacable and immemorial enemy—a great and cruel and dreadful monster to be evaded, hoodwinked, combated, stabbed in the dark if occasion offers? ... Is it an easy matter, on their coming over here, to make them feel themselves a part of [the government], and to imbue them with a loyalty to it?" One of the features of both these books is the figure, which was to become so familiar in the American fiction of this period, of the extravagant and socially ambitious woman who drives and sometimes ruins her hard-working husband. In *The Cliff-Dwellers*, the power behind everything, the wife of the owner of the office building, "a radiant, magnificent young creature, splendid, like all her mates, with the new and eager splendor of a long-awaited opportunity," appears, at an opera performance, only at the end of the book. A newly married husband in the audience has never seen her before, but "he knew that she was Cecilia Ingles, and his heart was constricted at the sight of her. It is for such a woman that one man builds a Clifton and that a hundred others are martyred in it."

*The Cliff-Dwellers*, which takes for its subject the accidental modern unit of the office building, the diversity of human beings who have it in common that they are thrown together by working there, was perhaps suggested by Zola, and it anticipates such similar books as Waldo Frank's *City Block* and Dos Passos's *Manhattan Transfer*. *With the Procession*, a better novel, is closer to the tradition of Howells—the low-keyed, prosaic domestic chronicle. But, having done his duty by Chicago in these studies of a social organism, the author, still involved with his city, went on to pieces of lesser scope, in which he is more himself and more enjoyable today than in either of these solider novels or in his fantasies of leisured Europeans.

Fuller said that he hated Chicago and that if it were not for his family interests he would leave it and go to live in Italy, and he advised Hamlin Garland, a young writer from Wisconsin, since Garland did not have to stay there, to leave. But he was not entirely unmoved by the cultural ambitions of the city, which was ridiculed in the East for some Chicagoan's statement that Chicago was going to "make culture hum." Chicago was to have its Art Institute and its Opera, both genuinely superior institutions. An excellent literary review, the *Dial*, to which Fuller often contributed, had been started in Chicago in 1880 and was to remain there till 1916; the *Chap-Book*, in the *Yellow Book* tradition, which ran from 1894 to 1898, published Yeats and Henry James; and *Poetry*, which printed the early work of Eliot, Pound, and other then unknown but later famous poets and to which Fuller acted as adviser, was started in 1912. In 1890, the University of Chicago had been founded, with Rockefeller money. Its first president, William R. Harper, of Ohio, a leading Hebrew scholar who had been teaching at Yale, was a man full of enthusiasm and innovating ideas, and he brought to the West an extraordinary faculty, which included, on the side of the humanities (the scientific side was equally remarkable): in English— Robert M. Lovett of Massachusetts and Harvard; William Vaughn Moody, the poet and dramatist, of Indiana and Harvard; Robert Herrick, the novelist, of Cambridge and Harvard; and John M. Manly, the Chaucerian scholar, of Alabama and Harvard; in Classics—Paul Shorey of Iowa and Harvard; and in History—Ferdinand Schevill of Ohio and Yale, and the Baltic outlaw H. E. von Holst, who became an authority on American history. Thorstein Veblen spent fourteen years and wrote *The Theory of the Leisure Class* at Chicago, and John Dewey was at one time director of the school of education. This group of scholars and writers combined the best of the East with the best of the Middle West who had been educated in the East. Some of them had studied in Europe, and many spent their vacations there. They equaled, if they did not surpass, the group that Woodrow Wilson not much later (1902) was able to recruit for Princeton. I have heard Robert Lovett tell of the missionary spirit with which these young men set out to create from scratch, in what had lately been a swampy waste, a great emporium of learning and inspiration—Robert Herrick, so thorough a New Englander, fastidious and rather thin-skinned, was to remain in Chicago thirty years, and in his entertaining novel *Chimes*, though putting on record the crudity and disorder of the university's early days and its struggles with its backers and trustees, he brings out the bold aims of the president and the courage and goodwill of the pioneering teachers. The university did provide an intellectual center for the competitive scramble that Fuller described, and he followed its activities with much interest, as he did the artistic activities of the city. He established close relations with the academic people, and he responded with lively interest to any manifestations of talent on the part of young painters or writers. His spirit seems to have been pervasive, and the tributes collected after his death by Anna Morgan, the manager of a little theater, are evidence of the gratitude of his colleagues, who felt the stimulus of the presence among them of a craftsman of very high standards who had put himself to school to the finest of the scholarship and art of the world. And the novelist, on his side, diverted himself by writing about these cultural exploits.

In 1901, Fuller published a group of three stories called *Under the Skylights*. Perhaps the best of these, "The Downfall of Abner Joyce," is based on the career of Hamlin Garland. Abner Joyce, on coming to Chicago, writes stark and indignant stories about the rigors of life on the Western farms and affects to despise the activities of what he regards as an effete intelligentsia, but when he finds himself taken up by them and given an entrée into the social life of Chicago he develops an appetite for it and is obviously very much gratified at becoming a fashionable figure. This characterization is amply confirmed by the four volumes of Garland's memoirs, in which he recounts at length his relations with many celebrities of the literary and political and moneyed worlds, whom he never missed a chance of seeing and whose kindness to and praise of himself he obviously loved to chronicle. He was always presiding at meetings of academies and getting up artists' clubs. When he organized such a club in Chicago and called it the Cliff-Dwellers, after Fuller's novel, Fuller—no doubt embarrassed—refused to become a member, or even, Garland says, so far as he knows, to accept an invitation to dine there. Yet it is evidence of Fuller's generosity where anyone of real talent was concerned that, in spite of his portrait of Garland as something of a bumpkinish climber, he should have remained on good terms with him all his life and that he did not forfeit Garland's respect. He was evidently, however, to return to the subject in another little comedy, called "Addolorata's Intervention." Here the character who represents Fuller and the character who represents Garland accidentally meet in Sicily. The former, a novelist who has never had much audience, cannot but feel that the latter, now a popular writer, is treating him with a cavalier condescension. He meets, also, a young lady fan of his own unpopular works, but he praises his rival to her, and she immediately attaches herself to the other, who eagerly snatches her up. The first writer, who is conscious of his superiority and really does not care about the girl, looks on at the whole comedy with a detachment not untinged by a certain disdainful envy.

It should be said at this point, in parenthesis, before we pass in review the more successful books of Fuller, that he was curiously unsuccessful and gave evidence of unexpectedly uncertain taste when he tried to work in any other form or vein than those of his ironic fiction. *The Puppet-Booth* (1896), which followed *With the Procession*, is a collection of little plays—with Maeterlinck somewhere in the background—that depart from the realistic without managing to achieve the poetic. And when the *Spoon River Anthology* of Edgar Lee Masters appeared in 1915, Fuller was excited by it and thought that this kind of epitaph in *vers libre* or broken prose had interesting possibilities. Two years later, he published a book of such epitaphs called *Lines Long and Short*, but they lack the grim pathos of Masters. Fuller here is simply sketching the same kind of characters that appear in his novels, but with much less telling effect. In the meantime, in 1899, he had been provoked by the war with Spain and our occupation of the Philippines to a quite uncharacteristic outbreak—a satire in verse called *The New Flag*. He was unable to find a publisher for what was thought, in that imperialistic era, an antipatriotic tirade and had it printed at his own expense. *The New Flag* is ill-written as verse and even rather coarse in its violence. Robert Lovett, in an article in *The New Republic* at the time of Fuller's death, expressed the opinion that this blast had a bad effect on Fuller's career: it made him unpopular in Chicago, and what was worse, it deranged and poisoned a temperament and a talent which were normally calm and aloof. McKinley's invasion of the Philippines, with its two years of war on the natives, was an act of gratuitous conquest that shocked men who had forgotten the Mexican War and accepted the Civil War—men such as Mark Twain and William Vaughn Moody, who protested with blistering bitterness. It is significant that the part-time expatriate Fuller, who ridiculed and deplored the tendencies of contemporary America, should still have retained enough of old-fashioned American idealism to flare up and give vent to such vituperation.

*Under the Skylights* was followed, in 1908, by *Waldo Trench and Others: Stories of Americans in Italy*, which exploits much more successfully the same materials as an earlier collection, of 1898, *From the Other Side: Stories of Transatlantic Travel*. The European figures of these earlier stories are the phantoms of a consolatory daydream, but the Americans abroad of *Waldo Trench* represent situations at home of which Fuller had had firsthand experience. In the story which gives the volume its title, a young man from Oklahoma is first seen much moved and excited at discovering, in downtown New York, a church which is 150 years old. "How it brings back the old Revolutionary days!" he exclaims. "I expect to see few things more impressive than this." But he is on his way to Europe, and when he gets there he discovers the Renaissance, by which he is even more excited. He is infatuated with Van Dyck and Raphael, Brunelleschi and Isabella d'Este, till someone puts him on to the Middle Ages, and he decides that Isabella d'Este is inferior to Dante's Beatrice and that he must go at once to Assisi. But then he is told by someone that classical Rome is the thing if one wants "to get the foundations of a good solid education," and while he is doing Rome, someone else tells him that "the Etruscans were the first schoolmasters of the Romans. They whipped those poor, uncouth creatures into shape and passed them on to the Greeks," so Trench goes to study the Etruscan cities. But poking among their ruins, he runs into an Englishman who exclaims to him scornfully, "Why, they're only Etruscan!" "What did you expect them to be?" "'I'm after the Pelasgians,' [the Englishman] returned in the sourest tone imaginable; 'what is this modern world to *me*?'" The next step back into the European past would be to explore the remains of the early Sicilian rock-dwellers, "called Sikelians or Sicanians." But a friend, with mischievous intent, explains at once to Waldo that these names belong to two different groups: "The distinction between them is an important one and well worthy of the best endeavors of an ambitious young *savant*." In the meantime, he has met a rich girl from Ohio, whose aunt, also rich, is pulsing with the spirit of Western enterprise and discourages Waldo's researches. She thinks that he is headed in the wrong direction: "That young man," she declares. "Such amazing vigor, such exhaustless driving power, such astonishing singleness of purpose! And all, at present, so misapplied. Think what such qualities are going to effect for him on those farms and in the civic life of his new commonwealth!" He gives up his ambition to penetrate the past, and marries the niece and returns to Oklahoma.

Another of these stories, "For the Faith," seems to me a comic masterpiece. It presents in a few pages a whole cultural shift in American life and might well be included in the reading list of a course in American history. A young schoolteacher from Stoneham Falls, Connecticut, is taking, with a couple of other girls, a vacation trip to Europe and writing to a friend at home. She finds herself on the boat with a very well-known "plutocrat," to whom she always refers with a proper New England scorn both snobbish and moralistic. But the plutocrat has with him an agreeable nephew, who pays the young lady compliments and seems to feel a real interest in her. She, however, maintains her attitude and, when she meets them again on her travels, insists to him that he and his uncle only want to buy up European art treasures and take them back to America: "Oh, leave those poor things alone! Let the land that originated them keep them a little longer. They were born here and they belong here. Restrain yourself. I'd much rather you went back to America and learned to rob your fellow-citizens." But Philippa, as in those days they used to say, has set her cap for young Thorpe. She has at first been writing of her plans for doing England in the usual guidebook way—"Salisbury and Winchester and Wells"— but she afterward manages an itinerary which enables her to keep up her acquaintance with the plutocrat and his nephew. Eventually, she bags her prey. The young man, when he gets back to the States, is going to have a job in one of his uncle's companies in Colorado, and she looks forward to being founder and president of the first women's club in the town. The modulation from her original point of view into complete acceptance of the millionaire is accomplished by Fuller with much humorous subtlety. Though her tone remains equally priggish, she now has a rationalization for her approval of everything she condemned before: "We cannot have an omelet without breaking a few eggs; we cannot bring a vast new country under the plough without turning under, at the same time, a certain number of innocent flowers; nor can a man seat himself at the apex of an enormous fortune without the charge of many minor injustices from a chorus of outspoken enemies. The old gentleman—whom I at last view not as a sociological abstraction but as a human creature like the rest of us—has probably had his beliefs and convictions, after all, and has in some degree suffered and sacrificed himself for them." What puts everything on a perfectly sound basis is discovering that the millionaire was, like herself, a product of the Naugatuck Valley: "He had been born on a farm *near* Stoneham Falls and been carried over into Fairfield County at the age of one."

Fuller published in the *Dial* in 1917 "A Plea for Shorter Novels," which is based, among other considerations, on the needlessness of writing descriptions of such places as everyone knows and of characters whom the reader will in any case identify with people he has seen. He "would sweep away . . . all laborious effort on stuff that is dragged in because someone will think it 'ought to be there'—clichés, conventional scenes and situations." In the next year, he published *On the Stairs*, which seems to me one of his best things. I used to amuse myself by telling foreign visitors that it was "the great American novel." (I find that James Huneker, in a letter to Fuller, calls it "the great Chicago novel.") *On the Stairs* deals with life in Chicago, but it dispenses with realistic trappings, and the author explains in a foreword that the book is an attempt at the kind of thing which he has recently been recommending. His device in this story is to tell it much as if he were an old Chicagoan recounting to another Chicagoan who takes the town and the milieu for granted the inside story of families that both of them have known. In the last quarter of the last century, two boys grow up in the city. One of them, Raymond Prince, is the son of a well-to-do family, who, like Fuller's, has come to the West, by way of New York State, from New England; the other, Johnny McComas, is the son of their stableman, who has lived with his family in the stable. Raymond breaks away, like Fuller, from the family background of banking and real estate, studies architecture and art, and spends a few years in Europe. In the meantime, Johnny has left school early, has worked hard, and soon becomes envied and admired as "the youngest bank-president in the 'Loop.'" We follow thereafter the progress of Johnny, as he grows more and more prosperous, and the gradual subsidence of Raymond, who has no interest in the family bank—it eventually goes into receivership—but never succeeds in doing anything of any worth in line with his artistic tastes. Raymond's discontented wife from the East, to his bitter humiliation, divorces him and marries Johnny, and Raymond is now so impoverished that he is obliged to let Johnny put his son through Yale. To make matters even worse from the point of view of Raymond, this son marries Johnny's daughter, a daughter by an earlier, very bourgeois wife. Now, in a story by Henry James, it would be made clear that Raymond had the finer values and that his frustration was not without nobility; in a story by Horatio Alger, Johnny would be a self-made hero who had achieved the kind of success that every American wants. But the point of Fuller's novel is that the two men are equally mediocre and that the social distinctions which originally divided them have in two generations disappeared. Raymond, to be sure, is pathetic, but we do not much sympathize with him. Johnny is relatively impressive by reason of his masculine vigor, and he behaves in a not ungenerous way, but he remains rather coarse and discomforting, and we do not like *him* much, either. Huneker compared *On the Stairs* to Flaubert's *Bouvard et Pécuchet*.

The futility of the young man who comes back to Chicago from Europe with greater sophistication and polish but enfeebled qualifications for making himself a place in the world of his origin has already been illustrated by Fuller in Truesdale Marshall of *With the Procession*. This is, in fact, with Fuller a recurrent theme—a kind of caricature of one aspect of himself. But he was not, of course, himself an ineffectual dilettante. Continuing to live in his native city and, as he once told Garland, with "no expectation of seeing satisfactory improvement in this town during my lifetime," he remained nevertheless indefatigable in his attempts to encourage anyone who showed any sign of serious cultural ambition. He put himself at the service of young painters and writers; with the latter, he read and criticized their manuscripts and even corrected their proofs. For years he conducted a book department in one of the daily papers. The volume of "Tributes to Henry B. from friends in whose minds and hearts he will always live" (the title on the cover is *Henry B. Fuller*), compiled by Anna Morgan, shows how many and what various people felt that they owed him a debt: Jane Addams, Louis Bromfield, Hamlin Garland, Lorado Taft, the sculptor; Bert Leston Taylor, the columnist; John T. McCutcheon, the cartoonist and illustrator; Harriet Monroe, the editor of *Poetry*; Thornton Wilder, Booth Tarkington, and other figures less well known. A good many of them seemed to feel that, less successful than some of them, he was somehow a little above them. At every gathering he was eagerly expected, though he did not always appear. Like many intelligent and affectionate born bachelors, he counted very much on his friends. He looked on sympathetically at their family relations and liked to amuse their children, with whom he was very popular and to whom he sometimes stood godfather; he would make the evenings gay by playing and enjoying old songs. But about his own life he was always guarded. He was supposed to have a room in his mother's house, but actually he seemed to live, says his biographer, Constance M. Griffin, "in a succession of rooming houses, where he could not be reached by telephone, and where no one would presume to call." No one ever knew his address, and he was regarded as something of a "mystery." This way of life is partly to be explained by his dislike of being disturbed, his scrupulous independence, and his resolute intention, so unaccountable in Chicago, not to have to make any money beyond his modest family income. In a society in which, as Fuller describes it, one's status depended on one's income and in which, as a consequence, this status was always precarious, he chose to maintain the cultural prestige to which he had been born in the city by accepting somewhat sordid conditions of living. Hamlin Garland complains of Fuller that he has "lived so long in restaurants that his table manners annoy me. He automatically polishes his coffee cup and wipes all the forks and knives on his napkin or on a corner of the tablecloth. He turns each piece of toast (looking for a possible fly) and peers into the milk or cream jug for a cockroach, all of which is funny for a time but comes to be an irritation at last—and yet he is the ablest, most distinctive, most intellectual of all our Western writers. He can be—and generally is—the most satisfactory of all my literary companions." Though Garland says in his memoirs that he was irked by Fuller's faultfinding, the adjective most often applied to him in the Morgan collection of tributes is "gentle." It is said of him that though his character was essentially steely, his manner in company was shy. Burton Rascoe thus described him in a "profile" of 1924: "In person Mr. Fuller is a furtive little fellow with a neatly trimmed white beard and white hair; his skin is smooth and white; his voice is soft and hesitant; his eyes gleam with amused inquisitiveness; and he is always perfectly shod and tailored. He is neat, gracious, charming, excessively quiet." In the photographs of Fuller in his later years, one notes always a slight look of anxiety.

There was perhaps another reason for the secrecy of Fuller's habits. He was evidently homosexual. This seems obvious throughout his work, in which he prefers to dwell on the splendid physiques of his young male characters rather than on the attractions of the women. He has a tendency, as in *On the Stairs*, to favor his vigorous vulgarians at the expense of his effete *raffinés*. On the death of Rudolph Valentino, Fuller wrote, but did not publish, a eulogy of this "Sheik" of the movies, who was apparently, according to Mencken's account of his curious interview with him, a genuinely sensitive fellow. Though certain conventionally desirable matings do occur in Fuller's novels, the situations that involve the affections are likely to be those in which some older man—it was apparently Fuller's problem—is trying to find a sympathetic younger man to live or travel with him. In his "Plea for Shorter Novels," he includes among elements to be eliminated "reluctant love passages" and "repellent sex discussions." But this emphasis was undoubtedly one of the reasons—together with his resolve to avoid "scenes of violence and bloodshed with which one may have no proper affinity" and "indelicate 'close-ups' which explore and exploit poor humanity beyond the just bounds of decorum"—for Fuller's lack of popularity. The novelists of that sentimental period—Owen Wister in *The Virginian* and George Cable in *The Cavalier*—were capable of glorifying virility in a way that probably flushed with pride their masculine readers as well as excited their large feminine audience, but Fuller was incapable of such specious romance: he is ironic about even his handsome young men. His books contain no sex interest of any kind. It is all the more startling, then, that he should suddenly, in *The Puppet-Booth*—in one of his short plays, called *At Saint Judas's*—have given such frank expression to that element of his personality. This rather absurd piece—Fuller is bad when he tries to be overtly dramatic—is concerned with the crisis that precedes a wedding, when the best man, the bridegroom's close friend, with whom he has been sharing rooms, turns up in the sacristy of the church in a state of hysterical emotion and tells the groom that he must not get married, that the prospective bride is a slut, that she has been going to bed with him, the best man. In this story, however, he soon breaks down, knowing well that the other will not believe it: "*I* am here. And *she* will never be. You may wait, but you shall wait in vain. *(He places his hand upon the other's shoulder.)* If she were to come, I should not let her have you. She shall not have you. Nobody shall have you." A horrible scene ensues—a scene too horrible for Fuller to handle. The friend attempts to bar the groom from entering the church. The groom says, "Stand aside. I hate you; I detest you; I despise you; I loathe you." "We have been friends always," the other replies. "I have loved you all my life. . . . The thought of *her* made me mad, made me desperate." He declares that one of the three shall die. The bridegroom invites him to "use your blade" (he evidently refers to a sword). The bride is coming up the aisle, and the groom enters the church. *"Upon the floor of the sacristy lies the body of a man in a pool of blood."* The trouble here is that Fuller is incapable of imagining at all convincingly such an outbreak of naked passion—especially between characters who are carrying swords. I agree with Miss Griffin when she says that the middle-aged Freiherr von Kaltenau, as he appears in *The Last Refuge*, traveling with an adored young man, is to be identified with Fuller when this character, taking stock of his life, concludes that it "had been indeed too free—too free from ties, from duties, from obligations, from restraints; too free from guidance, too free from the kindly pressure of any ordering hand. . . . The book of life had been opened wide before him, but he had declined to make the usual advance that leads straight on from chapter to chapter; rather had he fluttered the leaves carelessly, glanced at the end before reaching the middle, and thoroughly thwarted the aims and intentions of the great Author." I agree that the author identifies himself also with another of the people in this book, a novelist whose "principal concern was the portrayal of his contemporaries in works of fiction," when he confesses that his "participation in life has been, after all, but partial. I have always felt a slight reluctance about committing myself—a touch of dread about letting myself go. I have lived, in fact, by the seashore without ever venturing into the water. Others have gone in before my eyes, and I have recorded, to the best of my endeavor, the exhilarations they appeared to feel, the dangers they appeared to brave. But as soon as the waves have stolen up to my own toes, I have always stepped back upon the dry sands."

"There was in its deepest recesses," writes Harriet Monroe of Fuller's character, without assigning a specific cause, "an unconquerable reticence—Henry Fuller found it impossible to tell his whole story. He could not give himself away, and therefore it may be that the greatest book of which his genius was capable was never written, the book which would have brought the world to his feet in complete accord and delight." But one cannot imagine Fuller's writing such a book, and when he did reveal his secret, so far from bringing the world to his feet, he made it look the other way. In 1919, when he was sixty-two, he took the audacious step of publishing a novel, *Bertram Cope's Year*, with homosexual characters. His attitude about this at first is quite unabashed and cool: "I wrote," he tells Henry Kitchell Webster, another Illinois novelist, "in complete reaction from the love flummery of Holworthy Hall, et al. [Holworthy Hall was a pseudonym, the name of one of the Harvard dormitories, used by Harold Everett Porter, a writer for *Collier's* and *The Saturday Evening Post*.] Those fellows tire me. Perhaps I've gone too far the other way. While doing the job, I *did* think, now and then, of some of your own aberrations and perversions (Olga, Helena, et cet.)—but these in latter-day society are getting almost too common to be termed 'abnormal.' Lots of people must have read you in unperturbed innocency, and I hope a good many will read me that way, too. Certainly we are both 'Innocent Kids' compared with Cabell in *Jurgen*." And *Bertram Cope's Year*, though it involves homosexual situations, is not really a book about homosexuality. It has a kind of philosophic theme, which seems to me to raise it well above the fiction of social surfaces of the school of William Dean Howells. The story is made to take place in a Middle Western university town, which derives, Fuller admits, to some extent from Evanston, Illinois. Bertram Cope is a young instructor who is working for an M.A. in English. He is very good-looking, with yellow hair, and not stupid, though not strikingly intelligent, and he is found attractive by a number of persons. There is, first, Mr. Basil Randolph, a "scholar *manqué*," who works in the family brokerage business but is far more interested in collecting jades and other *objets d'art* and in hovering around the male students, who are likely themselves to be hovering around the quadrangle that houses the girls. There is also Medora Phillips, a well-to-do widow, who likes to have young people around her and has living in the house with her a niece, a girl secretary, and a girl boarder. All these people become infatuated with Bertram, who does not become attached to any of them.

He is said to be "an ebullient Puritan," with New England perhaps in the background, and he is interested only in making his way. The niece traps him into an engagement, from which he afterward manages to extricate himself; the more aggressive boarder, who is fearfully jealous of the niece, tries to ensnare him by painting his portrait; the secretary writes him sonnets which are considered by the older generation to go pretty far for a young girl. And Mrs. Phillips herself—though he regards her merely as a person to whose house he is glad to go— becomes much preoccupied with Bertram. The designs of Mr. Randolph are frustrated—he has taken new rooms, with an extra bed-room—when Bertram himself takes new rooms in order to accommodate a friend with whom he has been intimately corresponding and whom he brings on to keep him company. This friend, whose name is Arthur Lemoyne, Mr. Randolph does not at first want to meet and, when he does, immediately recognizes as the wrong kind of homosexual and resents as a dangerous rival: "His dark eyes were too liquid; his person was too plump," etc. Lemoyne, on his side, has brought pressure on Bertram to get out of his engagement with the niece, and he now pits himself against Randolph and all the ladies of the Phillips household. But nothing can dispel the enchantment which Bertram continues to exercise over all of them. When he tips over in a small sailboat, he is saved by his fiancée, who disentangles him from the mainsail and cordage, but he gets credit for having saved *her*; when the Phillips cottage on the dunes is broken into by an escaped convict, Bertram merely wakes up with a shriek while another man grapples with the burglar, but it is Bertram who becomes the hero. When he passes out at a dinner as the result of drinking wine, to which he is not accustomed, on top of a day of excessive work and a more or less empty stomach, he becomes the object of everyone's attention and everyone's solicitude. Mrs. Phillips's rather sour brother-in-law, crippled and half-blind, who plays the role of the detached observer and is completely aware of what is going on, growls that it all reminds him of a religious festival he once attended in an Italian hill town near Florence: "There was a kind of grotto in the church, under the high altar; and in the grotto was a full-sized figure of a dead man, carved and painted—and covered with wounds; and round that figure half the women and girls of the town were collected, stroking, kissing . . . Adonis all over again!"

This establishes the real point of the story, which is that Bertram's admirers all look to find in him a version of a semidivine ideal that he makes no attempt to live up to; that he is quite unconscious that his beauty and charm, together with a hard, self-sufficient core of character, have caused them to endow him with qualities which he does not at all possess. In the end, he simply gets his degree and leaves. But in the meantime he has been separated from Arthur Lemoyne. The latter has taken a feminine role in a college musical comedy and has had a unique success as a female impersonator; after the play, he has disgraced himself behind the scenes by making advances to a boy who has been playing a male part. His connection with the college is tenuous—something arranged by Bertram, through Randolph—and the authorities let him go. Bertram appeals to Randolph, who refuses to be helpful, and Arthur, with his bad reputation, is now a nuisance, anyhow, to Bertram. Bertram goes East and gets a better job in a better university. Randolph and Mrs. Phillips talk about him after he has left. She believes that when Bertram is earning enough, he will marry her secretary, the only one of his friends to whom he has written, though in a quite noncommittal way; Randolph, on the contrary, believes that Bertram will set up housekeeping with Arthur. At no point has the reader been given any clue as to Bertram's sexual inclinations. Fuller's rather difficult problem here has been to make Bertram intrinsically uninteresting and even rather comic, but at the same time to dramatize convincingly the spell of enchantment he is supposed to cast. This is seen in his effect on the other characters, but the reader is not made to feel it: Bertram is represented as behaving in an agreeable enough way, but in his self-centeredness, he never does anything that is made to seem really attractive. And the result, as in *On the Stairs*, is a kind of deliberate flatness.

This curious book, which is perhaps Fuller's best, seems never to have had adequate attention. The few people who have written about Fuller at any length have, so far as my reading goes, always treated it very gingerly. The only contemporary, so far as I know, who showed any real appreciation was James Huneker, who very much prided himself on his sophistication and lack of prudery and had previously applauded *At Saint Judas's*. He wrote Fuller of *Bertram Cope's Year* that he had read it three times: "Its portraiture and psychological strokes fill me with envy and also joy. *Ça y est*, I said to myself. And Chicago! It is as desolate, your dissection, as a lunar landscape. We are like that, not like Whitman's Camerados and his joyful junk. Why do you speak of your last book! You are only beginning, you implacable Stendhal of the lake!" But otherwise the effect of the novel was a slighting reproof or a horrified silence. André Gide had then only the prestige of a very limited cult; Proust had not yet been translated. Burton Rascoe wrote, "It may be said that *Bertram Cope's Year*, in so far as it was read and understood at all, shocked Mr. Fuller's friends so painfully that they silenced it into limbo. It is a story, delicately done with the most exquisite taste, of a "sublimated irregular affection. It received scant and unintelligent notice from the reviewers, and though it was filled with dynamite scrupulously packed, it fell as harmless as a dud, only to be whispered about here and there by grave people who wondered why Mr. Fuller should choose such a theme." But even this writer of the early twenties who wants to do justice to Fuller does not accurately describe the book. The central theme, as I have said above, is not "a sublimated irregular affection." Fuller has merely, in writing of the power exerted by a "charismic" personality, extended what was then the conventional range. The effect on poor Fuller himself of the reception of his book was terrible. He disparaged his own courage by saying that he wished he had never written it, and he burned up his manuscript and proofs. It was ten years before he ventured to publish another novel.

He returned in 1929, in *Gardens of This World*—of which I have already spoken—to his beloved group of Old World characters. "Such a goddam lovely little book," he says in a letter to one of his young friends. *Not on the Screen*, which was published in 1930, is the last of his Chicago novels and not only the most stripped but the palest of them; yet Fuller is always readable and always winning, through his dry sense of comedy. The book begins with a movie which a girl and a young man are watching. In the picture, there is a melodramatic situation. The rest of the novel is the story of the subsequent relations of the couple, which repeats the story of the film but is not at all melodramatic. The upstart young man from the country wins the hand of the rich young girl without any very stiff struggle. There are some rather disagreeable but not very dramatic encounters between this modest but successful young man and a socially well-situated and insolent young banker who is competing for the hand of the girl. The banker, who has power of attorney for the girl's widowed mother, resorts to unscrupulous practices in his efforts to gain his end, by threatening to ruin the family and attempting to send the young man to jail. But, although in the film the corresponding character is made to play the role of the villain, the character in the novel is not himself sent to jail. He is never melodramatically unmasked, but, in a quiet way, pressure is put upon him to restore the family fortunes. The mistress of the young banker, who would figure as the "vamp" in the picture, is a cheap and rather pathetic figure who, although she arouses suspicion by going out with the *jeune premier*, has never for a moment tempted him. The story is all told in terms of the social nuances of Chicago, of which Fuller was an amused observer, but the point of the whole thing is that in a Western city like Chicago—and perhaps, by implication, anywhere in the United States—these differences matter very little. You cannot get a thrilling drama out of them. This novel is another exercise in the art of making it flat—the quality of which art, of course, was appreciated little by the public and which accounts for the lessening interest in the books of Fuller's later years.

In this very late last burst of energy—Fuller was now seventy-two— he started still another novel, but he did not get far with this or see the publication of either *Not on the Screen* or *Gardens of This World*. He died alone in a rooming house in July 1929. One is reminded of the ending of one of the character sketches in *Lines Long and Short*, the portrait of a familyless bachelor who has tried to make a life for himself by his attentions to the families of friends and who is left with little consolation:

> Yes, perhaps he did
> Come through all right—
> With much or little sympathy—
> To take up, with what zest he could,
> The frantic role
> Of buying favors from a cooling world.
> Spend as you will,
> It's sad to be old, and alone.
> (Fudge! that's the very thing
> I tried hard not to say!)

The literature on Fuller is extremely meager. Besides the volume of tributes mentioned and a few other scattered memoirs, there is only the inadequate biography by Constance M. Griffin—evidently one of those theses which the estimable Arthur H. Quinn of the University of Pennsylvania, the author of comprehensive and useful books on American fiction and drama, induced his students to write on neglected American authors. We must be grateful to Mr. Quinn. If it had not been for him, we should have had nothing of value at all on such writers as Kate Chopin and Fuller. But something more searching and solid is needed, and now that the University of Chicago Press has reprinted *With the Procession*, I should like to suggest that it commission a life and letters of Fuller, as well as a volume of his uncollected pieces. He did a good deal of reviewing in his lifetime. I have just been through the articles he contributed to *The New Republic* during the twenties when he was not writing novels. They are always discriminating and conscientious, and it is interesting to know what he thought about Chekhov, Cabell, and Proust. Miss Griffin's selective bibliography includes many other items which awaken curiosity, as well as a long list of unpublished or uncollected stories. We know from those stories of Kate Chopin and Cable which were rejected by the conventional magazines of the nineties and the early 1900s that some of these authors' most interesting things were inacceptable to the squeamish editors. Fuller's early humorous writings for *Life* should also be investigated. I have looked up "A Transcontinental Episode, or, Metamorphoses at Muggins' Misery: A Cooperative Novel by Bret James and Henry Harte" (published in 1884). It is juvenile but not unamusing. A Jamesian young man who has lived abroad and is always slipping into French arrives in one of Harte's tough California settlements. He falls in love with the local belle and she with him, as the result of which he tries to transform himself into the kind of man he thinks she admires. But she, on her side, during an absence of his, has schooled herself to be refined. Fuller supplies two alternative endings, by each of the collaborators. In Harte's version, when her lover returns in the garb of a rugged Westerner, she casts off her elegant clothes and with a whoop leaps into his arms. In James's, she preserves the "finer" manners and dress to which her contact with the traveled young Easterner has raised her, but the question of whether they can ever now get together is left, in the Jamesian fashion, completely up in the air. This little skit foreshadows the theme of the constant conflict between the two states of American culture which was to occupy Fuller all his life.

—May 23, 1970

# BERTRAM COPE'S YEAR

# I

## Cope at a College Tea

WHAT is a man's best age? Peter Ibbetson, entering dreamland with complete freedom to chose, chose twenty-eight, and kept there. But twenty-eight, for our present purpose, has a drawback: a man of that age, if endowed with ordinary gifts and responsive to ordinary opportunities, is undeniably—a man; whereas what we require here is something just a little short of that. Wanted, in fact, a young male who shall seem fully adult to those who are younger still, and who may even appear the accomplished flower of virility to an idealizing maid or so, yet who shall elicit from the middle-aged the kindly indulgence due a boy. Perhaps you will say that even a man of twenty-eight may seem only a boy to a man of seventy. However, no septuagenarian is to figure in these pages. Our elders will be but in the middle forties and the earlier fifties; and we must find for them an age which may evoke their friendly interest, and yet be likely to call forth, besides that, their sympathy and their longing admiration, and later their tolerance, their patience, and even their forgiveness.

I think, then, that Bertram Cope, when he began to intrigue the little group which dwelt among the quadruple avenues of elms that led to the campus in Churchton, was but about twenty-four,—certainly not a day more than twenty-five. If twenty-eight is the ideal age, the best is all the better for being just a little ahead.

Of course Cope was not an undergraduate—a species upon which many of the Churchtonians languidly refused to bestow their regard. "They come, and they go," said these prosperous and comfortable burghers; "and, after all, they're more or less alike, and more or less unrewarding." Besides, the Bigger Town, with all its rich resources and all its varied opportunities, lay but an hour away. Churchton lived much of its real life beyond its own limits, and the student who came to be entertained socially within them was the exception indeed.

No, Bertram Cope was not an undergraduate. He was an instructor; and he was working along, in a leisurely way, to a degree. He expected to be an M.A., or even a Ph.D. Possibly a Litt.D. might be within the gift of later years. But, anyhow, nothing was finer than "writing"—except lecturing about it.

"Why haven't we known you before?" Medora T. Phillips asked him at a small reception. Mrs. Phillips spoke out loudly and boldly, and held his hand as long as she liked. No, not as long as she liked, but longer than most women would have felt at liberty to do. And besides speaking loudly and boldly, she looked loudly and boldly; and she employed a determined smile which seemed to say, "I'm old enough to do as I please." Her brusque informality was expected to carry itself off—and much else besides. "Of course I simply *can't* be half so intrepid as I seem!" it said. "Everybody about us understands that, and I must ask your recognition too for an ascertained fact."

"Known me?" returned Cope, promptly enough. "Why, you haven't known me because I haven't been here to *be* known." He spoke in a ringing, resonant voice, returning her unabashed pressure with a hearty good will and blazing down upon her through his clear blue eyes with a high degree of self-possession, even of insouciance. And he explained, with a liberal exhibition of perfect teeth, that for the two years following his graduation he had been teaching literature at a small college in Wisconsin and that he had lately come back to Alma Mater for another bout: "I'm after that degree," he concluded.

"Haven't been here?" she returned. "But you *have* been here; you must have been here for years—for four, anyhow. So why haven't we . . . ?" she began again.

"Here as an undergraduate, yes," he acknowledged. "Unregarded dust. Dirt beneath your feet. In rainy weather, mud."

"Mud!" echoed Medora Phillips loudly, with an increased pressure on his long, narrow hand. "Why, Babylon was built of mud—of mud bricks, anyway. And the Hanging Gardens . . . !" She still clung, looking up his slopes terrace by terrace.

Cope kept his self-possession and smiled brilliantly.

"Gracious!" he said, no less resonant than before. "Am I a landscape garden? Am I a stage-setting? Am I a———?"

Medora Phillips finally dropped his hand. "You're a wicked, unappreciative boy," she declared. "I don't know whether to ask you to my house or not. But you may make yourself useful in *this* house, at least. Run along over to that corner and see if you can't get me a cup of tea."

Cope bowed and smiled and stepped toward the tea-table. His head once turned, the smile took on a wry twist. He was no squire of dames, no frequenter of afternoon receptions. Why the deuce had he come to this one? Why had he yielded so readily to the urgings of the professor of mathematics?—himself urged in turn, perhaps, by a wife for whose little affair one extra man at the opening of the fall season counted, and counted hugely. Why must he now expose himself to the boundless aplomb and momentum of this woman of forty-odd who was finding amusement in treating him as a "college boy"? "Boy" indeed she had actually called him: well, perhaps his present position made all this possible. He was not yet out in the world on his own. In the background of "down state" was a father with a purse in his pocket and a hand to open the purse. Though the purse was small and the hand reluctant, he must partly depend on both for another year. If he were only in business—if he were only a broker or even a salesman—he should not find himself treated with such blunt informality and condescension as a youth. If, within the University itself, he were but a real member of the faculty, with an assured position and an assured salary, he should not have to lie open to the unceremonious hectorings of the socially confident, the "placed."

4

He regained his smile on the way across the room, and the young creature behind the samovar, who had had a moment's fear that she must deal with Severity, found that a beaming Affability—though personally unticketed in her memory—was, after all, her happier allotment. In her reaction she took it all as a personal compliment. She could not know, of course, that it was but a piece of calculated expressiveness, fitted to a particular social function and doubly overdone as the wearer's own reaction from the sprouting indignation of the moment before. She hoped that her hair, under his sweeping advance, was blowing across her forehead as lightly and carelessly as it ought to, and that his taste in marquise rings might be substantially the same as hers. She faced the Quite Unknown, and asked it sweetly, "One lump or two?"

"The dickens! How do *I* know?" he thought. "An extra one on the saucer, please," he said aloud, with his natural resonance but slightly hushed. And his blue eyes, clear and rather cold and hard, blazed down, in turn, on her.

"Why, what a nice, friendly fellow!" exclaimed Mrs. Phillips, on receiving her refreshment. "Both kinds of sandwiches," she continued, peering round her cup. "Were there three?" she asked with sudden shrewdness.

"There were macaroons," he replied; "and there was some sort of layer-cake. It was too sticky. These are more sensible."

"Never mind sense. If there is cake, I want it. Tell Amy to put it on a plate."

"Amy?"

"Yes, Amy. *My* Amy."

"Your Amy?"

"Off with you,—parrot! And bring a fork too."

Cope lapsed back into his frown and recrossed the room. The girl behind the samovar felt that her hair was unbecoming, after all, and that her ring, borrowed for the occasion, was in bad taste. Cope turned back with his plate of cake and his fork. Well, he had been promoted from a "boy" to a "fellow"; but must he continue a kind of methodical dog-trot through a sublimated butler's pantry?

"That's right," declared Mrs. Phillips, on his return, as she looked lingeringly at his shapely thumb above the edge of the plate. "Come, we will sit down together on this sofa, and you shall tell me all about yourself." She looked admiringly at his blue serge knees as he settled down into place. They were slightly bony, perhaps; "but then," as she told herself, "he is still quite young. Who would want him anything but slender?—even spare, if need be."

As they sat there together,—she plying him with questions and he, restored to good humor, replying or parrying with an unembarrassed exuberance,—a man who stood just within the curtained doorway and flicked a small graying moustache with the point of his forefinger took in the scene with a studious regard. Every small educational community has its scholar *manqué*—its haunter of academic shades or its intermittent dabbler in their charms; and Basil Randolph held that rôle in Churchton. No alumnus himself, he viewed, year after year, the passing procession of undergraduates who possessed in their young present so much that he had left behind or had never had at all, and who were walking, potentially, toward a promising future in which he could take no share. Most of these had been commonplace young fellows enough—noisy, philistine, glaringly cursory and inconsiderate toward their elders; but a few of them—one now and then, at long intervals—he would have enjoyed knowing, and knowing intimately. On these infrequent occasions would come a union of frankness, comeliness and *élan*, and the rudiments of good manners. But no one in all the long-drawn procession had stopped to look at him a second time. And now he was turning gray; he was tragically threatened with what might in time become a paunch. His kind heart, his forthreaching nature, went for naught; and the young men let him walk under the elms and the scrub-oaks neglected. If they had any interest beyond their egos, their fraternities, and (conceivably) their studies, that interest dribbled away on the quadrangle that housed the girl students. "If they only realized how much a friendly hand, extended to them from middle life, might do for their futures . . . !" he would sometimes sigh. But the youthful egoists, ignoring him still, faced their respective futures, however uncertain, with much more confidence than he, backed by whatever assurances and accumulations he enjoyed, could face his own.

"To be young!" he said. "To be young!"

Do you figure Basil Randolph, alongside his portière, as but the observer, the *raisonneur*, in this narrative? If so, you err. What!—you may ask,—a rival, a competitor? That more nearly.

It was Medora Phillips herself who, within a moment or two, inducted him into this rôle.

A gap had come in her chat with Cope. He had told her all he had been asked to tell—or all he meant to tell: at any rate he had been given abundant opportunity to expatiate upon a young man's darling subject—himself. Either she now had enough fixed points for securing the periphery of his circle or else she preferred to leave some portion of his area (now ascertained approximately) within a poetic penumbra. Or perhaps she wished some other middle-aged connoisseur to share her admiration and confirm her judgment. At all events———

"Oh, Mr. Randolph," she cried, "come here."

Randolph left his doorway and stepped across.

"Now you are going to be rewarded," said the lady, broadly generous. "You are going to meet Mr. Cope. You are going to meet Mr.———" She paused. "Do you know,"—turning to the young man,—"I haven't your first name?"

"Why, is that necessary?"

"You're not ashamed of it? Theodosius? Philander? Hieronymus?"

"Stop!—please. My name is Bertram."

"Never!"

"Bertram. Why not?"

"Because that would be too exactly right. I might have guessed and guessed———!"

"Right or wrong, Bertram's my name."

"You hear, Mr. Randolph? You are to meet Mr. Bertram Cope."

Cope, who had risen and had left any embarrassment consequent upon the short delay to Basil Randolph himself, shot out a hand and summoned a ready smile. Within his cuff was a hint for the construction of his fore-arm: it was lean and sinewy, clear-skinned, and with strong power for emphasis on the other's rather short, well-fleshed fingers. And as he gripped, he beamed; beamed just as warmly, or just as coldly—at all events, just as speciously—as he had beamed before: for on a social occasion one must slightly heighten good will,—all the more so if one be somewhat unaccustomed and even somewhat reluctant.

Mrs. Phillips caught Cope's glance as it fell in all its glacial geniality.

"He looks down on us!" she declared.

"How down?" Cope asked.

"Well, you're taller than either of us."

"I don't consider myself tall," he replied. "Five foot nine and a half," he proceeded ingenuously, "is hardly tall."

"It is we who are short," said Randolph.

"But really, sir," rejoined Cope kindly, "I shouldn't call you short. What is an inch or two?"

"But how about me?" demanded Mrs. Phillips.

"Why, a woman may be anything—except too tall," responded Cope candidly.

"But if she wants to be stately?"

"Well, there was Queen Victoria."

"You incorrigible! I hope I'm not so short as that! Sit down, again, we must be more on a level. And you, Mr. Randolph, may stand and look down on us both. I'm sure you have been doing so, anyway, for the past ten minutes!"

"By no means, I assure you," returned Randolph soberly.

Soberly. For the young man had slipped in that "sir." And he had been so kindly about Randolph's five foot seven and a bit over. And he had shown himself so damnably tender toward a man fairly advanced within the shadow of the fifties—a man who, if not an acknowledged outcast from the joys of life, would soon be lagging superfluous on their rim.

Randolph stood before them, looking, no doubt, a bit vacant and inexpressive. "Please go and get Amy," Mrs. Phillips said to him. "I see she's preparing to give way to some one else."

Amy—who was a blonde girl of twenty or more—came back with him pleasantly and amiably enough; and her aunt—or whatever she should turn out to be—was soon able to lay her tongue again to the syllables of the interesting name of Bertram.

Cope, thus finally introduced, repeated the facial expressions which he had employed already beside the tea-table. But he added no new one; and he found fewer words than the occasion prompted, and even required. He continued talking with Mrs. Phillips, and he threw an occasional remark toward Randolph; but now that all obstacles were removed from free converse with the divinity of the samovar he had less to say to her than before. Presently the elder woman, herself no whit offended, began to figure the younger one as a bit nonplused.

"Never mind, Amy," she said. "Don't pity him, and don't scorn him. He's really quite self-possessed and quite chatty. Or"—suddenly to Cope himself—"have you shown us already your whole box of tricks?"

"That must be it," he returned.

"Well, no matter. Mr. Randolph can be nice to a nice girl."

"Oh, come now,——"

"Well, shall I ask you to my house, after this?"

"No. Don't. Forbid it. Banish me."

"Give one more chance," suggested Randolph sedately.

"Why, what's all this about?" said the questioning glance of

Amy. If there was any offense at all, on anybody's part, it lay in making too much of too little.

"Take back my plate, somebody," said Mrs. Phillips.

Randolph put out his hand for it.

"This sandwich," said Amy, reaching for an untouched square of wheat bread and pimento. "I've been so busy with other people . . ."

"I'll take it myself," declared Mrs. Phillips, reaching out in turn. "Mr. Randolph, bring her a nibble of something."

"*I* might——" began Cope.

"You don't deserve the privilege."

"Oh, very well," he returned, lapsing into an easy passivity.

"Never mind, anyway," said Amy, still without cognomen and connections; "I can starve with perfect convenience. Or I can find a mouthful somewhere, later."

"Let us starve sitting," said Randolph, "Here are chairs."

The hostess herself came bustling up brightly.

"Has everybody . . . ?"

And she bustled away.

"Yes; everybody—almost," said Mrs. Phillips to her associates, behind their entertainer's back. "If you're hungry, Amy, it's your own fault. Sit down."

And there let us leave them—our little group, our cast of characters: "everybody—almost," save one. Or two. Or three.

# 2

## *Cope Makes a Sunday Afternoon Call*

MEDORA PHILLIPS was the widow of a picture-dealer, now three years dead. In his younger days he had been something of a painter, and later in life as much a collector as a merchandizer. Since his death he had been translated gradually from the lower region proper to mere traffickers on toward the loftier plane which harbored the more select company of art-patrons and art-amateurs. Some of his choicer ventures were still held together as a "gallery," with a few of his own canvases included; and his surviving partner felt this collection gave her good reason for holding up her head among the arts, and the sciences, and humane letters too.

Mrs. Phillips occupied a huge, amorphous house some three-quarters of a mile to the west of the campus. It was a construction in wood, with manifold "features" suggestive of the villa, the bungalow, the chateau, the palace; it united all tastes and contravened all conventions. In its upper story was the commodious apartment which was known in quiet times as the picture-gallery and in livelier times as the ball-room. It was the mistress' ambition to have the lively times as numerous as possible—to dance with great frequency among the pictures. Six or eight couples could gyrate here at once. There was young blood under her roof, and there was young blood to summon from outside; and to set this blood seething before the eyes of visiting celebrities in the arts and letters was her dearest wish. She had more than one spare bedroom, of course; and the Eminent and the Queer were always welcome for a sojourn of a week or so, whether they came to read papers and deliver lectures or not. She was quite as well satisfied when they didn't. If they would but sit upon her wide veranda in spring or autumn, or before her big open fire-place in winter and "just talk," she would be as open-eyed and open-eared as you pleased.

"This is much nicer," she would say. Nicer than what, she did not always make clear.

Yes, the house was nearly three-quarters of a mile to the west of the campus, but it was twice as far as if it had been north or south. Trains and trolleys, intent on serving the interests of the great majority, took their own courses and gave her guests no aid. If the evening turned cold or blustery or brought a driving rain she would say:

"You can't go out in this. You must stay all night. We have room and to spare."

If she wanted anybody to stay very much, she would even add:

"I can't think of your walking toward the lake with such a gale in your face,"—regardless of the fact that the lake wind was the rarest of them all and that in nine cases out of ten the rain or snow would be not in people's faces but at their backs.

If she didn't want anybody to stay, she simply ordered out the car and bundled him off. The delay in the offer of the car sometimes induced a young man to remain. Tasteful pajamas and the promise of a suitably early breakfast assured him that he had made no mistake.

Cope's first call was made, not on a tempestuous evening in the winter time, but on a quiet Sunday afternoon toward the end of September. The day was sunny and the streets were full of strollers moving along decorously beneath the elms, maples and catalpas.

"Drop in some Sunday about five," Medora Phillips had said to him, "and have tea. The girls will be glad to meet you."

"The girls"? Who were they, and how many? He supposed he could account for one of them, at least; but the others?

"You find me alone, after all," was her greeting. "The girls are out walking—with each other, or their beaux, or whatever. Come in here."

She led him into a spacious room cluttered with lambrequins, stringy portières, grilles, scroll-work, bric-à-brac. . . .

"The fine weather has been too much for them," she proceeded. "I was relying on them to entertain you."

"Dear me! Am I to be entertained?"

"Of course you are." Her expression and inflection indicated to him that he had been caught up in the cogs of a sizable machine, and that he was to be put through it. Everybody who came was entertained—or helped entertain others. Entertainment, in fact, was the one object of the establishment.

"Well, can't you entertain me yourself?"

"Perhaps I can." And it almost seemed as if he had been secured and isolated for the express purpose of undergoing a particular course of treatment.

"——in the interval," she amended. "They'll be back by sunset. They're clever girls and I know you'll enjoy them."

She uttered this belief emphatically—so emphatically, in truth, that it came to mean: "I wonder if you will indeed." And there was even an overtone: "After all, it's not the least necessary that you should."

"I suppose I have met one of them already."

"You have met Amy. But there are Hortense and Carolyn."

"What can they all be?" He wondered to himself: "daughters, nieces, cousins, co-eds, boarders . . . ?"

"Amy plays. Hortense paints. Carolyn is a poet."

"Amy plays? Pardon me for calling her Amy, but you have never given me the rest of her name."

"I certainly presented you."

"To 'Amy'."

"Well, that was careless, if true. Her name is Amy Leffingwell; and Hortense's name is——"

"Stop, please. Pay it out gradually. My poor head can hold only what it can. Names without people to attach them to . . ."

"The people will be here presently," Medora Phillips said, rather shortly. Surely this young man was taking his own tone. It was not quite the tone usually taken by college boys on their first call. Her position and her imposing surroundings—yes, her kindliness in noticing him at all—might surely save her from informalities that almost shaped into impertinences. Yet, on the other hand, nothing bored one more than a young man who openly showed himself intimidated. What was there behind this one? More than she had thought? Well, if so, none the worse. Time might tell.

"So Miss Leffingwell plays?" He flared out his blue-white smile. "Let me learn my lesson page by page."

"Yes, she plays," returned Medora Phillips briefly. "Guess what," she continued presently, half placated.

They were again side by side on a sofa, each with an elbow on its back and the elbows near together. Nor was Medora Phillips, though plump, at all the graceless, dumpy little body she sometimes taxed herself with being.

"What? Oh, piano, I suppose."

"Piano!"

"What's wrong?"

"The piano is common: it's assumed."

"Oh, she performs on something unusual? Xylophone?"

"Be serious."

"Trombone? I've seen wonders done on that in a 'lady orchestra'."

"Don't be grotesque." She drew her dark eyebrows into protest. "What a sight!—a delicate young girl playing a trombone!"

"Well, then,—a harp. That's sometimes a pleasant sight."

"A harp needs an express wagon. Though of course it *is* pretty for the arms."

"Arms? Let me see. The violin?"

"Of course. And that's probably the very first thing you thought of. Why not have mentioned it?"

"I suppose I've been taught the duty of making conversation."

"The duty? Not the pleasure?"

"That remains to be . . ." He paused. "So she has arms," he pretended to muse. "I confess I hadn't quite noticed."

"She passed you a cup of tea, didn't she?"

"Oh, surely. And a sandwich. And another. And a slice of layer cake, with a fork. And another cup of tea. And a macaroon or two——"

"Am I a glutton?"

"Am I? Some of all that provender was for me, as I recall."

They were still side by side on the sofa. Both were cross-kneed, and the tip of her russet boot almost grazed that of his Oxford tie. He did not notice: he was already arranging the first paragraph of a letter to a friend in Winnebago, Wisconsin. "Dear Arthur: I called,—as I said I was going to. She is a scrap-per. She goes at you hammer and tongs    pretending to quarrel as a means of entertaining you . . ."

Medora Phillips removed her elbow from the back of the sofa, and began to prod up her cushions. "How about your work?" she asked. "What are you doing?"

He came back. "Oh, I'm boning. Some things still to make up. I'm digging in the poetry of Gower—the 'moral Gower'."

"Well, I see no reason why poetry shouldn't be moral. Has he been publishing anything lately that I ought to see?"

"Not—lately."

"I presume I can look into some of his older things."

"They are all old—five hundred years and more. He was a pal of Chaucer's."

She gave him an indignant glance. "So that's it? You're laying traps for me? You don't like me! You don't respect me!"

One of the recalcitrant cushions fell to the floor. They bumped heads in trying to pick it up.

"Traps!" he said. "Never in the world! Don't think it! Why, Gower is just a necessary old bore. Nobody's supposed to know much about him—except instructors and their hapless students."

He added one more sentence to his letter to "Arthur": "She pushes you pretty hard. A little of it goes a good way . . ."

"Oh, if *that's* the case . . ." she said. "How about your thesis?" she went on swiftly. "What are you going to write about?"

"I was thinking of Shakespeare."

"Shakespeare! There you go again! Ridiculing me to my very face!"

"Not at all. There's lots to say about him—or them."

"Oh, you believe in Bacon!"

"Not at all—once more. I should like to take a year and spend it among the manor-houses of Warwickshire. But I suppose nobody would stake me to that."

"I don't know what you have in mind; some wild goose chase, probably. I expect your friends would like it better if you spent your time right here."

"Probably. I presume I shall end by doing a thesis on the 'color-words' in Keats and Shelley. A penniless devil was no luck."

"Anybody has luck who can form the right circle. Stay where you are. A circle formed here would do you much more good than a temporary one four thousand miles away."

Voices were heard in the front yard. "There they come, now," Mrs. Phillips said. She rose, and one more of the wayward cushions went to the floor. It lay there unregarded,—a sign that a promising tête-à-tête was, for the time being, over.

# 3

## Cope Is "Entertained"

Mrs. Phillips stepped to the front door to meet the half dozen young people who were cheerily coming up the walk. Cope, looking at the fallen cushions with an unseeing eye, remained within the drawing-room door to compose a further paragraph for the behoof of his correspondent in Wisconsin:

"Several girls helped entertain me. They came on as thick as spatter. One played a few things on the violin. Another set up her easel and painted a picture for us. A third wrote a poem and read it to us. And a few sophomores hung about in the background. It was all rather too much. I found myself preferring those hours together in dear old Winnebago . . ."

Only one of the sophomores—if the young men were really

of that objectionable tribe—came indoors with the young ladies. The others—either engaged elsewhere or consciously unworthy—went away after a moment or two on the front steps.
Perhaps they did not feel "encouraged." And in fact Mrs. Phillips
looked back toward Cope with the effect of communicating the
idea that she had enough men for to-day. She even conveyed to
him the notion that he had made the others superfluous.
But——

"Hum!" he thought; "if there's to be a lot of 'entertaining,'
the more there are to be entertained the better it might turn
out."

He met Hortense and Carolyn—with due stress laid on their
respective patronymics—and he made an early acquaintance
with Amy's violin.

And further on Mrs. Phillips said:

"Now, Amy, before you really stop, do play that last little
thing. The dear child," she said to Cope in a lower tone, "composed it herself and dedicated it to me."

The last little thing was a kind of "meditation," written very
simply and performed quite seriously and unaffectedly. And it
gave, of course, a good chance for the arms.

"There!" said Mrs. Phillips, at its close. "Isn't it too sweet?
And it inspired Carolyn too. She wrote a poem after hearing it."

"A copy of verses," corrected Carolyn, with a modest catch in
her breath. She was a quiet, sedate girl, with brown eyes and
hair. Her eyes were shy, and her hair was plainly dressed.

"Oh, you're so sweet, so old-fashioned!" protested Mrs.
Phillips, slightly rolling her eyes. "It's a poem,—of course it's a
poem. I leave it to Mr. Cope, if it isn't!"

"Oh, I beg——" began Cope, in trepidation.

"Well, listen, anyway," said Medora.

The poem consisted of some six or seven brief stanzas. Its title was read, formally, by the writer; and, quite as formally, the dedication which intervened between title and first stanza,—a dedication to "Medora Townsend Phillips."

"Of course," said Cope to himself. And as the reading went on, he ran his eyes over the dusky, darkening walls. He knew what he expected to find.

Just as he found it the sophomore standing between the big padded chair and the book-case spatted his hands three times. The poem was over, the patroness duly celebrated. Cope spatted a little too, but kept his eye on one of the walls.

"You're looking at my portrait!" declared Mrs. Phillips, as the poetess sank deeper into the big chair. "Hortense did it."

"Of course she did," said Cope under his breath. He transferred an obligatory glance from the canvas to the expectant artist. But———

"It's getting almost too dark to see it," said his hostess, and suddenly pressed a button. This brought into play a row of electric bulbs near the top edge of the frame and into full prominence the dark plumpness of the subject. He looked back again from the painter (who also had black hair and eyes) to her work.

"I am on Parnassus!" Cope declared, in one general sweeping compliment, as he looked toward the sofa where Medora Phillips sat with the three girls now grouped behind her. But he made it a boreal Parnassus—one set in relief by the cold flare and flicker of northern lights.

"Isn't he the dear, comical chap!" exclaimed Mrs. Phillips, with unction, glancing upward and backward at the girls. They smiled discreetly, as if indulging in a silent evaluation of the sincerity of the compliment. Yet one of them—Hortense—formed her black brows into a frown, and might have spoken resentfully, save for a look from their general patroness.

"Meanwhile, how about a drop of tea?" asked Mrs. Phillips suddenly. "Roddy"—to the sophomore—"if you will help clear that table . . ."

The youth hastened to get into action. Cope went on with his letter to "Arthur":

"It was an afternoon in Lesbos—with Sappho and her band of appreciative maidens. Phaon, a poor lad of nineteen, swept some pamphlets and paper-cutters off the center-table, and we all plunged into the ocean of Oolong—the best thing we do on this island . . ."

He was lingering in a smiling abstractedness on his fancy, when——

"Bertram Cope!" a voice suddenly said, "do you do nothing—nothing?"

He suddenly came to. Perhaps he had really deserved his hostess' rebuke. He had not offered to help with the tea-service; he had proferred no appropriate remark, of an individual nature, to any of the three *ancillae* . . .

"I mean," proceeded Mrs. Phillips, "can you do nothing whatever to entertain?"

Cope gained another stage on the way to self-consciousness and self-control. Entertainment was doubtless the basic curse of this household.

"I sing," he said, with naïf suddenness and simplicity.

"Then, sing—do. There's the open piano. Can you play your own accompaniments?"

"Some of the simpler ones."

"Some of the simpler ones! Do you hear that, girls? He is quite prepared to wipe us all out. Shall we let him?"

"That's unfair," Cope protested. "Is it my fault if composers *will* write hard accompaniments to easy airs?"

"Will you sing before your tea, or after it?"

"I'm ready to sing this instant,—during it, or before it."

"Very well."

The room was now in dusk, save for the bulbs which made the portrait shine forth like a wayside shrine. Roddy, the possible sophomore, helped a maid find places for the cups and saucers; and the three girls, still formed in a careful group about the sofa, silently waited.

"Of course you realize that this is not such a very large room," said Mrs. Phillips.

"Meaning . . . ?"

"Well, your speaking voice *is* resonant, you know."

"Meaning, then, that I am not to raise the roof nor jar the china. I'll try not to."

Nor did he. He sang with care rather than with volume, with discretion rather than with abandon. The "simple accompaniments" went off with but a slight hitch or two, yet the "resonant voice" was somehow, somewhere lost. Possibly Cope gave too great heed to his hostess' caution; but it seemed as if a voice essentially promising had slipped through some teacher's none too competent hands, or—what was quite as serious—as if some temperamental brake were operating to prevent the complete expression of the singer's nature. Lassen, Grieg, Rubinstein— all these were carried through rather cautiously, perhaps a little mechanically; and there was a silence. Hortense broke it.

"Parnassus, yes. And finally comes Apollo." She reached over and murmured to Mrs. Phillips: "None too skillful on the lyre, and none too strong in the lungs . . ."

Medora spoke up loudly and promptly.

"Do you know, I think I've heard you sing before."

"Possibly," Cope said, turning his back on the keyboard. "I sang in the University choir for a year or two."

"In gown and mortar-board? 'Come, Holy Spirit,' and all that?"

"Yes; I sang solos now and then."

"Of course," she said. "I remember now. But I never saw you before without your mortar-board. That changes the forehead. Yes, you're yourself," she went on, adding to her previous pleasure the further pleasure of recognition. "You've earned your tea," she added. "Hortense," she said over her shoulder to the dark girl behind the sofa, "will you——? No; I'll pour, myself."

She slid into her place at table and got things to going. There was an interval which Cope might have employed in praising the artistic aptitudes of this variously gifted household, but he found no appropriate word to say,—or at least uttered none. And none of the three girls made any further comment on his own performance.

Mrs. Phillips accompanied him, on his way out, as far as the hall. She looked up at him questioningly.

"You don't like my poor girls," she said. "You don't find them clever; you don't find them interesting."

"On the contrary," he rejoined, "I have spent a delightful hour." Must he go on and confess that he had developed no particular dexterity in dealing with the younger members of the opposite sex?

"No, you don't care for them one bit," she insisted. She tried to look rebuking, reproachful; yet some shade of expression conveyed to him a hint that her protest was by no means sincere: if he really didn't, it was no loss—it was even a possible gain.

"It's you who don't care for me," he returned. "I'm *vieux jeu*."

"Nonsense," she rejoined. "If you have a slight past, that only makes you the more atmospheric. Be sure you come again soon, and put in a little more work on the foreground."

Cope, on his way eastward, in the early evening, passed, near the trolley tracks, the Greek lunch-counter, without a thought; he was continuing his letter to "Dear Arthur":

"I think," he wrote, with his mind's finger, "that you might as well come down. I miss you—even more than I thought I should. The term is young, and you can enter for Spanish, or Psychology, or something. There's nothing for you up there. The bishop can spare you. Your father will be reasonable. We can easily arrange some suitable quarters . . ."

And we await a reply from "Dear Arthur"—the fifth and last of our little group. But no; there are two or three others—as you have just seen.

# 4

## *Cope Is Considered*

A FEW DAYS after the mathematical tea, Basil Randolph was taking a sedate walk among the exotic elms and the indigenous oaks of the campus; he was on his way to the office of the University registrar. He felt interested in Bertram Cope and meant to consult the authorities. That is to say, he intended to consult the written and printed data provided by the authorities,—not to make verbal inquiries of any of the college officials themselves. He was, after all, sufficiently in the academic tradition to prefer the consultation of records as against the employment of *viva voce* methods; and he saw no reason why his new interest should be widely communicated to other individuals. There was an annual register; there was an album of loose sheets kept up by the members of the faculty; and there was a card-catalogue, he remembered, in half a dozen little drawers. All this ought to remove any necessity of putting questions by word of mouth.

The young clerk behind the broad counter annoyed him by no offer of aid, but left him to browse for himself. First, the printed register. This was crowded with professors—full, head, associate, assistant; there were even two or three professors emeritus. And each department had its tale of instructors. But no mention of a Bertram Cope. Of course not; this volume, it occurred to him presently, represented the state of things during the previous scholastic year.

Next the card-catalogue. But this dealt with the students only—undergraduate, graduate, special. No Cope there.

Remained the loose-leaf faculty-index, in which the members of the professorial body told something about themselves in a great variety of handwriting: among other things, their full names and addresses, and their natures in so far as penmanship might reveal it. Ca; Ce; Cof; Collard, Th. J., who was an instructor in French and lived on Rosemary Place; Copperthwaite, Julian M., Cotton . . . No Cope. He looked again, and further. No slightest alphabetical misplacement.

"You are not finding what you want?" asked the clerk at last. The search was delaying other inquirers.

"Bertram Cope," said Randolph. "Instructor, I think."

"He has been slow. But his page will be in place by to-morrow. If you want his address . . ."

"Yes?"

"——I think I can give it to you." The youth retired behind a screen. "There," he said, returning with a bit of pencilling on a scrap of paper.

Randolph thanked him, folded up the paper, and put it in his pocket. A mere bit of ordinary clerkly writing; no character, no allure. Well, the actual chirography of the absentee would be made manifest before long. What was it like? Should he himself ever have a specimen of it in a letter or a note?

That evening, with his after-dinner cigarette, he strolled casually through Granville Avenue, the short street indicated by the address. It was a loosely-built neighborhood of frame dwellings, with yards and a moderate provision of trees and shrubs— a neighborhood of people who owned their houses but did not spend much money on them. Number 48 was a good deal like the others. "Decent enough, but commonplace," Randolph pronounced. "Yet what could I have been expecting?" he added; and his whimsical smile told him not to let himself become absurd.

There were lighted windows in the front and at the side. Which of these was Cope's, and what was the boy doing? Was he deep in black-letter, or was he selecting a necktie preliminary to some evening diversion outside? Or had he put out his light— several windows were dark—and already taken the train into town for some concert or theatre?

"Well," said Randolph to himself, with a last puff at his cigarette, "they're not likely to move out and leave him up in the air. I hope," he went on, "that he has more than a bedroom merely. But we know on what an incredibly small scale some of them live."

He threw away his cigarette and strolled on to his own quarters. These were but ten minutes away. In his neighborhood, too, people owned their homes and were unlikely to hurry you out on a month's notice. You could be sure of being able to stay on; and Randolph, in fact, had stayed on, with a suitable family, for three or four years.

He had a good part of one floor: a bedroom, a sitting room, with a liberal provision of bookshelves, and a kind of large closet which he had made into a "cabinet." There are all sorts of cabinets, but this was a cabinet for his "collection." His collection was not without some measure of local fame; if not strictly valuable, it was at least comprehensive. After all, he collected to please himself. He was a collector in Churchton and a stockbroker in the city itself. The satirical said that he was the most important collector in "the street," and the most important stockbroker in the suburbs. He was a member of a somewhat large firm, and not the most active one. His interest had been handed down, in a manner, from his father; and the less he participated the better his partners liked it. He had no one but himself, and a sister on the far side of the city, miles and miles away. His principal concern was to please himself, to indulge his nature and tastes, and to get, in a quiet way, "a good deal out of life." But nobody ever spoke of him as rich. His collection represented his own preferences, perseverance and individual predilections. Least of all had it been brought together to be "realized on" after his death.

"I may be something of a fool, in my own meek fashion," he acknowledged, "but I'm no such fool as that."

He had a few jades and lacquers—among the latter, the ordinary inkwells and sword-guards; a few snuff-boxes; some puppets in costume from Mexico and Italy; a few begrimed vellum-bound books in foreign languages (which he could not always read); and now and then a friend who was "breaking up" would give him a bit of Capo di Monte or an absurd enigmatic musical instrument from the East Indies. And he had a small department of Americana, dating from the days of the Civil War.

"Miscellaneous enough," pronounced Medora Phillips, on once viewing his cabinet, "but not altogether"—she proceeded charitably—"utter rubbish."

And it was felt by others too that, in the lack of any wide opportunity, he had done rather well. Churchton itself was no nest of antiquities; in 1840 it had consisted merely of a log tavern on the Green Bay road, and the first white child born within its limits had died but recently. Nor was the Big Town just across the "Indian Boundary" much older. It had "antique shops," true; but one's best chances were got through mousing among the small scattered troups of foreigners (variegated they were) who had lately been coming in pell-mell, bringing their household knick-knacks with them. There was a Ghetto, there was a Little Italy, there were bits of Bulgaria, Bohemia, Armenia, if one had tired of dubious Louis Quinze and Empire. In an atmosphere of general newness a thing did not need to be very old to be an antique.

The least old of all things in Randolph's world were the students who flooded Churchton. There were two or three thousand of them, and hundreds of new ones came with every September. Sometimes he felt prompted to "collect" them, as contrasts to his older curios. They were fully as interesting, in their way, as brasswork and leatherwork, those products of peasant natures and peasant hands. But these youths ran past one's eye, ran through one's fingers. They were not static, not even stable. They were restless birds of passage who fidgeted through their years, and even through the days of which the years were made: intent on their own affairs and their own companions; thankless for small favors and kind attentions—even unconscious of them; soaking up goodwill and friendly offices in a fashion too damnably taken-for-granted. . . . You gave them an evening among your books, with discreet things to drink, to smoke, to play at, or you offered them a good dinner at some good hotel; and you never saw them after. . . . They said "Yes, sir," or "Yep;" but whether they pained you by being too respectful or rasped you by being too rowdyish, it all came to the same: they had little use for you; they readily forgot and quickly dropped you.

"I wonder whether instructors are a shade better," queried Basil Randolph. "Or when do sense and gratitude and savoir-faire begin?"

A few days later he had returned to the loose-leaf faculty. Cope's page was now in place, with full particulars in his own hand: his interest was "English Literature," it appeared. "H'm! nothing very special in that," commented Randolph. But Cope's penmanship attracted him. It was open and easy: "He never gave *his* instructor any trouble in reading his themes." Yet the hand was rather boyish. Was it formed or unformed? "I am no expert," confessed Randolph. He put Cope's writing on a middle ground and let it go at that.

He recalled the lighted windows and wondered near which

one of them the same hand filled note-books and corrected students' papers.

"Rather a dreary routine, I imagine, for a young fellow of his age. Still, he may like it, possibly."

He thought of his own early studies and of his own early self-sufficiencies. He felt disposed to find his earlier self in this young man—or at least an inclination to look for himself there.

The next afternoon he walked over to Medora Phillips. Medora's upper floor gave asylum to a half-brother of her husband's—an invalid who seldom saw the outside world and who depended for solace and entertainment on neighbors of his own age and interests. Randolph expected to contribute, during the week, about so many hours of talk or of reading. But he would have a few words with Medora before going up to Joe.

Medora, among her grilles and lambrequins, was only too willing to talk about young Cope.

"A charming fellow—in a way," she said judicially. "Frank, but a little too self-assured and self-centered. Exuberant, but possibly a bit cold. Yet—charming."

"Oh," thought Randolph, "one of the cool boys, and one of the self sufficing. Probably a bit of an ascetic at bottom, with good capacity for self-control and self-direction. Not at all an uninteresting type," he summed it up. "An ebullient Puritan?" he asked aloud.

"That's it," she declared, "—according to my sense of it."

"Yet hardly a New Englander, I suppose?"

"Not directly, anyhow. From down state—from Freeford, I think he said. I judge that there's quite a family of them."

"Quite a family of them," he repeated inwardly. A drawback indeed. Why could an interesting young organism so seldom be detached from its milieu and enjoyed in isolation? Prosy parents; tiresome, detrimental brothers . . . He wondered if she had any idea what they were all like. It might be just as well, however, not to know.

"And, judging from the family name, and from their taste at christenings, I should say there might be some slant toward England itself. A nomenclature not without distinction. 'Bertram'; rather nice, eh? And there is a sister who teaches in one of the schools, I understand; and her name is Rosalind, or Rosalys. Think of that! I gather that the father is in some business," she concluded.

"Well, well," thought Randolph; "more than one touch of gentility, of fine feeling." If the father was in "some business," most likely it was some one else's business.

"He sings," said Medora, further. "Entertained us the other Sunday afternoon. Cool and correct, but pleasant. No warmth, no passion. No special interest in any of my poor girls. I didn't feel that he was drawing any of them too near the danger-line."

"Mighty gratifying, that. Where does one learn to sing without provoking danger?"

"In a church choir, of course. He sang last year in the cathedral at Winnebago."

"Oh, in Wisconsin. And what took us to Winnebago, I wonder?"

"We were teaching in a college there."

"I see."

The talk languished. Basil Randolph had learned most that he wanted to know, and had learned it without asking too many direct questions. He began to pick at the fussy fringe on the arm of his chair and to cast an empty eye on the other fussy things that filled the room. The two had exhausted long ago all the old subjects, and he did not care to show an eagerness—still less, a continuing eagerness—for this new one: much could be picked up by indirection, even by waiting.

Medora felt him as distrait. "Do you want to go up and see Joe for a little while before you leave us?"

"I believe I will. Not that I've brought anything to read."

"I doubt if he cares to be read to this time—Carolyn gave him the headlines this forenoon. He's a bit restless; I think he'd rather talk. If you have nothing more to say to me, perhaps you can find something to say to him."

"Oh, come! I'm sure we've had a good enough little chat. Aren't you a bit restless yourself?"

"Well, run along. I've heard his chair rolling about up there for the last half hour."

# 5

## *Cope Is Considered Further*

RANDOLPH took the stairs to the second floor, and presently his footfalls were heard on the bare treads that led from the second to the third. At the top landing he paused and looked in through the open door of the picture-gallery.

Over the varnished oak floor of this roomy apartment a middle-aged man who wore a green shade above his eyes was propelling himself in a wheeled chair. Thus did Joseph Foster cover the space where the younger and more fortunate sometimes danced, and thus did he move among works of art which, even on the brightest days, he could barely see.

He knew the step. "Brought anything?" he asked.

He depended on Randolph for the latest brief doings in current fiction; and usually in the background—and often long in abeyance—was something in the way of memoirs or biography, many-volumed, which could fill the empty hours either through retrospect or anticipation.

"Only myself," replied the other, stepping in. Foster dextrously manœuvred his chair toward the entrance and reached out his hand.

"Well, yourself is enough. It's good to have a man about the place once in a while. Once in a while, I said. It gets tiresome, hearing all those girls slithering and chattering through the halls." He put his bony hands back on the rims of his wheels. "Where have you been all this time?"

"Oh, you know I come when I can." Randolph ran his eye over the walls of the big empty room. The pictures were all in place—landscapes, figure-pieces, what not; everything as familiar as the form of words he had just employed to meet an oft-repeated query implying indifference and neglect.

"How is it outside? I haven't been down on the street for a month."

"Oh, things are bright and pleasant enough." Through the wide window there appeared, half a mile away, the square twin towers of the University library, reminiscent of Oxford and Ely. Round them lesser towers and gables, scholastic in their gray stone, rose above the trees of the campus. Beyond all these a level line of watery blue ran for miles and provided an eventless horizon. A bright and pleasant enough sight indeed, but nothing for Joe Foster.

"Well, let me by," he said, "and we'll get along to my own

room." The resonant bigness of the "gallery" was far removed from the intimate and the sociable.

To the side of this bare place, with its canvases which had become rather démodé—or at least had long ceased to interest—lay two bed-chambers: Foster's own, and one adjoining, which was classed as a spare room. It was sometimes given over to visiting luminaries of lesser magnitudes. Real celebrities—those of national or international fame—were entertained in a sumptuous suite on the floor below. Casual young bachelors, who sometimes happened along, were lodged above and were expected to adjust themselves, as regarded the bathroom, to the use and wont of the occupant adjoining.

Foster's own room was a cramped omnium gatherum, cluttered with the paraphernalia of daily living. It was somewhat disordered and untidy—the chamber of a man who could never see clearly how things were, or be completely sure just what he was about.

"There's Pepys up there," he said, pointing to his bookshelf, as he worked out of his chair and tried to dispose himself comfortably on a couch. "I hope we're going to get along a little farther with him, some time."

"As to that, I *have* been getting along a little farther;—I've been to the Library, looking somewhat ahead in the completer edition. I find that 'Will,' who flung his cloak over his shoulder, 'like a ruffian,' and got his ears boxed for it, was no mere temporary serving-man, but lived on with Pepys for years and became the most intimate and trusted of his friends. And 'Gosnell,' who lasted three days, you remember, as Mrs. Pepys' maid, turns up a year or two later as an actress at 'the Duke's house.' and 'Deb,' that other maid whose name we have noted farther along—well, there's a deal more about her than exactly tends to edification. . . ."

"Good. I hope we shall have some more of it pretty soon."

"To-day?"

"Not exactly to-day. I've got some other things to think about."

"Such as?"

"Well, I expect you're going to be invited here to dinner pretty soon?"

"So? I've been invited here to dinner before this."

"But another day has come. A new light has risen. I haven't seen it, but I've heard it. I've heard it sing."

"A light singing? Aren't you getting mixed?"

"Oh, I don't know. There was Viollet-le-Duc and the rose-window of Notre Dame. They took him there as a child for a choral service, and he thought it was the rose itself that sang. And there was Petrarch, and the young Milton—both talking about 'melodious tears'—and something of the same sort in 'The Blessed Damosel.' And ——"

"A psychological catch for which there ought to be a name. Perhaps there *is* a name."

"Well, as I say, the light rose, shone, and sang. I didn't see it—I never see anybody. But his voice came up here quite distinctly. It seemed good to have a man in the house. Those everlasting girls—I hope he wasn't bothering to sing for *them*."

"He probably was. How did it go?"

"Very well indeed."

"What kind of voice?"

"Oh, baritone, I suppose you'd call it."

"And he sang sentimental rubbish?"

"Not at all. Really good things."

"With passion?"

"Well, hardly. With cool correctness. An icicle on Diana's temple—that would be my guess."

"An icicle? No wonder the young ladies don't quite fancy him."

"I understand he took them all in a lump—so far as he took them at all. Treated them all exactly alike; Hortense was quite scornful when she brought up my lunch-tray. Of course that's no way for a man to do."

"On the contrary. For certain purposes it might be a very good way."

"'On the contrary,' if you like; since frost may perform the effects of fire. Medora herself is beginning to see him as a tall, white candle, burning in some niche or at some shrine. Sir Galahad—or something of that sort."

Randolph grimaced at this.

"Oh, misery! I hope she hasn't mentioned her impression to *him*! Imagine whether a man would enjoy being told a thing like that. I hope, I'm sure, that no 'Belle Dame sans Merci' will get on his tracks!"

"If he goes in too much for 'palely loitering' he may be snatched."

"Poor fellow! They'd better leave him to his studies and his students. He has his own way to make, I presume, and will need all his energies to get ahead. For, as some one has said, 'There are no tea-houses on the road to Parnassus.' Neither do tea-fights boost a man toward the Porch or Academe."

"He's going in for teas?"

"I won't say that. But it was at a tea that I met him. A trigonometry tea at little Mrs. Ryder's."

"You've seen him then. You have the advantage of me. What's he like?"

"Oh, he has points in his favor. He has looks; a trim figure, even if spare; well-squared shoulders; and manners with a breezy, original tang. The kind of young fellow that people are likely enough to like."

"What kind of manners did he have for you?"

"Well, there you rather get me. He called me 'sir,' with a touch of deference; yet somehow I felt as if I were standing too close to an electric fan."

"Yes, even when they indulge a show of deference, they contrive to blow our gray hairs about our wrinkled temples."

"Don't talk about gray hairs. You have none; and mine are not always seen at first glance."

"Medora begins to tax me with a few. Don't you see any?"

"Not one. I concentrate on my own. Tush, you're only forty-seven."

"Or fifty-seven, or sixty-seven, or seventy-seven . . ." Foster adjusted his green shade and attempted an easier disposition of his twisted limbs on the couch. "Well, forty-seven, as you suggest,—as you insist. How old is this young fellow?"

"Twenty-four or twenty-five."

"Well, they can make us seem either younger or older. That rests with ourselves. It's all in how we take them, I expect."

"Better take them so as to make ourselves younger."

"Then the other question."

"How they take us?"

"Yes. We're lucky, in this day and generation, if they take us at all."

"You may be right," assented Randolph ruefully. "Yet there are gleams of hope. The more thoughtful among them have a kind of condescending pity to bestow———"

"And the thoughtless?"

"They can find uses for us. One of the faculty was telling me how he tried to give two or three of his juniors an outing at his cottage over in Michigan. Everything he gave they took for granted. And if anything was lacking they took—exceptions. Monopolized the boats; ignored the dinner-hour . . . Sometimes I think that even the thoughtless are thoughtful in their own way and use us, if we happen to have lands and substance, purely as practical conveniences. I've been almost glad to think that I possess none myself."

"Don't stay here and talk like that. This is one of my blue days."

"I wish I had brought a novelette. Sure you don't want to hear a little more about the Countess of Castlemaine and the rascalities of the Navy Office?"

"No; some other time, when I feel a bit more robust. It isn't every day that the mind can digest such a period with comfort."

"Are we two old fogies beginning to wear on each other?"

"I hope not. But when you go down, stop for Medora a minute and see if she hasn't got something to say."

Medora—when he finally got down stairs—had.

She laid some knitting on the drawing-room table and came out into the hall.

"No reading this afternoon, I judge. What I heard, or seemed to hear, was a broken flow of talk."

"No reading. Restless."

"So I was afraid. I'd rather have one good steady voice purring along for him, and then I know he's all right. Carolyn has been too busy lately. What seems to have unsettled him?"

"Oh, I don't know. Young life, possibly."

"Well, I've asked and asked the girls not to be quite so gay and chattery in the upper halls."

"You can't keep girls quiet."

"I don't want to—not everywhere and at all times."

"I have an idea that a given number of girls make more noise in a house than the same number of young fellows. I know that they do in boarding-houses and rooming-houses, and I believe it's so as between sororities and fraternities. Put a noise-gauge in the main hall of the Alpha-Alpha house and another in the main hall of the Beta-Beta house, and the girls would run the score above the boys every time. If ever I build a sorority house, it will be for the Delta-Iota-Nus, and a statue of the great goddess DIN herself shall stand just within the entrance."

"You discourage me. I was going to give a dinner."

"Go ahead. A few remarks from me won't stop the course of your hospitality. Neither would a few orations. Neither would a few deliberative bodies assembled for a month of sessions, with every member talking from nine till six."

"You think I indulge in too many?"

"Too many what? Festivals? Puns?"

Medora paused, a bit puzzled.

"Puns? Why, I never, never——— Oh, I see!"

"Too many dinners? No. Who could?"

"This one was to be a young people's dinner. I was going to invite you."

"Thanks. Thanks. Thanks."

"Still, if you think my girls are noisy . . ."

"I was speaking of girls in numbers."

"Well, Bertram Cope didn't find them so."

"Why not?"

"Why not, indeed? They collected in a silent little group behind my sofa . . ."

"Puzzled? Awed?"

"Fudge! Well, save Thursday."

"Is he coming?"

"I trust so."

"Then they do need a constabulary to keep them quiet?"

"Oh, hush!"

"How many are you expecting to have? You know I don't enjoy large parties."

"Could you stand ten?"

"I think so."

"Thursday, then," she said, with a definitive hand on the knob of the door.

Randolph went down the front walk with a slight stir of elation—a feeling that had come to be an infrequent visitor enough. He hoped that the company would be not only predominantly youthful, but exclusively so—aside from the hostess and himself. And even she often had her young days and her young spots. It would doubtless be clamorous; yet clamor, understood and prepared for, might be met with composure.

# 6

## *Cope Dines—and Tells About It*

CO P E pushed away the last of the themes and put the cork back in the red-ink bottle. Here was a witless girl who seemed to think that Herrick and Cowper were contemporaries. The last sense to develop in the Western void was apparently the sense of chronology—unless, indeed, it were a sense for the shades of difference which served to distinguish between one age and another and provided the raw material that made chronology a matter of consequence at all.

"If there were only one more," muttered Cope, looking at the pile of sheets under the gas-globe, "I should probably learn that Chaucer derived from Beaumont and Fletcher."

He reached up and jerked the gas-jet to a different angle. The flame lit, through its nicked, pale-pink globe, a bedroom cramped in size and meagre in furnishings: a narrow bed, dressed to look like a lounge; two stiff-backed oak chairs, not lately varnished; a bookshelf overhead, with some dozen of the more indispensable aids to our tongue's literature. The table at which he sat was one of plain deal, covered with some Oriental-seeming fabric which showed here and there inkspots that ante-dated his own pen. He threw up this covering as it fell over the front edge of the table, pulled out a drawer, laid a sheet of paper in the bettered light, and uncorked a black-ink bottle.

"Dear Arthur," he began.

He looked across to the other chair, with its broken spindles and obfuscated varnish. With things as he wanted them, his cor-respondent would be sitting there and letter-writing would be unnecessary.

"Dear Arthur," he repeated aloud, and set himself to a gen-eral sketch of the new land and the "lay" of it.

"Three-quarters of them are of course girls," he presently found himself writing, "which is the common proportion al-most everywhere, I presume, except in engineering and den-tistry. However, there are four or five men. I've been pretty careful, and they still treat me with respect. I'm afraid my course is regarded as a 'snap.' Everybody, it seems, can grasp En-glish literature (and produce it). And almost anybody, I begin to fear, can teach it. Judging, that is, from the pay. I'm afraid the good folks at Freeford will find themselves pinched for another year still."

He glanced across toward the pile of corrected themes. He felt that not everybody was "called," as a matter of course, to write English, and he stubbornly nourished the belief that toiling over others' imperfections was more of a job than boards of trustees always realized.

"Of course," he presently resumed, "things are rather changed from what they were before. I find more in the way of social opportunities and greater interest shown by the middle-aged. It is no disadvantage to cultivate people who have their own homes; the lunch-rooms round the fountain-square are numerous enough, but not so good as they might be. And I don't know but that an instructor may lose caste by eating among a miscellany of undergraduates. Anyhow, it's no plan to pursue for long."

He sat for a moment, lost in thought over recent social experiences.

"One very good house has lately been opened to me," he continued. "I dined there last Thursday evening. It's really quite a mansion—a great many large rooms: picture-gallery, ball-room, and all that; and the dinner itself was very handsomely done. You know my theory,—a theory rather forced upon me, in truth, by circumstances,—that the best way to enjoy a good meal is to have had a string of poor ones. Well, since coming back, and with no permanent arrangements made, I have had plenty of chance for getting into position to appreciate the really first-class. There was a color-scheme in pale pink—ribbons of that color, pink icing on the cakes, and so on. The same thing could be done, and done charmingly, in light green—with pistache ice-cream. Of course the candle-shades were pink too."

His eye wandered toward a small triangular closet, made off from the room by a flimsy and faded calico-print curtain.

"I had my dress-suit cleaned and pressed, but the lapels of the coat came out rather shiny, and I thought it better to hire one for the occasion. There was no trouble about a fit——I have standardized shoulders, as you know.

"Of course I miss you all the time, and I assuredly missed you just here. If it is really true, as you write, that you are holding your summer gains and weigh twelve pounds more than you did at the end of June, and if you are thinking of getting a new suit, please bear in mind that my own won't last much longer. I have the chance, now, to go out a good deal and to meet influential, worth-while people. In the circumstances I ask you not to bant. One rather spare man in a pair of men is enough.

"My hostess, a Mrs. Phillips, I met at a tea during my first week. This tea was given by a lady in the mathematical department, and she and her husband were at the dinner. They are people in the early or middle thirties, I judge, and were probably put in as a connecting link between the two sections of the party. Mrs. Phillips herself is a rich widow of forty-odd—forty-five or six, possibly,—though I am not the very best judge in such matters: no need to tell you that, on such a point, my eye and my general sense are none too acute. The only other middle-aged (or elderly) person present was a Mr. Randolph, who is perhaps fifty, or a little beyond, yet who appears to have his younger moments. There were some girls, and there were two young men in business in the city—neighbors and not connected with the University at all. 'For which relief,' etc.,—

since it *is* a bit benumbing to move in academic circles exclusively;—I should hate to feel that a really professorial manner was stealing over me. Well, everybody was lively and gay, except at first Ryder (he's the math. man); but even he limbered up finally. Mrs. Phillips herself has a great deal of action and vivacity—seemed hardly more than thirty. Well, I could be pretty gay too with a lot of money behind me; and I think that, for another year or so, I can contrive to be gay without it. But after that . . .

"I wish you had been there instead of Ryder. If you are really going to be twenty-seven in November—as I figure it—you might yourself have served as a connecting link between youth and age. No, no; I take it back; I didn't mean it. I wouldn't have you seem older for anything, and you know it.

"There were three girls. They all live in the house itself, forming a little court: Mrs. P. seems to need young life and young attentions. So not one of them had to be taken home— there's usually *that* to do, you know. Not that it would have mattered much, as the distances would have been short and the night was clear starlight. But they could all stay where they were, and I walked home in quite different company."

Cope threw back his Oriental table-cover once more and drew out a few additional sheets of paper.

"One of them is an artist. She paints portraits, and possibly other things. Oh, I was going to say there is an art-gallery at the top of the house. Her husband—I mean Mrs. Phillips'—was a painter and collector himself; and after dinner we went up there, and a curious man came in, propelling a wheeled chair— a sort of death's-head at the feast. . . . But don't let me get too far away from the matter in hand. She is dark and a bit tonguey—the artist-girl; and I believe she would be sarcastic and witty if she weren't held down pretty well. I think she's a niece: the relationship leaves her free, as I suppose she feels, to express herself. If you like the type you may have it; but wit in a woman, or even humor, always makes me uncomfortable. The feminine idea of either is a little different from ours.

"Another girl is a musician. She plays the violin—quite tolerably. Yes, yes, I recall your views about violin-playing: it's either good or bad—nothing between. I'll say this, then: she played some simple and unpretentious things and did them very deftly. Simple, unpretentious: oddest thing in the world, for she is a recent graduate of our school of music and began this fall as an instructor. Wouldn't you have expected to find her demanding a chance to perform a sonata at the least, or pining miserably for a concerto with full orchestra? Well, this young lady I put down as a plain boarder—you can't maintain a big house on memories and a collection of paintings. She's a nice child, and I dare say makes as good a boarder as any nice child could.

"The third girl—if you want to hear any more about them—seems to be a secretary. Think of having the run of a house where a social secretary is required! I'm sure she sends out the invitations and keeps the engagement-book. Besides all that, she writes poetry—she is the minstrel of the court. She does verses about her châtelaine—is quite the mistress of self-respecting adulation. *She* would know the difference between Herrick and Cowper!" . . .

Cope pulled out his watch. Then he resumed.

"It's half past ten, but I think I'll run on for a few moments longer. If I don't finish, I can wind up to-morrow.—Mr. Randolph sat opposite me. He looked at me a lot and gave attention to whatever I said—whether said to him, or to my neighbors right and left, or to the whole table. I didn't feel him especially clever, but easy and pleasant—and friendly. Also a little shy—even after we had gone up to the ball-room. I'm afraid that made me more talkative than ever; you know how shyness in another man makes me all the more confident and rackety. Be sure that voice of mine rang out! But not in song. There was a piano up stairs, of course, and that led to a little dancing. Different people took turns in playing. I danced—once—with each of the three girls, and twice with my hostess; then I let Ryder and the two young business-men do the rest. Randolph danced once with Mrs. Phillips, and that ended it for him. My own dancing, as you know, is nothing to brag of: I think the young ladies were quite satisfied with the little I did. I'm sure *I* was. You also know my views on round dances. Why dancing should be done exclusively by couples arranged strictly on the basis of contrasted sexes . . . ! I think of the good old days of the Renaissance in Italy, when women, if they wanted to dance, just got up and danced—alone, or, if they didn't want to dance alone, danced together. I like to see soldiers or sailors dance in pairs, as a straightforward outlet for superfluous physical energy. Also, peasants in a ring—about a Maypole or something. Also, I very much like square dances and reels. There were enough that night for a quadrille, with somebody for the piano and even somebody to 'call off,'—but whoever sees a quadrille in these days? However, I mustn't burn any more gas on this topic.

"I sat out several dances between Mrs. Phillips and Mr. Randolph. He thought he had done enough for her, and she thought I had done enough for them all. And one of the young business-men did enough for that springy, still-young Mrs. Ryder. Once, indeed, Mrs. Phillips asked me if I wouldn't like to try a third dance with her (she goes at it with a good deal of old-time vivacity and vim); but I told her she must know by this time that I was something of a bungler. 'I wouldn't quite say that,' she returned, smiling; but we continued to sit there side by side on a sort of bench built against the wall, and she seemed as well pleased to have it that way as the other. She did, however, speak about a little singing. I told her that she must have found me something of a bungler there, too, and reminded her that I couldn't play the accompaniments of my best songs at all. Arthur, my dear boy, I depend on *you* for that, and you must come down here and do it.

"No singing, then. But Mrs. Phillips was not quite satisfied. Wouldn't I recite something? Heavens! Well, of course I know lots of poems—*c'est mon métier*. I repeated one. Then other volunteers were called upon—it was entertaining with a vengeance! The young ladies had to chip in also—though they, of course, were prepared to. And one of the young business-men did some clever juggling; and Mrs. Ryder sang a little French ballade; and Mr. Randolph—poor man!—was suddenly routed out of his placidity, and responded as well as he could with one or two little stories, not very pointed and not very well told. But I judge he makes no great claim to being a *raconteur*—he was merely paying an unexpected tax as gracefully as he could.

"Well, as I was saying, the man in the wheeled chair came in. Of course he hadn't been down to dinner—I think I saw a tray for him carried along the hall. As he was working his way through the door, I suppose I must have been talking and laughing at my loudest; and that big, bare room, done in hard wood, made me seem noisier still. He sort of stopped and twitched, and appeared to shrink back in his chair: I presume my tones went straight through the poor twisted invalid's head. He must have fancied me (from the racket I was making) as a sort of free-and-easy Hercules (which is not quite the case), if not as the whole football squad rolled into one. Whether he really saw me, then or thereafter, I don't know; he wore a sort of green shade over his eyes. Of course I met him in due form. I tried not to give his poor hand too much of a wring (another of my bad habits); but he took all I gave and even seemed to hang on for a little more. He sat quietly to one side for a while, and I tried not to act the bull of Bashan again. Anyhow, he didn't start a second time. Presently he pulled out rather unceremoniously: the two young business-men had begun a sort of burlesque fandango, and their feet were pretty noisy on the bare floor. He started off after looking toward the piano and then toward me; and Mrs. Phillips glanced about as if to hint that any display of surprise or of indulgence would be misplaced. Poor chap!—well, I'm glad he didn't see me dancing.

"We broke up about eleven, and Mr. Randolph suggested that, as we lived in the same general direction, we might walk homeward together. Great heaven! it's eleven—and five after—now! Enough, in all conscience, for to-night. You shall have the rest to-morrow."

# 7

## Cope Under Scrutiny

AN EVENING or two later Cope again corked his red ink and uncorked his black.

"As I have said, Mr. Randolph and I walked home together. He stopped for a moment in front of his place. Another large, handsome house. He told me he had the use of his quarters as long as his landlord's lease ran, and asked me to come round some time and see how he was fixed. Then he said suddenly that the evening was fine and the night young and that he would walk on with me to *my* quarters, if I didn't mind. Of course I didn't— he seemed so friendly and pleasant; but I let him learn for himself that I was far from being lodged in any architectural monument. Well, we went on for the necessary ten minutes, and he didn't seem at all put out by the mediocre aspect of the house where I have put up. He sort of took it all for granted—as if he knew about it already. In fact, on the way from his place to mine, I no more led him (as I sense it now) than he led me. He hesitated at no corner or crossing. 'I am an old Churchtonian,' he said incidentally—as if he knew everything and everybody. He also mentioned, just as incidentally, that he had a brother-in-law on our board of trustees. Of course I promised to go round and see him. I presume that I shall drop in on him some time or other. Come down here, and you shall have one more house of call.

"He stopped for a moment in front of my diggings, taking my hand to say goodnight and taking his own time in dropping it. Enough is enough. 'You have the small change needed for paying your way through society,' he said, with a sort of smile. 'I must cultivate a few little arts myself,' he went on; 'they seem necessary in some houses. But I'm glad, after all, that I didn't remember to-night that a tribute was likely to be levied; it would have taken away my appetite and have made the whole evening a misery in advance. As things went, I had, on the whole, a pleasant time. Only, I understood that you sang; and I was rather hoping to hear you.' 'I do best with my regular accompanist,' I returned—meaning you, of course. I hope you don't mind being degraded to that level. 'And your regular accompanist is not——not——?' 'Is miles away," I replied. 'A hundred and fifty of them,' I might have added, if I had chosen to be specific. Now, if he had wanted to hear me, why hadn't he asked? He would have needed only to second Mrs. Phillips herself; and there he was, just on the other side of me. In consequence of his reticence I was driven—or drove myself—to blank verse. And that other man, the one in the chair; he may have had his expectations too. Arthur, Arthur, try to grasp the situation! You must come down here, and you must bring your hands with you. Tell the bishop and the precentor that you are needed elsewhere. They will let you off. Of course I know that a village choir needs every tenor it can get—and keep; but come. If they insist, leave your voice behind; but do bring your hands and your reading eye. Don't let me go along making my new circle think I'm an utter dub. Tell your father plainly that he can never in the world make a wholesale-hardware-man out of you. Force him to listen to reason. What is one year spent in finding out just what you are fit for? Come along; I miss you like the devil; nobody does my things as sympathetically as you do. Give up your old anthems and your old tinware and tenpennies and come along. I can bolt from this hole at a week's notice, and we can go into quarters together: a real bed instead of an upholstered shelf, and a closet big enough for two wardrobes (if mine really deserves the name). We could get our own breakfast, and you could take a course in something or other till you found out just what the Big Town could do for you. In any event you would be bearing me company, and your company is what I need. So pack up and appear."

The delay in the posting of this appeal soon brought from Winnebago a letter outside the usual course of correspondence. It was on a fresh sheet and under a new date-line that Cope continued. After a page of generalities and of attention to particular points in the letter from Wisconsin, Cope took up his own line of thought.

"I had meant, of course, to look in on him within a few

days,—no great hurry about it. But on Sunday evening he wrote and asked if he might not call round on me instead. My name is not in the telephone-book; neither, as I found out, was his. So I used up a sheet of paper, an envelope, and a stamp—just such as I am now using on you—to tell him that he might indeed. I put in the 'indeed' for cordiality, hoping he wouldn't think I had slighted *his* invitation. On Monday evening he came round—I must have reached him by the late afternoon delivery. Need I say that he had to take this poor place as he found it? But there was no sign of the once-over—no tendency to inventory or appraise. He sat down beside me on the couch just as if he had no notion that it was a bed (and a rather rocky one, at that), and talked about my row of books, and about music and plays, and about his own collection of curios—all in a quiet, contained way, yet intent on me if not on my outfit. Well, it's pleasant to be considered for what you are rather than for what you have (or for what few poor sticks your landlady may have); and I rather liked his being here. Certainly he was a change from my students, who sometimes seem to exclude better timber.

"Needless to say, he repeated his invitation, and last evening I shunted Middle English (in which I have a lot to catch up) and walked round to him. Very adequately and handsomely lodged. Really good bachelor quarters (I hadn't known for certain whether he was married or not). A stockbroker of a sort, I hear,—but not enough to hurt, I should guess. He has a library and a sitting-room. Like me, he sleeps three-quarters, but he doesn't have to sit on his bed in the daytime. And he has a bathrobe of just the sort I shall have, when I can afford it. He has got together a lot of knick-knacks and curios, but takes them lightly.

'Sorry I've only one big arm-chair,' he said, handing me his cigarette-case and settling me down in comfort; 'but I entertain very seldom. I should like to be hospitable,' he went on; '—I really think it's in me; but that's pretty much out of the question here. I have no chef, no dining-room of my own, no ball-room, certainly. . . . Perhaps, before very long, I shall have to make a change.'

"He asked me about Freeford, and I didn't realize until I was on my way back that he had assumed my home town just as he had assumed my lodging. Well, all right; I never resent a friendly interest. He sat in a less-easy chair and blew his smoke-rings and wondered if I had been a small-town boy. 'I'm one, too,' he said; '—at least Churchton, forty years—at least Churchton, thirty years ago, was not all it is to-day. It has always had its own special tone, of course; but in my young—in my younger days it was just a large country village. Fewer of us went into town to make money, or to spend it.' . . .

"And then he asked me to go into town, one evening soon, and help him spend some. He suggested it rather shyly; *à tâtons*, I will say—though French is not my business. He offered a dinner at a restaurant, and the theatre afterwards. Did I accept? Indeed I did. Think, Arthur! after all the movies and restaurants round the elms and the fountain (tho' you don't know them yet)! I will say, too, that his cigarettes were rather better than my own. . . .

"I suppose he is fully fifty; but he has his young days, I can see. Certainly his age doesn't obtrude,—doesn't bother me at all, though he sometimes seems conscious of it himself. He wears eye-glasses part of the time,—for dignity, I presume. He had them on when I came in, but they disappeared almost at once, and I saw them no more.

"He asked me about my degree,—though I didn't remember having spoken of it. I couldn't but mention 'Shakespeare'—as the word goes; and you know that when I mention him, it always makes the other man mention Bacon. He did mention Bacon, and smiled. 'I've studied the cipher,' he said. 'All you need to make it go is a pair of texts—a long one and a short one—and two fonts of type, or their equivalent in penmanship. Two colors of ink, for example. You can put anything into anything. See here.' He reached up to a shelf and brought down a thin brown square note-book. 'Here's the alphabet,' he said; 'and here'— opening a little beyond—'is my use of it: one of my earliest exercises. I have put the first stanza of "Annabel Lee" into the second chapter of "Tom Jones."' He ignored the absent eye-glasses and picked out the red letters from the black with perfect ease. 'Simplest thing in the world,' he went on; 'anybody can do it. All it needs is time and patience and care. And if you happen to be waggishly or fraudulently inclined you can give yourself considerable entertainment—and can entertain or puzzle other people later. You don't really believe that "Bacon wrote Shakespeare"?'

"Of course I don't, Arthur,—as you very well know. I picked out the first line of 'Annabel Lee' by arranging the necessary groupings among the odd mixture of black and red letters he exhibited, and told him I didn't believe that Bacon wrote Shakespeare—nor that Shakespeare did either. 'Who did, then?' he naturally asked. I told him that I would grant, at the start and for a few seasons, a group of young noblemen and young gentlemen; but that some one of them (supposing there to have been more than that one) soon distanced all the rest and presently became the edifice before which the manager from Stratford was only the façade. He—this 'someone'—was a noble and a man of wide reach both in his natural endowments and in his acquired culture. But he couldn't dip openly into the London cesspool; he had his own quality to safeguard against the contamination of a new and none too highly-regarded trade. 'I don't care for your shillings,' he said to Shaxper, 'nor for the printed plays afterward; but I do value your front and your footing and the services they can render me on my way to self-expression.' He was an earl, or something such, with a country-seat in Warwick, or on the borders of Gloucestershire; 'and if I only had a year and the money to make a journey among the manor-houses of mid-England,' I said, 'and to dig for a while in their muniment-rooms . . .' Well, you get the idea, all right enough.

"He came across and sat on the arm of the big easy-chair. 'If you went over there and discovered all that, the English scholars would never forgive you.' As of course they wouldn't: look at the recent Shaxper discoveries by Americans in London! 'And wouldn't that be a rather sensational thesis,' he went on, 'from a staid candidate for an M.A., or a Ph.D., or a Litt.D., or whatever it is you're after?' It would, of a verity; and why shouldn't it be? 'Don't go over there,' he ended with a smile, as he dropped his hand on my shoulder; 'your friends would rather have you here.' 'Never fear!' I returned; 'I can't possibly manage it. I shall just do something on "The Disjunctive Conjunctions in 'Paradise Lost,'" and let it go at that!'

"He got up to reach for the ash-receiver. 'They tell me,' he

said, 'that a degree isn't much in itself—just an *étape* on the journey to a better professional standing.' 'Yes,' said I, '—and to better professional rewards. It means so many more hundreds of
dollars a year in pay.' But you know all about that, too.

"I'm glad your dramatic club is getting forward so well with
the rehearsals for its first drive of the season; glad too that, this
time at least, they have given you a good part. Tell me all about
it before the big stars in town begin to dim your people in my
eyes—and in your own; and don't let them cast you for the next
performance in January. You will be here by then.

"Yours,
"B.L.C."

# 8

## *Cope Undertakes an Excursion*

TWO OR THREE days later, Randolph met Medora Phillips in front of the bank. This was a neat and solemn little edifice opposite the elms and the fountain; it was neighbored by dry-goods stores, the offices of renting agencies, and the restaurants where the unfraternized undergraduates took their daily chances. Through its door passed tradesmen's clerks with deposits, and young housewives with babies in perambulators, and students with their small financial problems, and members of the faculty about to cash large or small checks. Mrs. Phillips had come across from the dry-goods store to pick up her monthly sheaf of vouchers,—it was the third of October.

"Don't you want to come in for a minute?" she asked Randolph. "Then you can walk on with me to the stationer's. Carolyn tells me that our last batch of invitations reduced us to nothing. How did *your* dinner go?"

Randolph followed her into the cool marble interior. "Oh, in town, you mean? Quite well, I think. I'm sure my young man took a good honest appetite with him!"

"I know. We don't do half enough for these poor boys."

"Yes, he rose to the food. But not to the drinks. I took him, after all, to my club. I innocently suggested cocktails; but, no. He declined—in a deft but straightforward way. Country principles. Small-town morals. He made me feel like a—well, like a corrupter of youth."

"You didn't mind, though,—of course you didn't. You liked it. Wasn't it noble! Wasn't it charming! So glad that *we* had nothing but Apollinaris and birch beer! Still, it would have been a pleasure to hear him refuse."

The receiving-teller gave her her vouchers. She put them in her handbag and somehow got round a perambulator, and the two went out on the street.

"And how did your 'show' go?" she continued. "That's about as much as we can call the drama in these days."

"That, possibly, didn't go quite so well. I took him to a 'comedy,'—as they nowadays call their mixture of farce and funniment. 'Comedy'!—I wish Meredith could have seen it! Well, he laughed a little, here and there,—obligingly, I might say. But there was no 'chew' in the thing for him,—nothing to fill his intellectual maw. He's a serious youngster, after all,—exuberant as he seems. I felt him appraising me as a gay old irresponsible. . . ."

"'Old'—you are not to use that word. Come, don't say that he—that he venerated you!"

"Oh, not at all. During the six hours we were together—train, club, theatre, and train again—he never once called me 'sir'; he never once employed our clumsy, repellent Anglo-Saxon mode of address, 'mister'; in fact, he never employed any mode of address at all. He got round it quite cleverly,—on system, as I soon began to perceive; and not for a moment did he forget that the system was in operation. He used, straight through, a sort of generalized manner—I might have been anywhere between twenty and sixty-five."

They were now in front of the stationer's show-window, and there were few people in the quiet thoroughfare to jostle them.

Medora smiled.

"How clever; how charming!" she said. "Leaving you altogether free to pick your own age. I hope you didn't go beyond thirty-five. You must have been quite charming in your early thirties."

"That's kind of you, I'm sure; but I don't believe that I was ever 'charming' at *any* age. I think you've used that word once too often. I was a quiet, studious lad, with nice notions, but possibly something of a prig. I was less 'charming' than correct. The young ladies had the greatest confidence in me,—not one of them was ever 'afraid'."

"Why, how horrid! How utterly unsatisfactory! Nor their mothers?"

"No. And I'm still single, as you're advised. And I'm not sure that the young gentlemen cared much more for me. If I had had a little more 'gimp' and *verve*, I might have equalled the particular young gentleman of whom we have been discoursing. But . . ."

His obviously artificial style of speech concealed, as she guessed, some real feeling.

"Oh, if you insist on disparaging yourself . . . !"

"I was quite as coolly correct as I apprehend him to be; and if I could only have contrived to compass the charming, as well, who knows what——?"

"You don't like my word. Is there a better, a more suitable?"

"No. You have the *mot juste*."

He threw a finger through the wide pane of glass. "Is that the sort of thing you are after? Those boxes of pale gray are rather good."

"I never buy from the show-window. Come in, and help me choose."

"I love to shop," he said, in a mock ecstasy. "With others," he added. "I like to follow money in—and to contribute taste and experience."

Over the stationer's counter she said:

"Save Sunday. We are going out to the sand-hills."

"Thank you. Very well. Most glad to."

"And you are to bring him."

"Him?"

"Bertram Cope."

"Why, I've given him six hours within two or three days. And now you're asking me to give him sixteen."

"Sixteen—or more. But you're not giving them to him. You're giving them to all of us. You're giving them to me. The day is likely to be fine and settled, and I'd recommend your catching the 8:30 train. I shall have my full load in the car. And more, if I have to take along Helga. Try to reach us by one, or a quarter past."

Mrs. Phillips had lately taken on a house among the sand dunes beyond the state line. This singular region had recently acquired so wide a reputation for utter neglect and desolation that—despite its distance from town, whether in miles or in hours—no one could quite afford to ignore it. Picnics, pageants, encampments and excursions all united in proclaiming its remoteness, its silence, its vacuity. Along the rim of ragged slopes which put a term to the hundreds of miles of water that spread from the north, people tramped, bathed, canoed, motored and week-ended. Within a few seasons Duneland had acquired as great a reputation for "prahlerische Dunkelheit"—for ostentatious obscurity—as ever was enjoyed even by Schiller's Wallenstein. "Lovers of Nature" and "Friends of the Landscape" moved through its distant and inaccessible purlieus in squads and cohorts. Everybody had to spend there at least one Sunday in the summer season. There were enthusiasts whose interest ran from March to November. There were fanatics who insisted on trips thitherward in January. And there were one or two superfanatics—ranking ahead even of the fishermen and the sanddiggers—who clung to that weird and changing region the whole year through.

Medora Phillips' house was several miles beyond the worst of the hurly-burly. There were no tents in sight, even in August. Nor was the honk of the motor-horn heard even during the most tumultuous Sundays. The spot was harder to reach than most others along the twenty miles of nicked and ragged brim which helped enclose the wide blue area of the Big Water, but was better worth while when you got there. Her little tract lay beyond the more prosaic reaches that were furnished chiefly in the light green of deciduous trees; it was part of a long stretch thickly set for miles with the dark and sombre green of pines. Our nature-lover had taken, the year before, a neglected and dilapidated old farmhouse and had made it into what her friends and habitués liked to call a bungalow. The house had been put up—in the rustic spirit which ignores all considerations of landscape and outlook—behind a well-treed dune which allowed but the merest glimpse of the lake; however, a walk of six or eight minutes led down to the beach, and in the late afternoon the sun came with grand effect across the gilded water and through the tall pine-trunks which bordered the zig-zag path. Medora had added a sleeping-porch, a dining-porch and a lean-to for the car; and she entertained there through the summer lavishly, even if intermittently and casually.

"No place in the world like it!" she would declare enthusiastically to the yet inexperienced and therefore the still unconverted. "The spring arrives weeks ahead of our spring in town, and the fall lingers on for weeks after. Come to our shore, where the fauna and flora of the whole country meet in one. All the wild birds pass in their migrations; and the flowers!" Then she would expatiate on the trailing arbutus in April, and the vast sheets of pale blue lupines in early June, and the yellow, sunlike blossoms of the prickly-pear in July, and the red glories of painter's-brush and bittersweet and sumach in September. "No wonder," she would say, "that they have to distribute handbills on the excursion-trains asking people to leave the flowers alone!"

"How shocking!" Cope had cried, with his resonant laugh, when this phase of the situation was brought to his attention. "Are the automobile people any better?"

Randolph had told him of some of the other drawbacks involved in the excursion. "It's a long way to go, even when you pass up the trolley and make a single big bolt by train. And it leads through an industrial region that is mighty unprepossessing—little beauty until almost the end. And even when you get there, it may all seem a slight and simple affair for the time and trouble taken—unless you really like Nature. And lastly," he said, with a sidelong glance at Cope, "you may find yourself, as the day wears on, getting a little too much of my company."

"Oh, I hope that doesn't mean," returned Cope, with another ingenuous unchaining of his native resonance, "that you are afraid of getting a little too much of mine! I'm fond of novelty, and nobody can frighten me."

"If that's the case, let's get away as early in the day as we can. Breakfasts, of course, are late in every household on Sunday. So let's meet at the Maroon-and-Purple Tavern at seven-thirty, and make a flying start at eight."

Sunday morning came clear and calm and warm to the town,—a belated September day, or possibly an early intimation of Indian summer,—and it promised to be even more delightful in the favored region toward which our friends were journeying. After they had cleared many miles of foundries and railroad crossings, and had paralleled for a last half-hour a distant succession of sandhills, wooded or glistening white, they were set down at a small group of farmhouses, with a varied walk of five miles before them. Half a mile through a shaded country lane; another half-mile along a path that led across low, damp ground through thickets of hazel and brier; a third half-mile over a light soil, increasingly sandy, beneath oaks and lindens and pines which cloaked the outlines of the slopes ahead; and finally a great mound of pure sand that slanted up into a blue sky and made its own horizon.

"We've taken things easy," said Randolph, who had been that way before, "and I hope we have enough breath left for our job. There it lies, right in front of us."

"No favor asked here," declared Cope. He gave a sly, sidewise glance, as if to ask how the other might stand as to leg-muscles and wind.

"Up we go," said Randolph.

# 9

## *Cope on the Edge of Things*

THE ADVENTURER in Duneland hardly knows, as he works his way through one of the infrequent "blow-outs," whether to thank Nature for her aid or to tax her with her cruelty. She offers few other means of reaching the water save for these nicks in the edges of the great cup; yet it is possible enough to view her as a careless and reckless handmaiden busily devastating the cosmical china-closet. The "blow-out" is a tragedy, and the cause of further tragedy. The north winds, in the impetus gathered through a long, unimpeded flight over three hundred miles of water, ceaselessly try and test the sandy bulwarks for a slightest opening. The flaw once found, the work of devastation and desolation begins; and, once begun, it continues without cessation. Every hurricane cuts a wider and deeper gash, fills the air with clouds of loose sand, and gives sinister addition to the white shifting heaps and fields that steal slowly yet unrelentingly over the green hinterland of forest which lies below the southern slopes. Trees yet to die stand in passive bands at their feet; the stark, black trunks of trees long dead rise here and there in spots where the sand-glacier has done its work of ruin and passed on.

After some moments of scrambling and panting our two travelers gained the divide. Below them sloped a great amphitheatre of sand, falling in irregular gradations; and at the foot of all lay the lake, calmly azure, with its horizon, whether near or far— for it was almost impossible to say—mystically vague. On either hand rose other hills of sand, set with sparse pines and covered, in patches, with growths of wild grape, the fruit half ripened. Within the amphitheatre, at various levels, rose grimly a few stumps and shreds of cedars long dead and long indifferent to the future ravages of the enemy. The whole scene was, to-day, plausibly gentle and inert. It was indeed a bridal of earth and sky, with the self-contained approval of the blue deep and no counter-assertion from any demon wind.

"So far, so good," said Randolph, taking off his hat, wiping his forehead, and breathing just a little harder than he liked. "The rest of our course is plain: down those slopes, and then a couple of miles along the shore. Easy walking, that; a mere promenade on a boulevard."

Cope stood on the height, and tossed his bare head like a tireless young colt. The sun fell bright on his mane of yellow hair. He took in a deep breath. "It's good!" he declared. "It's great! And the water looks better yet. Shall we make it in a rush?"

He began to plunge down the long, broken sand-slope. Each step was worth ten. Randolph followed—with judgment. He would not seem young enough to be a competitor, nor yet old enough to be a drag. On the shore he wiped and panted a little more—but not to the point of embarrassment, and still less to the point of mortification. After all, he was keeping up pretty well.

At the bottom Cope, with his shoes full of sand, turned round and looked up the slope down which his companion was coming. He waved his arms. "It's almost as fine from here!" he cried.

The beach, once gained, was in sight both ways for miles. Not a human habitation was visible, nor a human being. Two or three gulls flew a little out from shore, and the tracks of a sand-piper led from the wet shingle to the first fringe of sandgrass higher up.

"Where are the crowds?" asked Cope, with a sonorous shout.

"Miles behind," replied Randolph. "We haven't come this long distance to meet them after all. Besides," he continued, looking at his watch, "this is not the time of day for them. At twelve-fifteen people are not strolling or tramping; they're thinking of their dinner. We have a full hour or more for making less than two easy miles before we reach *ours*."

"No need to hurry, then."

The beach, at its edge, was firm, and they strolled on for half a mile and cooled off as they went. The air was mild; the noon-day sun was warm; both of them had taken off their coats.

They sat down under a clump of basswoods, the only trees beyond the foot of the sand-slope, and looked at the water.

"It's like a big, useless bathtub," observed Randolph.

"Not so much useless as unused."

"Yes, I suppose the season *is* as good as over,—though this end of the lake stays warm longer than most other parts."

"It isn't so much the warmth of the water," remarked Cope sententiously. "It's more the warmth of the air."

"Well, the air seems warm enough. After all, the air and the sun are about the best part of a swim. Do you want to go in?"

Cope rose, walked to the edge of the water, and put in a finger or two. "Well, it might be warmer; but, as I say . . ."

"We could try a ten-minute dip. That would get us to our dinner in good time and in good trim."

"All right. Let's, then."

"Only, you'll have to do most of the swimming," said Randolph. "My few small feats are all accomplished pretty close to shore."

"Never mind. Company's the thing. A fellow finds it rather slow, going in alone."

Cope whisked off his clothes with incredible rapidity and piled them—or flung them—under the basswoods: the suddenly resuscitated technique of the small-town lad who could take avail of any pond or any quiet stretch of river on the spur of the moment. He waded in quickly up to his waist, and then took an intrepid header. His lithe young legs and arms threw themselves about hither and yon. After a moment or two he got on his feet and made his way back across a yard of fine shingle to the sand itself. He was sputtering and gasping, and the long yellow hair, which usually lay in a flat clean sweep from forehead to occiput, now sprawled in a grotesque pattern round his temples.

"B-r-r! It *is* cold, sure enough. But jump in. The air will be all right. I'll be back with you in a moment."

Randolph advanced to the edge, and felt in turn. It *was* cold. But he meant to manage it here, just as he had managed with the sand-slopes.

Two heads bobbed on the water where but one had bobbed before. Ceremonially, at least, the rite was complete.

"It's never so cold the second time," declared Cope encouragingly. "One dip doesn't make a swim, any more than one swallow——"

He flashed his soles in the sunlight and was once again immersed, gulping, in a maelstrom of his own making.

"Twice, to oblige you," said Randolph. "But no more. I'll leave the rest to the sun and the air."

Cope, out again, ran up and down the sands for a hundred feet or so. "I know something better than this," he declared presently. He threw himself down and rolled himself in the abundance of fine, dry, clean sand.

"An arenaceous ulster—speaking etymologically," he said. He came back to the clump of basswoods near which Randolph was sitting on a short length of drift wood, with his back to the sun, and sat down beside him.

"You're welcome to it," said Randolph, laughing; "but how are you going to get it off? By another dip? Certainly not by the slow process of time. We have some moments to spare, but hardly enough for that. Meanwhile . . ."

He picked up a handful of sand and applied it to a bare shoulder-blade which somehow had failed to get its share of protection.

"Thanks," said Cope: "the right thing done for Polynices. Yes, I shall take one final dip and dry myself on my handkerchief."

"I shall dry by the other process, and so shall be able to spare you mine."

"How much time have we yet?"

Randolph reached for his trousers, as they hung on a lower branch of one of the basswoods. "Oh, a good three-quarters of an hour."

"That's time enough, and to spare. I wonder whom we're going to meet."

"There's a 'usual crowd': the three young ladies, commonly; one or two young men who understand how to tinker the oil-stove—which usually needs it—and how to prime the pump. They once asked me to do these things; but I've discovered that younger men enjoy it more than I do, so I let them do it. Besides these, a number of miscellaneous people, perhaps, who come out by trolley or in their own cars."

"The young ladies always come?" asked Cope, brushing the sand from his chest.

"Usually. Together. The Graces. Otherwise, what becomes of the Group?"

"Well, I hope there'll be enough fellows to look after the stove and the pump—and them. I'm not much good at that last."

"No?"

"There's a knack about it—a technique—that I don't seem to possess. Nor do I seem greatly prompted to learn it."

"Of course, there is no more reason for assuming that every man will make a good lover than that every woman will make a good mother or a good housekeeper."

"Or that every adult male will make a good citizen, desiring the general welfare and bestirring himself to contribute his own share to it. I don't feel that I'm an especially creditable one."

"So it runs. We ground our general life on theories, and then the facts come up and slap us in the face." Randolph rose and relieved the basswood of the first garments. "Are you about ready for that final dip?"

Cope made his last plunge and returned red and shivering to use the two handkerchiefs.

"Well, we have thirty minutes," said Randolph, as they resumed their march. On the one hand the ragged line of dunes with their draping, dense or slight, of pines, lindens and oaks; on the other the unruffled expanse of blue, spreading toward a horizon even less determinate than before.

"No, I'm not at all apt," said Cope, returning to his theme; "not even for self-defense. I suppose I'm pretty sure to get caught some time or other."

"Each woman according to her powers and gifts. Varying degrees of desire, of determination, of dexterity. To be just, I might add a fourth d—devotion."

"You've run the gauntlet," said Cope. "You seem to have come through all right."

"Well," Randolph returned deprecatingly, "I can't really claim ever to have enlisted any woman's best endeavors."

"I hope I shall have the same good luck. Of your four *d's*, it's the dexterity that gives me the most dread."

"Yes, the appeal (not always honest) to chivalry,—though devotion is sometimes a close second. You're manœuvred into a position where you're made to think you 'must.' I've known chaps to marry on that basis. . . . It's weary waiting until Madame dies and Madonna steps into her place."

"Meanwhile, safety in numbers."

"Yes, even though you're in the very midst of wishing or of wondering—or of a careful concern to cloak either."

"Don't dwell on it! You fill me with apprehensions."

Randolph put up his arm and pointed. A roof through a notch between two sandhills beyond a long range of them, was seen, set high and half hidden by the spreading limbs of pines. "There it is," he said.

"So close, already?" Such, indeed, it appeared.

"Not so close as it seems. We may just as well step lively."

Cope, with an abundance of free action, was treading along on the very edge of things, careless of the rough shingle and indifferent to the probability of wet feet, and swinging his hat as he went. In some such spirit, perhaps, advanced young Stoutheart to the ogre's castle. He even began to foot it a little faster.

"Well, I can keep up with you yet," thought Randolph. Aloud, he said: "You've done very well with your hair. Quite an inspiration to have carried a comb."

Cope grimaced.

"I trust I'm free to comb myself on Sunday. There are plenty of others to do it for me through the week."

# 10

## *Cope at His House Party*

"You look as fit as two fiddles," said Medora Phillips, at the top of her sandhill.

"We are," declared Randolph. "Have the rest of the orchestra arrived?"

"Most of us are here, and the rest will arrive presently. Listen. I think I hear a honk somewhere back in the woods."

The big room of the house, made by knocking two small rooms together, seemed fairly full already, and other guests were on the back porch. The Graces were there, putting the finishing-touches to the table—Helga had not come, after all, but had gone instead, with her young man, to spend a few sunny afternoon hours among the films. And one of the young business-men present at Mrs. Phillips' dinner was present here; he seemed to know how to handle the oil-stove and the pump (with the coöperation of the chauffeur), and how to aid the three handmaidens in putting on the knives, forks, plates and napkins that Helga had decided to ignore. The people in the distant motor-car became less distant; soon they stopped in a clearing at the foot of the hill, and before long they appeared at the top with a small hamper of provisions.

"Oh, why didn't you ask *us* to bring something!" cried Cope. Randolph shrugged his shoulders: he saw himself lugging a basket of eatables through five miles of sand and thicket.

"You've brought yourself," declared Mrs. Phillips genially. "That's enough."

There was room for the whole dozen on the dining-porch. The favored few in one corner of it could glimpse the blue plane of the lake, or at least catch the horizon; the rest could look over the treetops toward the changing colors of the wide marshes inland. And when the feast was over, the chauffeur took his refreshment off to one side, and then amiably lent a hand with the dishes.

"Let me help wipe," cried Cope impulsively.

"There are plenty of hands to help," returned his hostess. She seemed to be putting him on a higher plane and saving him for better things.

One of the better things was a stroll over her tumultuous domain: the five miles he had already covered were not enough.

"I'll stay where I am," declared Randolph, who had taken this regulation jaunt before. He followed Cope to the hook from which he was taking down his hat. "Admire everything," he counselled in a whisper.

"Eh?"

"Adjust yourself to our dominant mood without delay or reluctance. Praise promptly and fully everything that is ours."

The party consisted of four or five of the younger people and two or three of the older. Most of them had taken the walk before; Cope, as a novice, became the especial care of Mrs. Phillips herself. The way led sandily along the crest of a wooded amphitheatre, with less stress on the prospect waterward than might have been expected. Cope was not allowed, indeed, to overlook the vague horizon where, through the pine groves, the blue of sky and of sea blended into one; but, under Medora Phillips' guidance, his eyes were mostly turned inland.

"People think," she said, "that 'the Dunes' means nothing beyond a regular row of sandhills following the edge of the water; yet half the interest and three-quarters of the variety are to be found in behind them. See my wide marsh, off to the southeast, with those islands of tamarack here and there, and imagine how beautiful the shadows are toward sunset. Look at that thick wood at the foot of the slope: do you think it is flat? No, it's as humpy and hilly as anything ever traversed. Only this spring a fascinating murderer hid there for weeks, and last January we could hear the howls of timber-wolves driven down from Michigan by the cold. And see those tall dead pines rising above it all. I call them the Three Witches. You'll get them better just a few paces to the left. This way." She even placed her hand on his elbow to make sure that her tragic group should appear to highest advantage. Yes, he was an admirable young man, giving admirable attention; thrusting out his hat toward prospects of exceptional account and casting his frank blue eyes into her face between-times. Charmingly perfect teeth and a wonderful sweep of yellow hair. A highly civilized faun for her highly sylvan setting. Indifferent, perhaps, to her precious Trio; but there were other young fellows to look after *them*.

Cope praised loudly and readily. The region was unique and every view had its charm—every view save one. Beyond the woods and the hills and the distant marshes which spread behind all these, there rose on the bluish horizon a sole tall chimney, with its long black streak of smoke. Below it and about it spread a vast rectangular structure with watch-towers at its corners. The chimney bespoke light and heat and power furnished in quantities—power for many shops, manned by compulsory workers: a prison, in short.

"Why, what's that?" asked Cope tactlessly.

Medora Phillips withheld her eyes and sent out a guiding finger in the opposite direction. "Only see the red of those maples!" she said; "and that other red just to the left—the tree with the small, fine leaves all aflame. Do you know what it is?"

"I'm afraid not."

"It's a tupelo. And this shrub, right here?" She took between her fingers one large, bland indented leaf on a small tree close to the path.

Cope shook his head.

"Why, it's a sassafras. And this?"—she thrust her toe into a thick, lustrous bed of tiny leaves that hugged the ground. "No, again? That's kinnikinnick. Oh, my poor boy, you have everything to learn. Brought up in the country, too!"

"But, really," said Cope in defense, "Freeford isn't so small as *that*. And even in the country one may turn by preference to books. Try me on primroses and date-palms and pomegranates!"

Medora broke off a branch of sassafras and swished it to and fro as she walked. "See," she said; "three kinds of leaves on the same tree: one without lobes, one with a single lobe, and one with two."

"Isn't Nature wonderful," replied Cope easily.

Meanwhile the young ladies sauntered along—before or behind, as the case might be—in the company of the young business-man and that of another youth who had come out independently on the trolley. They appeared to be suitably accompanied and entertained. But shiftings and readjustments ensued, as they are sure to do with a walking-party. Cope presently found himself scuffling through the thin grass and the briery thickets alongside the young business-man. He was a clever, companionable chap, but he declared himself all too soon, even in this remote Arcadia, as utterly true to type. Cope was not long in feeling him as operating on the unconscious assumption— unconscious, and therefore all the more damnable—that the young man in business constituted, ipso facto, a kind of norm by which other young men in other fields of endeavor were to be gauged: the farther they deviated from the standard he automatically set up, the more lamentable their deficiencies. A few condescending inquiries as to the academic life, that strange aberration from the normality of the practical and profitable course which made the ordinary life of the day, and the separation came. "Enough of *him!*" muttered Cope to himself presently, and began to cast about for other company. Amy Leffingwell was strolling along alone: he caught a branch of haw from before her meditative face and proffered a general remark about the beauty of the day and the interest in the changing prospect.

Amy's pretty pink face brightened. "It *is* a lovely day," she said. "And the more of this lovely weather we have in October—and especially in November—the more trouble it makes."

"Surely you don't want rain or frost?"

"No; but it becomes harder to shut the house up for good and all. Last fall we opened and closed two or three times. We even tried coming out in December."

"In mackintoshes and rubber boots?"

"Almost. But the boots are better for February. At least, they would have been last February."

"It seems hard to imagine such a future for a place like this,—or such a past."

"Things can be pretty rough, I assure you. And the roads are not always as good as they are to-day." And when the pump froze, she went on, they had to depend upon the lake; and when the lake froze they had to fall back on melted snow and ice. And even when the lake didn't freeze, the blowing waters and the flying sands often heaped up big ridges that quite cut them off from the open sea. Then they had to prospect along those tawny hummocks for some small inlet that would yield a few buckets of frozen spray,—keeping on the right side of the deep fissures that held the threat of icebergs to be cast loose at any moment; "and sometimes," she added, in search of a little thrill, "we would get back toward shore to find deep openings with clear water dashing beneath—we had been walking on a mere snow-crust half the time."

"Most interesting," said Cope accommodatingly. He saw no winter shore.

"Yes, February was bad, but Mrs. Phillips wanted to make sure, toward the end of the winter, that the house hadn't blown away,—nor the contents; for we have housebreakers every so often. And Hortense wanted to make some 'color-notes.' I believe she's going to try for some more to-day."

"To-day is a good day—unless the October tints are too obvious."

"She says they are not subtle, but that she can use them."

Well, here he was, talking along handily enough. But he had no notion of talking for long about Hortense. He preferred returning to the weather.

"And what does such a day do for you?" he asked.

"Oh, I suppose it helps me in a general way. But *my* notes, of course, are on paper already."

Yes, he was walking alongside her and holding his own—thus far. She seemed a pretty enough, graceful enough little thing; not so tall by an inch or so as she appeared when seated behind that samovar. On that day she had been reasonably sprightly—toward others, even if not toward him. To-day she seemed meditative, rather; even elegiac—unless there was a possible sub-acid tang in her reference to Hortense's color-notes. Aside from that possibility, there was little indication of the "dexterity" which Randolph had asked him to beware.

"On paper already?" he repeated. "But not all of them? I

know you compose. You are not saying that you are about to give composition up?" A forced and awkward "slur," perhaps; but it served.

She gave a little sigh. "Pupils don't want *my* pieces," she said. "Scales; exercises . . ."

"I know," he returned. "Themes,—clearness, mass, unity . . . It's the same."

They looked at each other and smiled. "We ought not to think of such things to-day," she said.

Mrs. Phillips came along, shepherding her little flock for the return. "But before we *do* turn back," she adjured them, "just look at those two lovely spreading pines standing together alone on that far hill." The small group gazed obediently—though to many of them the prospect was a familiar one. Yes, there stood two pines, one just a little taller than the other, and just a little inclined across the other's top. "A girl out here in August called them Paolo and Francesca. Do you think," she asked Cope, "that those names are suitable?"

"Oh, I don't know," he replied, looking at the trees thoughtfully. "They seem rather—static; and Dante's lovers, if I recollect, had considerable drive. They were '*al vento*'—on the wind—weren't they? It might be less violent and more modern to call your trees Pelleas and Melisande, or——"

"That's it. That's the very thing!" said Medora Phillips heartily. "Pelleas and Melisande, of course. That girl had a very ordinary mind."

"I've felt plenty of wind on the dunes, more than once," interjected Hortense.

"Or Darby and Joan," Cope continued. "Not that I'm defending that poor creature, whoever she was. They seem to be a pretty staid, steady-going couple."

"Don't," said Medora. "Too many ideas are worse than too few. They confuse one."

And Amy Leffingwell, who had seemed willing to admire him, now looked at him with an air of plaintive protest.

"'Darby and Joan'!" muttered Hortense into a sumach bush. "You might as well call them Jack and Jill!"

"They're Pelleas and Melisande," declared Mrs. Phillips, in a tone of finality. "Thank you so much," she said, with a smile that reinstated Cope after a threatened lapse from favor.

# I I

## Cope Enlivens the Country

As THEY DREW near the house they heard the tones of a gramophone. This instrument rested flatly on a small table and took the place of a piano, which would have been a fearful thing to transport from town and back. It was jigging away merrily enough, with a quick, regular rhythm which suggested a dance-tune; and when the party re-entered the big room it was seen that a large corner of the center rug was still turned back. Impossible that anybody could have been dancing on the Sabbath; surely everybody understood that the evangelical principles of Churchton were projected on these occasions to the dunes. Besides, the only women left behind had been two in their forties;

the men in their company were even older. Medora Phillips looked at Randolph, but he was staring inexpressively at the opposite wall. She found herself wondering if there were times when the mere absence of the young served automatically to make the middle-aged more youthful.

"Well, we've had a most lovely walk," she declared. She crossed to the far corner of the room, contriving to turn down the rug as she went, and opened up a new reservoir of records. She laid them on the table rather emphatically, as if to say, "*These are suited to the day.*"

"I hope you're all rested up," she continued, and put one of the new records on the machine. The air was from a modern opera, true; but it was slow-going and had even been fitted out with "sacred" words. Everybody knew it, and presently everybody was humming it.

"It ought not to be hummed," she declared; "it ought to be sung. You can sing it, Mr. Cope?"

"Oh yes, indeed," replied Cope, readily enough. "I have the breath left, I think,—or I can very soon find it."

"Take a few minutes. I'll fill in with something else."

They listened to an inconclusive thing by a wobbling soprano, and then Mrs. Phillips put the other record back.

The accompaniment to the air was rather rich and dense, and the general tone-quality was somewhat blatant. But Cope stood up to it all, and had the inspiration to treat the new combination as a sort of half-joke. But he was relieved from the bother of accompanying himself; his resonance overlaid in some measure the cheap quality of the record's tone; he contrived to master a degree of momentum—to let himself go; and the general result was good,—much better than his attempt at that tea. Hortense and Carolyn looked at him with a new respect; and Amy, who had been willing to admire, now admired openly. Cope ended, gave a slight grimace, and sauntered away from the table and the instrument. He knew that he had done rather well.

"Bravo!" loudly cried one of the ladies, who felt that she was under suspicion of having taken a step or two in the dance. And, "Oh, my dear," said Mrs. Phillips to her, sotto voce, "isn't he utterly charming!"

Cope wiped his brow. The walk had made him warm, and the singing had made him warmer. One or two of the women were using chance pamphlets as fans (despite Mrs. Phillips' ill-concealed doubts), and everybody showed a willingness to keep in the draught from the open windows.

"Is it close here?" asked the hostess anxiously. "The day is almost like summer. If the water is anywhere nearly as warm as the air is . . . Let me see; it's a quarter to four. I have a closetful of bathing suits, all sizes and shapes and several colors, if anybody cares to go in."

"Don't!" cried Cope explosively.

She looked at him with interest. "Have you been trying it?"

"I have. On the way along the shore. I assure you, however warm the air may be, the bathing season is over."

"Well, I rather thought something had been happening to you. Mr. Randolph, is it as bad as he says?"

"I'll take his word," replied Randolph. "And I think all of us had better do the same."

"We might go down to the beach, anyway," she said. "Hortense wants to make her color-notes, and the color will be good from now on."

Several of the party threaded their way down over the sliding sandy path which led through the pines and junipers. Cope was willing to go with the others—on the present understanding. He objected to promiscuous bathing even more strongly than he objected to promiscuous dancing.

There were some new cumuli in the east, out above the water, and they began to take the late afternoon sun. Hortense cast about for just the right point of view, with Carolyn to help on "atmosphere" and two young men to be superserviceable over campstool, sketch-block and box of colors. She brought back a few dabs which may have served some future use;—at all events they served as items in a social record.

Cope and Amy, with some of the others, strolled off in the opposite direction. The water remained smooth, and some of the men idly skipped stones. One of them dipped in his hand. "Cold?" he exclaimed; "I should say!"

Amy looked admiringly at Cope, as one who had braved, beyond season, the chill of the great deep, and he tried to reward her with a "thought" or two. He had skipped stones himself between dips, and Randolph had made a reflection which he could now revise and employ.

"See!" he said, as a flat, waveworn piece of slate left the hand of the young business-man and careered over the water; "one, two, three—six, eight—ten, thirteen; and then down, down, after all,—down to the bottom. And so we end—every one of us. The great thing is to crowd in all the action we can before the final plunge comes—to go skipping and splashing as hard and long and fast and far as we may!"

A valuable thought, possibly, and elaborated beyond Randolph's sketchy and casual utterance; but Amy looked uncomfortable and chilled and glanced with little favor at a few other flat stones lying at her feet. "Please don't. Please change the subject," she seemed to ask.

She changed it herself. "You sang beautifully," she said, with some return of warmth—even with some approach to fervor.

"Oh, I can sing," he returned nonchalantly, "if I can only have my hands in my pockets, or waving in the air, or anywhere but on a keyboard."

"I wish you had let them persuade you to sing another." She was not only willing to admire, but desirous: conscientious amends, perhaps, for an earlier verdict. "One or two more skips, you know, after getting started."

"Oh, once was enough. A happy coincidence. The next might have been an unhappy one."

"You have never learned to accompany yourself?"

"As you've seen, I'm a rather poor hand at it; I've depended a good deal on others. Or, better, on another."

She looked at him earnestly. "Have you ever sung to an obbligato?"

"None of my songs, thus far, has called for one. An obbligato? Never so much honored. No, indeed. Why, to me it would seem almost like singing with an orchestra. Imagine a 'cello. Imagine a flute—still I'm not a soprano going mad. Or imagine a saxophone; that might be droll."

He gave out a sort of dragging bleat. She did not smile; perhaps she felt such an approach to waggery unworthy of him. Perhaps she was holding him up to the dignity of the natural scene, and to the importance of the occasion as she conceived it.

Cope had no desire to figure as a comique, and at once regained sobriety. "Of course," he admitted, "we are not at a *thé dansant* or a cabaret. Such things ought not to be thought of—here."

She turned her eyes on him again, with a new look of sympathy and understanding. Perhaps understanding between them had failed or lapsed but a moment before.

"How all of this shames the town!" she said.

"And us—if we misbehave," he added.

Mrs. Phillips came scurrying along, collecting her scattered guests, as before. "Tea!" she said. "Tea for one or two who must make an early start back to town. Also a sip and a bite for those who stay."

She moved along toward Hortense and her little group. Hortense's "color-notes" did not appear to amount to much. Hortense seemed to have been "fussed"—either by an excess of company and of help, or by some private source of discontent and disequilibrium.

"Come," Mrs. Phillips cried to her, "I need every Martha to lend a hand." Hortense rose, and one of her young men picked up her campstool.

"So glad you haven't got to go early," said Mrs. Phillips to Randolph and Cope. "In fact, you might stay all night. It will be warm, and there are cots and blankets for the porch."

"Thanks, indeed," said Cope. "But I have a class at eight-fifteen to-morrow morning, and they'll be waiting to hear about the English Novel in the Eighteenth Century, worse luck! Fielding and Richardson and——"

"Are you going to explain Pamela and Clarissa to them?" asked Hortense. She was abrupt and possibly a bit scornful.

Cope seemed to scent a challenge and accepted it. "I am. The women may figure on the covers, but the men play their own strong part through the pages."

"I seem to recall," contributed Mrs. Phillips, "that Sir Charles Grandison figured both ways."

"That prig!" said Hortense.

"Well, if you can't stay overnight," Mrs. Phillips proceeded, "at least stay a few hours for the moonlight. The moon will be almost full to-night, and the walk across the marshes to the trolley-line ought to be beautiful. Or Peter could run you across in eight or ten minutes."

She did not urge Randolph to remain in the absence of Cope, though Randolph's appearance at his office at ten in the morning would have surprised no one, and have embarrassed no one.

Tea was served before the big fireplace in which a small flame to heat the kettle was rising. Randolph set his empty cup on the shelf above.

"Notice," said Mrs. Phillips to him, "that poem of Carolyn's just behind your cup: 'Summer Day in Duneland'." It was a bit of verse in a narrow black frame, and the mat was embellished with pen-and-ink drawings of the dunes, to the effect of an etching. An etcher, in fact, a man famous in his field, had made them, Mrs. Phillips explained.

"And at the other end of the shelf," she advised him, "is a poem in free verse, done by a real journalist who was here in

June. See: 'Homage to Dunecrest'——written with a blue pencil on a bit of driftwood."

"Sorry *we* can't leave any souvenir behind," said Cope, who had stolen up and was looking at the "poem" over Randolph's shoulder. "But one must (first) be clever; and one must (second) know how to put his cleverness on record."

"I shall remember *your* record," she returned with emphasis. Cope smiled deprecatingly; but he felt sure that he had sung well.

The moonlight, when it came, was all that Medora Phillips had promised. There was another stroll on the beach, with Cope between Medora and Carolyn. Then he and Randolph took the causeway across the marsh, stopped the trolley by burning a newspaper on the track, and started on the long trip home.

As the car ran along jerkily from station to station, the earlier void of Duneland became peopled indeed. The extraordinarily mild day had drawn out hundreds—had given the moribund summer-excursion season a new lease of life. Every stoppage brought so many more young men in soiled khaki, with shape-less packs on their backs, and so many more wan maidens, no longer young, who were trying, in little bands, to capture from Nature the joys thus far denied by domestic life; and at one sta-tion a belated squad of the "Lovers of Landscape"—some forty or fifty in all—came flooding in with the day's spoils: masses of asters and goldenrod, with the roots as often as not; festoons of bittersweet, and sheaves of sumach and golden glow; and one ardent spirit staggered in under the weight of an immense brown paper bag stuffed with prickly pear. As the tight-packed company slid along, children drowsed or whimpered, short-tempered young men quarreled with the conductor, elderly folk sat in squeezed, plaintive resignation. . . . Soon the lights of foundry fires began to show on the sky; then people started dropping off in the streets of towns enlivened by the glitter of many saloons and an occasional loud glare from the front of a moving-picture theater. . . .

Through these many miles Randolph and Cope sat silent: there seemed to be a tacit agreement that they need no longer exert themselves to entertain each other. Cope reached home shortly before midnight. By next morning many of the doings of the previous day had quite passed from his mind. Yet a few firm impressions remained. He had had a good swim, if but a brief one, with a companion who had been willing, even if not bold; he had imposed an acceptable nomenclature upon a somewhat anonymous landscape; and, in circumstances slightly absurd, or at least unfavorable, he had done his voice and his method high credit in song. All else went for next to nothing.

# 12

## *Cope Amidst Cross-Purposes*

NEXT morning's mail brought Cope a letter from Arthur Lemoyne. The letter was short—at least when compared with Cope's own plentiful pennings; but it gave our young instructor a few points to think about while he was illuminating Clarissa Harlowe and making some careful comments on Joseph Andrews. Released toward noon, he read the letter over again; and he ran over it again during lunch. Lemoyne possessed a variety of gifts, but the gift of letter-writing, in an extended form, was not among them. He said all he had to say in four moderate pages.

"Yours received," he wrote. "Am glad the year has opened up

so interestingly for you. Of course I want to come down as soon as I can, *if* I can, and be with you."

Well, the "if," as the latter part of the letter indicated, was not likely to prove insurmountable. The assurance that he wanted to come was grateful, though superfluous: who had supposed for a moment that he didn't? Still, the thing, put down in plain black and white, had its look of comfort.

"Of course the business is not gaining much through my connection with it. I expect father begins to see *that*, pretty plainly. As for the cathedral choir and the dramatic club and all the rest, I am willing to throw them over—expecting that larger interests can be opened to me by you." . . .

Cope paused on these points. He had suggested that Lemoyne enroll as a student in some slight course or other, with the hope that his voice might lead to his wearing cap and gown at chapel services and that his dramatic experience might give him some rôle in the annual operetta. In either of these quarters a good tenor voice was usually to seek. And as for the business . . . Well, he had once overheard the elder Lemoyne's partner audibly wonder whether Arthur would ever learn how to ship a keg of nails out of their back door, even.

Cope pushed away his coffee-cup and asked the young Greek for a cut of pie.

"I sort of sounded father the other day, but he was pretty huffy. I'll try again, soon; but I doubt if I can manage to come down until after the holidays. You begin a new term, then, I suppose. The fact is, I took a week off in the middle of September, and father hasn't forgiven it. One of our fellows in the choir had just bought a little roadster, and he invited me for a trip to

Green Bay and beyond. We dipped along through Fish Creek, Ephraim, and so on. Good weather, good roads, good scenery, good hotels; and a pleasant time was had by all—or, rather, by both." . . .

Cope dwelt darkly on this passage. Arthur was flighty; Arthur was volatile; Arthur was even fickle, when the mood took him. Some arrangement that partook more of the hard-and-fast was needed. But there was comfort—of a kind—in the next passage.

"Though father, at best, will do very little, and though I have just now little enough of my own, there may be somebody or other among your faculty or trustees who could find me a niche in the college library or in the registrar's office. Or have all such posts been snapped up by Johnnys-on-the-spot? A small weekly stipend would rather help our *ménage,—hein?*"

This definite inquiry (which carried its own answer) seemed to drive one or two brass tacks with some definiteness. Cope himself was eking out his small salary with a small allowance from home; next year, with the thesis accomplished, better pay in some better place. A present partner and pal ought to be a prop rather than a drag: however welcome his company, he must bear his share.

"Look about a bit for quarters," Lemoyne went on, drawing toward his conclusion. "I presume room-rent is little more for two than for one. Possibly," he put down in an afterthought, "I might get a job in the city;" and then, "with warm regards," he came to a close as "Art."

Cope finished his lunch and walked out. If Arthur could do

one thing better than another, it was to make coffee; his product was assuredly better than the Greek's. The two had camped out more than once on the shores of Lake Winnebago, and Arthur had deftly managed the commissariat. They had had good times together and had needed no other company. How had it been on Green Bay—at Eagle Cliff and Apron Bluff and all the other places lately celebrated in lithographed "folders" and lately popularized by motorists? And who was the particular "fellow" who ran the roadster?

Late that afternoon Cope chanced upon Randolph among the fantastic basins and floral parterres of the court in front of the Botany building: Randolph had had a small matter for one of the deans. Together they sauntered over to the lake. From the edge of the bluff they walked out upon the concrete terrace above the general boiler-room and its dynamos. Alongside this, the vast tonnage of coal required for the coming winter was beginning to pile up. The weather was still mild and sunny and the lake was as valiantly blue as ever.

"It doesn't look like the same body of water, does it?" said Cope.

"It might be just as beautiful in its own way, here, as we found it yesterday, out there," returned Randolph. "I've asked my brother-in-law, I don't know how many times, why they can't do better by this unfortunate campus and bring it all up to a reasonable level of seemliness. But———"

"You have a relative among the———?"

"Yes, my sister's husband is one of the University trustees. But he lives miles from this spot and hardly ever sees it. Besides, his æsthetic endowments are not beyond those of the average university trustee. Sometimes they're as hard on Beauty as they are on Free Speech."

"I see they're hard on beauty; and I may live to find free speech mauled, too."

"Well, you're not in Sociology or Economics. Still, don't trifle with a long-established aesthetic idol either. Trustees—and department heads—are conservative."

"Oh, you mean about——?"

"About your immortal William. He wrote them. Don't try to rob him. Don't try to knock him off his pedestal."

"Oh, you're thinking about my thesis. What I said about Warwickshire was just a little flight of fancy, I guess,—a bit of doorstep travel. I'm likely enough to stay where I am."

"Well, how about the thesis, really?"

"I think I shall end by digging something out of Here and Now. 'Our Middle-West School of Fiction,'—what would you think of that?"

"H'm! If you can make it seem worth while . . ."

"Well, can't I?"

"Your work, from the very nature of it, must be critical. Now the critic, nine times out of ten, takes down a volume from its established shelf, dusts it off, ruffles the leaves a bit, and then puts it back where it was. The ruffling is sometimes very nice and interesting and often gives the ruffler a good position in the glorious company of earlier rufflers——"

"I shouldn't be satisfied with anything like that. Things have got to move. I want to take some recent, less-known men and put *them* on the shelves."

"Yet you don't want to waste work on material which time may show as of transient value, or of none."

"A fellow must chance it. Who gives quickly gives twice;—I suppose that applies to praise as well as to money. It irks me to find more praise bestowed on the praised-enough,—even on groups of secondary importance, sometimes just because they are remote (in England, perhaps), and so can be treated with an easy objectivity. To dig in your own day and your own community is harder, but I should feel it more rewarding."

"But aren't the English books really better? Haven't they more depth, substance and background?"

"Possibly,—according to the conventions they themselves have established—and according to the society they depict."

"Well, Academe hasn't nailed you yet!"

"No; and I hope it won't. I should like to write a whole book about our new men."

"But don't write a thesis and then expect to publish it with profit *as* a book. That's a common enough expectation—or temptation."

They turned away from the lake terrace and the imposing coal pile. Cope, Randolph saw, was in quite a glow; a generous interest had touched him, putting fresh light into his eyes and a new vigor into his step. He had displayed a charming enthusiasm, and a pure, disinterested one. Randolph, under a quiet exterior, was delighted. He liked the boy better than ever, and felt more than ever prompted to attach him to himself.

"How are you pleased with your present quarters?" he asked, as they returned through the Botany court. He thought of the narrow couch, the ink-spotted cover on the deal table, the few coats and shoes (they *couldn't* be many) behind that calico curtain.

"None too well," replied Cope. "I shall soon begin to look for another room. I rather expect to change about holiday time."

"I am thinking of making a change too," declared Randolph.

"Why, could you better yourself?" asked Cope, in a tone of surprise. "I never knew a bachelor to be better fixed."

"I need a little wider margin of room. I can afford it, and ought to have had it long ago. And I learn that the lease of the people I'm with expires in the spring. My collection is growing; and I ought to have another bedroom. Think of not being able to put a man up, on occasion! I shall take a small apartment on my own account, catch some Oriental who is studying frogs' legs or Occidental theology; and then—open house. In a moderate measure, of course."

"That listens good—as the young fellows say," replied Cope. "A not uncommon ideal, possibly; but I'm glad that some man, now and then, is able to realize it."

"I should hope to see you there," said Randolph intently.

"Thank you, indeed. Yes, while my time lasts. But my own lease is like your landlord's—short. Next year,—who knows where?"

"Why not here?"

"Oh!" Cope shrugged, as if conscious of the need of something better, and of presently deserving it. "Some big university in the East?" wondered Randolph to himself. Well, the transfer, if it came, was still a long way ahead.

As he walked home to dinner he entertained himself by imagining his new régime. There would be an alert, intelligent Jap, who, in some miraculous way, could "do for him" between his studies. There would be a cozy dining-room where three or four fellows could have a snug little dinner, with plenty of good talk during it and after it. There would be, finally, a convenient little spare room, wherein a young knight, escaped from some "Belle Dame sans Merci," might lean his sword against the wardrobe, prop his greaves along the baseboard, lay his steel gauntlets neatly on the top of the dresser, fold his hands over the turned-down sheet of a neat three-quarter-width brass bedstead, and with a satisfied sigh of utter well-being pass away into sleep. Such facilities, even if they scarcely equaled a chateau on the Ridge or a villa among the Dunes, might serve.

Cope, on his own way to dinner, indulged in parallel imaginings. He saw a larger room than his present, with more furniture and better; a bookcase instead of a shelf; a closet, and hot and cold water in some convenient alcove; a second table, with a percolator on it, at which Arthur, who was a light sleeper and willingly an early riser, might indulge his knack for coffee-making to the advantage of them both. And Arthur had the same blessed facility with toast.

Then his thoughts made an excursion toward Randolph. Here was a man who was in business in the city, and who was related, by marriage, to the board of trustees. How soon might one feel sufficiently well acquainted with him to ask his friendly offices in behalf of the new-comer,—the man who might reasonably be expected the first week in January?

# 13

## *Cope Dines Again—and Stays After*

MEDORA PHILLIPS' social activities ran through several social strata and her entertainments varied to correspond. Sometimes she contented herself with mere boy-and-girl affairs,
which were thrown together from material gathered within her
own household and from the humbler walks of undergraduate
life. Sometimes she entertained literary celebrities, and invited
the head professors and their wives to meet them. And two or
three times a season she gave real dinners to "society," sum-
moning to Ashburn avenue, from homes even more architectural than her own, the banking and wholesale families whose
incomes were derived from the city, but who pillared both the

university and the many houses of worship in Churchton itself. And sometimes, when she passed over the older generation of these families in favor of the younger, her courses were more "liberal" than Churchton's earlier standards quite approved.

On such formal occasions her three young ladies were dispensed with. They were encouraged to go to some sorority gathering or to some fudge-party. On the occasion now meditated she had another young person in mind. This was the granddaughter of one of the banking families; the girl might come along with her father and mother. She was not very pretty, not very entertaining; however, Mrs. Phillips needed one girl, and if she were not very attractive, none the worse. The one girl was for the one young man. The one young man was to be Bertram Cope. Our fond lady meant to have him and to show him off, sure that her choicest circle could not but find him as charming as she herself did. Most of us, at one time or another, have thrust forward our preferences in the same confident way.

Cope made less of an impression than his patroness had hoped for. Somehow his lithe youthfulness, his fine hair and teeth and eyes, the rich resonance of his voice counted for little—except, perhaps, with the granddaughter. The middle-aged people about him were used to young college men and indifferent to them. Cope himself felt that he was in a new environment, and a loftier one. Several of these were important people, with names familiar through the town and beyond. He employed a caution that almost became inexpressiveness. He also found Mrs. Phillips a shade more formal and stately than her wont. She herself, in her furtive survey of the board, was disappointed to find that he was not telling. "Perhaps it's that girl," she thought; "she may be even duller than I supposed." But never mind; all would be made right later. Some music had been arranged and there would be an accompanist who would help him do himself full justice.

"They'll enjoy him," she thought confidently.

She had provided an immensity of flowers. There was an excess of light, both from electric bulbs and from candles. And there was wine.

"I think I can have just one kind, for once," she had said to herself. "I know several houses where they have two,—Churchton or not,—and at least one where they sometimes have three. If this simple town thinks I can put grape-juice and Apollinaris before such people as these . . ." Besides, the interesting Cope might interestingly refuse!

As the many courses moved on, Cope smelt the flowers, which were too many, and some of them too odoriferous; he blinked at the lights and breathed the heavy thickening air; and he took—interestingly—a few sips of burgundy,—for he was now in Rome, and no longer a successful Protestant in some lesser town of the empire. He had had a hard, close day of it, busy indoors with themes and with general reading; and he recalled being glad that the dinner had begun with reasonable promptitude,—for he had bothered with no lunch beyond a glass of milk and a roll. To-night there had been everything,— even to an unnecessary entrée. He laid down a spoon on his plate, glad that the frozen pudding—of whatever sort—was disposed of. Too much of everything after too little. The people opposite were far away; their murmuring had become a mumbling, and he wished it was all over. The granddaughter at his elbow was less rewarding than ever, less justificatory of the effortful small-talk which he had put forth with more and more labor, and which he could scarcely put forth now at all. What was it he was meaning to do later? To sing? Absurd! Impossible! His head ached; he felt faint and dizzy . . .

"We will leave you gentlemen to your cigars," he heard a distant voice saying; and he was conscious for an instant that his hostess was looking down the table at him with a face of startled concern. . . .

"Don't try to lead him out," a deep voice said. "Lay him on the floor."

He felt himself lowered; some small rug was doubled and redoubled and placed under his head; a large, firm hand was laid to his wrist; and something—a napkin dipped in a glass of water and then folded?—was put to his forehead.

"His pulse will come up in a minute," he heard the same deep voice say. "If he had taken a step he would have fainted altogether."

"My poor, dear boy! Whatever in the world . . . !" Thus Medora Phillips.

"Better not be moved for a little," was the next pronouncement.

Cope lay there inert, but reasonably conscious of what was going on. His eyes gave him no aid, but his ears were open. He heard the alarmed voice of Medora Phillips directing the disconcerted maids, and the rustle and flutter of the garments of other daughters of Eve, who had found him interesting at last. They remarked appreciatively on his pallor; and one of them said, next day, before forgetting him altogether, that, with his handsome profile (she mentioned especially his nose and chin) and with his colorlessness, he looked for a moment like an ancient cameo.

He knew, now, that he was not going to faint, and that he was in better case than he seemed. In the circumstances he found nothing more original to say than: "I shall be all right in no time; just a touch of dizziness . . ." He was glad his dress-coat could stand inspection, and hoped nobody would notice that his shoes had been half-soled . . .

After a little while he was led away to a couch in the library. The deep-voiced doctor was on one side of him and Medora Phillips on the other. Soon he was left alone to recuperate in the dark,—alone, save for one or two brief, fluttery appearances by Mrs. Phillips herself, who allowed the coffee to be passed without any supervision on her own part.

On the second of these visitations he found voice to say:

"I'm so sorry for this—and so ashamed. I can't think how it could have happened."

He *was* ashamed, of course. He had broken up an entertainment pretty completely! Servants running about for him when they had enough to do for the company at large! All the smooth conventions of dinner-giving violently brushed the wrong way! He had fallen by the roadside, a young fellow who had rather prided himself on his health and vigor. Pitiful! He was glad to lie in the dark with his eyes shut tight, tight.

If he had been fifteen or twenty years older he might have taken it all rather more lightly. Basil Randolph, now—— But Randolph had not been invited, though his sister and her husband were of the company. Yet had it been Randolph, he would have smiled a wan smile and tried for a mild joke, conscious that he had made an original and picturesque contribution to the affair,—had broken the bland banality of routined dinner-giving and had provided woman with a mighty fine chance to "minister" and fuss: a thing she rather enjoyed doing, especially if a hapless, helpless man had been delivered into her hands as a subject.

But there was no such consolation for poor abashed Cope. He had disclosed himself, for some reason or other, a weakling; and he had weakened at a conspicuously wrong time and in a conspicuously mistaken place. He had hoped, over the cigars and coffee, to lay the foundation of an acquaintance with the brother-in-law who was a trustee,—to set up an identity in this influential person's mind as a possible help to the future of Arthur Lemoyne. But the man now in the dining-room, or the drawing-room, or wherever, might as well be in the next state.

There came a slight patter of rain on the bay-window near his head. He began to wonder how he was to get home.

Meanwhile, in the drawing-room, among the ladies, Mrs. Phillips was anxiously asking: "Was the room too warm? Could the wine have been too much for him?" And out in the dining-room itself, one man said, "Heaven knows just how they live," and another, "Or what they eat, or don't eat;" and a third, "Or just how hard these young beginners are driven."

"Ought he to go out to-night, Doctor?" asked Mrs. Phillips in a whisper, appearing in the dining-room door.

"He might better stay if he can," replied the authority, who happened to be at the nearer end of the table.

"Of course he can," she returned. Of course there was a room for him.

When the party finally reassembled in the drawing-room

Cope had disappeared. Mrs. Phillips could now enlarge on his attractiveness as a singer, and could safely assure them—what she herself believed—that they had lost a really charming experience. "If you could only have heard him that Sunday!" she concluded.

Cope had said, of course, "I can get home perfectly well," and, "It's a shame for me to be putting you out this way," and so on and on,—the things you yourself would have said in the circumstances; but he said them with no particular spirit, and was glad, as he walked uncertainly up stairs, that he had not far to go.

Mrs. Phillips indeed "had a room for him." She had rooms a-plenty. There was the chintz chamber on the third floor, where the Irish poet (who seemed not to expect very much for himself) had been put; and there was the larger, handsomer chamber on the second floor, where the Hindoo philosopher (who had loomed up big and important through a vague Oriental atmosphere) had been installed in state. It was a Louis Quinze room, and the bed had a kind of silken canopy and a great deal too much in the way of bolsters and lace coverings. It was thought that the Hindoo, judging from the report of the maid next morning, had been moved by some ascetic impulse to sleep not in the bed but on the floor beside it. This was the room now destined for Cope; surely one flight of stairs was enough. But there must be no further practice of asceticism,—least of all by a man who was really ill; so Mrs. Phillips, snatching a moment from her guests, herself saw the maid remove the lace pillow-shams and coverlet, and turn down the sheets, and set the thermos-bottle on the stand beside the reading lamp . . .

"Don't get up a moment earlier than you feel like doing," she said, at the door. "Breakfast——"

"To-morrow is one of my busy days," replied Cope wanly. "Goldsmith, Sheridan . . ."

"Well, we have other wage-workers in the house, you know. At seven-thirty, then, if you must."

"Seven-thirty, if you please. Thank you."

By the time Mrs. Phillips had returned to her guests, the first of the limousines was standing before the house; its wet top shone under an electric globe. Her own car, meanwhile, obdurately reposed in its garage. Presently a second limousine joined the first, and a third the second; and in another quarter of an hour her guests were well on their way to dispersal. She bade them all goodnight in the best of good humor.

"You've never before had quite such an evening as this, I'm sure!" she said, with great gaiety.

"Isn't it wonderful how she took it all!" said one lady to another, on the back seat of her car. "Anything like that would have thrown me off completely."

The other lady laughed amusedly. She often found our Medora "great fun."

Meanwhile, Cope, up stairs, was sinking deeper and deeper into his big, wide, overupholstered bed. And as his body sank, his spirit sank with it. He felt poor, unimportant, ill at ease. In especial, he felt greatly subordinated; he wished that he might have capitulated to a man. Then the mystery of handsome houses and of handsome furnishings came to harass him. Such things were everywhere: how were they got, how were they kept? Should he himself ever——? But no; nothing ahead for years, even in the most favorable of circumstances, save an assistant professorship, with its inconceivably modest emoluments . . .

And Medora Phillips, in the stir of getting her guests out of the house, had her first vision of him as sinking off to sleep. Somehow or other his fine, straight yellow hair retained its backward sweep with no impairment by reason of turnings and tossings; his clear profile continued to keep itself disengaged from any depression in the pillows; his slender hands were laid in quiet symmetry over the wide edge of the down-turned coverlet. A decorous, unperturbed young old-master . . . Van Eyck . . . Carpaccio . . .

Cope came down to breakfast a little pale, a little shame-faced; but he felt pretty well revived and he made up in excess of speech and action what he essentially lacked in spirit. Mrs. Phillips descended as early as the three girls,—earlier, in fact, than Hortense, who entered informally through the butler's pantry and apparently in full possession of last night's facts. Carolyn inquired civilly after his condition; Amy Leffingwell, with her blue eyes intent upon him, expressed concern and sympathy; Hortense, with her lips closely shut in a satirical smile, said nothing at all: a possible exhibition of self-control which gave her aunt some measure of solicitude. It was not always well when she talked, and it was not always well when she kept silent. Mrs. Phillips pressed the toast upon him and recommended the grape-fruit. He took both with satisfaction, and a second cup of coffee. With that he felt he could easily walk to his class-room; and the walk itself, in the fresh morning air, would brace him further for his hours of routine with his students.

"What a regular nuisance I've made of myself!" he said, on leaving the house.

"Oh, haven't you, just!" exclaimed Mrs. Phillips joyously.

"Your name as an entertainer will be all over town! I'm sure you gave some of those poky people a real touch of novelty!"

Amy Leffingwell was in the front hall at the same time, with her music-roll. They were going the same way, to substantially the same place, to meet about the same hour in the day's schedule. They went along the street together.

The morning air was brisk and cool after last night's shower. Like the trees under which they passed, it gave the first decided intimation of autumn. They set off at a lively pace toward the college towers and the lake.

Cope was soon sailing along with his head high, his trim square shoulders much in action, and his feet throwing themselves spiritedly here and there. Amy, who was not very tall, kept up as well as she could.

"This isn't too fast for you . . . ?" she asked presently.

"No; but it may be a little too fast for you. Excuse me; I've never learned to keep pace with a woman. But as for myself, I never felt better in my life. Every yard toward the good old lake"—the wind was coming down from the north in a great sweep—"makes me feel finer."

He slowed up appreciably.

"Oh, not for me!" she said in deprecation. "I like a brisk morning walk as well as anybody. Did you sing at all?" she asked.

"Not a note. They put the soft pedal on me. They 'muted' me," he amended, in deference to her own branch of the profession.

"We came in by the side door about half past nine. It was a dull meeting. I listened for you. Somebody was playing."

Cope gave a sly smile.

"It must have been the poor disappointed woman who was to have accompanied me. She had had a list of three or four of my things—to run them over in her own album, I suppose. Think just how disappointed she must have been to find that she had the whole field to herself!"

"Oh, musicians—even we poor, despised professionals—are not all like that. If it had been arranged for me to accompany you with an obbligato, I shouldn't have been pleased if opportunity had failed me."

"Your contribution would have been more important than hers. And your substitution for my failure would have given added interest."

The talk, having reached the zone of arid compliment, tended to languish. They had now reached Learning's side of the trolley-tracks, and rills in the great morning flood of the scholastic life were beginning to gather about them and to unite in a rolling stream which flowed toward the campus.

Two or three streets on, the pair separated, she to her work, he to his. For him the walk had been a nothing in particular—he would a little have preferred taking it alone. For her it had been—despite the low level of expressiveness reached on either side—a privilege which had been curtailed much too soon.

Meanwhile, back in the house, Hortense was detailing the events of the previous evening to Joe Foster; the general access of activity on the morning after had made it desirable that she help with his breakfast.

She went at it with a will.

"Why," she said, as Foster sat at his coffee, boiled egg and toast, "he keeled over like a baby."

"Hum!" said Foster darkly. It was as if a shaping ideal had dissipated. Or as if a trace of weakness in one seemingly so young and strong was not altogether unacceptable as a source of consolation.

However, Cope, at half past four that afternoon, was on the faculty tennis-courts, with a racquet in his hand. But one set was enough. "I seem to be a day ahead of my schedule," he said, pulling out and strolling along homeward.

# 14

## *Cope Makes an Evasion*

Two or three days later, Randolph put a book of essays in his pocket and went round to spend an hour with Joseph Foster. Foster sat in his wheeled chair in his own room. He was knitting. The past year or two had brought knitting-needles into countenance for men, and he saw no reason why he should not put a few hanks of yarn into shape useful for himself. He might not have full command of his limbs nor of his eyes, but he did have full command of his fingers. He had begun to knit socks for his own use; and even a muffler, in the hope that on some occasion, during the coming months, he might get outside.

As Randolph entered, Foster looked up from under his green

shade with an expression of perplexity. "Have I dropped a stitch here or not?" he asked. "I wish you knew something about knitting; I don't like to call Medora or one of the girls away up here to straighten me out. Look; what do you think?"

"They count all right," said Randolph; and he sat down on the couch opposite. "I've brought a book."

"I hope it's poetry!" said Foster, with a fierce promptness. "I hope it's about Adonis, or Thammuz, whose mishap 'in Lebanon' set all the Syrian females a-going. I could stand a lot more of that,——or perhaps I couldn't!"

"Why, Joe, what's gone wrong?"

"I suppose you know that your young friend got up a great to-do for us the other evening?"

"Yes; I've heard something about it." He looked at Foster's drawn face, and heard with surprise the rasping note in his voice. "Was it as bad as that?"

Foster drew his shade down farther over his eyes and clashed his needles together.

"I remember how, when I was in Florence, we went out to a religious festival one evening at some small hill-town near by. This was twenty years ago, when I *could* travel. There was a kind of grotto in the church, under the high altar; and in the grotto was a full-sized figure of a dead man, carved and painted—and covered with wounds; and round that figure half the women and girls of the town were collected, stroking, kissing . . . Adonis all over again!"

"Oh, come, Joe; don't get morbid."

Foster lifted one shoulder.

"Well, the young fellow began by roaring through the house

like a bull of Bashan, and he ended by toppling over like a little wobbly calf."

He spoke like a man who had imagined a full measure of physical powers and had envied them . . . had been exasperated by the exuberant presentation of them . . . had felt a series of contradictory emotions when they had seemed to fail . . .

"It was only a moment of dizziness," said Randolph. "I imagine he was fairly himself next day."

"Well, I've heard too much about it. Medora came up here and——"

"Need we go into that?"

"There were plenty more to help," Foster went on doggedly. "One dear creature, who was old enough to be more cautious, spilt water down the whole front of her dress——"

"I expect," said Randolph, "that the poor chap has been overworked; or careless about his meals; or worried in his classes—for he may not be fully settled in his new place; or some emotional strain may have set itself up——"

"I vote for the emotional strain," said Foster bluntly.

"A guess in the dark," commented Randolph, and paused. He himself knew little enough of Cope as a complex. He had met him but a few times, and could not associate him with his unknown background. He knew next to nothing of Cope's family, his connections, his intimates, his early associations and experiences. Nor had he greatly bestirred himself to learn. He had done little more than go to a library in the city and turn over the leaves of the Freeford directory. This publication, like most of those dealing with the smaller cities, gave separately the names of all the members of a family; and repetitions of the same address helped toward the arrangement of these individuals (disposed alphabetically) into family groups. Freeford had no great number of Copes, and several of them lived at 1636 Cedar Street. "Elm, Pine, Locust, Cedar," had thought Randolph; "the regular set." And, "One of the good streets," he surmised, "but rather far out. Cedar!" he repeated, and thought of Lebanon and the Miltonic Adonis. Of these various Copes, "Cope, David L., bookpr," might be the father,—unless "Cope, Leverett C., mgr" were the right man. If the former, he was employed by the Martin & Graves Furniture Company, and the Martins were probably important people who lived far out—and handsomely, one might guess—on a Prospect Avenue. . . . Then there was "Cope, Miss Rosalys M., schooltchr," same address as "David": she was likely his daughter. "H'm!" Randolph had thought, "these pickings are scanty,—enough anatomical reconstruction for to-day. . . ." And now he was thinking, as he sat opposite Foster, "If I had only picked up another bone or two, I might really have put together the domestic organism. Yet why should I trouble? It would all be plain, humdrum prose, no doubt. Glamour doesn't spread indefinitely. And then—men's brothers . . ."

"Well," asked Foster sharply, "are you mooning? Medora sat in the same place yesterday, and she talked for awhile too and then fell into a moonstruck silence. What's it all about?"

Randolph came out of his reverie. "Oh, I was just hoping the poor boy was back on his pins all right again."

Then he dropped back into thought. He was devising an outing designed to restore Cope to condition. If Cope could arrange for a free Saturday, they might contrive a week-end from Friday afternoon to Monday morning. It was too late for the north and too late for the opposite Michigan shore; but there was "down state" itself, where the days grew warmer and the autumn younger the farther south one went. There was a trip down a certain historic river,—historic, as our rivers went, and admirably scenic always. He recalled an exceptional hotel on one of its best reaches; one overrun in midsummer, but doubtless quiet at this season. It stood in the midst of some striking cliffs and gorges; and possibly one of the little river-steamers was in commission, or could be induced to run . . .

Foster dropped his muffler pettishly. "Read,—if you won't talk!"

"I can talk all right," returned Randolph. "In fact, I have a bit of news for you."

"What is it?"

"I'm going to move."

Foster peered out from under his shade.

"Move? What for? I thought you were all right where you are."

"All right enough; except that I want more room—and a house of my own."

"Have you found one?"

"I've about decided on an apartment. And I expect to move into it early next month."

"Top floor, of course?"

"No; first floor, not six feet above the street level."

"Good. If they'll lend me a hand here, to get down and out, I'll come and see you, now and then."

"Do so."

"That will give me a chance to wear this muffler, after all."

"So it will."

"Well, be a little more cordial. You expect to see your friends, don't you?"

"Of course. That's what it's for. Have I got to exert myself," he added, "to be cordial with *you*?"

"What's the neighborhood?"

"Oh, this one, substantially. The next street from where I am now."

"Housckeeper?"

"I think I'll have a Jap alone, at first."

"Dinners?"

"A few small try-outs, perhaps."

"Mixed parties?"

"Not at the beginning, anyhow."

"Oh; bachelor's hall."

"About that."

Foster readjusted his shade, and drove his needles into his ball of yarn.

"Complete new outfit?"

"Well, I have some things in storage."

"How about the people you're with now?"

"Their lease is up in the spring. They may go on; they may not. Fall's the time to change."

Foster drew out his needles again and fell to work.

"You ought to have seen Hortense the next morning. She put my tray on the table, and then went down in a heap on the floor—or it sounded like that. She was fainting away at dinner, she said."

"She found it amusing?"

"I don't know *how* she found it," returned Foster shortly. "If ever *I* do anything like that at your house, run me home."

"Not if it's raining. I shall be able to tuck you away somewhere."

"Don't. I never asked to be a centre of interest."

"Well," returned Randolph merely, and fell silent.

Foster resumed work with some excess of vigor, and presently got into a snarl. "Dammit!" he exclaimed, "have I dropped another?"

Randolph leaned over to examine the work. "Something's wrong."

"Well, let it go. Enough for now. Read."

There followed a half hour of historical essay, during which Foster a few times surreptitiously fingered his needles and yarn.

"Shall you have a reading-circle at your new diggings?" he asked after a while.

"If two can be said to make a circle,—and if you will really come."

"I'm coming. But I never understood that only two points could establish a circle. Three, anyway."

"Circle!" exclaimed Randolph. "Don't worry the word to death."

He went away presently, and as he walked his thoughts returned to Indian Rock. The excursion seemed a valid undertaking at an advantageous time; and he could easily spare a couple of days from the formation of his new establishment. He called on Cope that evening. Cope felt sure he could clear things for Saturday, and expressed pleasure at the general prospect. He happened to be writing to Lemoyne that evening and passed along his pleasure at the prospect to his friend. A few jaunts, outings or interludes of that kind, together with his week at his home in Freeford, over Christmas, would agreeably help fill in the time before Arthur's own arrival in January.

Randolph received Cope's response with gratification; it was pleasant to feel oneself acceptable to a younger man. In the intervals between his early looking at rugs and napery he collected timetables and folders, made inquiries, and had some correspondence with the manager of the admirable hotel. He had a fondness for well-kept hostelries just before or just after the active season. It was a pleasure to breakfast or dine in some far corner of a large and almost empty dining-room. It would be a pleasure to stroll through those gorges, which would be reasonably certain to be free from litter, and to perch on the crags, which would be reasonably certain to be free from picnic parties. It would be agreeable also to sleep in a chamber far from town noises and grimes, with few honks from late excursionists and but little early morning clatter from a diminished staff. And the river boats were still running on Sunday.

"It will brace him for the rest of his fall term," thought Randolph, "and me for my confounded shopping. And during some one of our boat-rides or rambles, I shall tell him of my plans for the winter."

The departure, it was agreed upon, should take place late on Friday afternoon. On Friday, at half past eleven, Randolph at his office in the city, received a long-distance call from Churchton. Cope announced, with a breathless particularity not altogether disassociated from self-conscious gaucherie, that he should be unable to go. Some unexpected work had been suddenly thrown upon him . . . He rather thought that one or two of his family might be coming to town for over Sunday . . .

The telephone, as a conveyor of unwelcome message, strikes a medium between the letter by mail and the face-to-face interview. If it does not quite give chance for the studied guardedness and calculated plausibility of the one, it at least obviates some of the risk involved in personal presence and in the introduction of contradictory evidence often contributed by manner and by facial expression. And a long distance interview must be brief,— at least there can be no surprise, no indignation, if it is made so.

"Very well," said Randolph, in reply to Cope's hurried and indistinct words. "I'm sorry," he added, and the brief talk was over. "You are feeling all right, I hope," he would have added, as the result of an afterthought; but the connection was broken.

Randolph left the instrument. He felt dashed, a good deal disappointed, and a little hurt. He took two or three folders from a pigeon-hole and dropped them into a waste-basket. Well, the boy doubtless had his reasons. But a single good one, frankly put forth, would have been better than duplicate or multiple reasons. He hoped that, on Sunday, a cold drizzle rather than a flood of sunlight might fall upon the autumn foliage of Indian Rock. And he would turn to-morrow to good account by looking, for an hour or two, at china.

Sunday afternoon was gorgeously bright and autumnal in Churchton, whatever it may have been along the middle reaches of the Illinois river; and at about four o'clock Randolph found himself in front of Medora Phillips' house. Medora and her young ladies were out strolling, as was inevitable on such a day;

but in her library he found Foster lying on a couch—the same piece of furniture which, at a critical juncture, had comforted Cope.

"Peter brought me down," said the cripple. "I thought I'd rather look at the backs of books than at the fronts of all those tedious pictures. Besides, I'm beginning to practice for my call at your new quarters." Then, with a sudden afterthought: "Why, I understood you were going somewhere out of town. What prevented?"

"Well, I changed my plans. I needed a little more time for my house-furnishing. I was looking yesterday at some table-ware for your use; am wondering, in fact, if Mrs. Phillips couldn't arrange to give me the benefit of her taste to-morrow or Tuesday . . ."

"She likes to shop," replied Foster, "and taste is her strong suit. I'll speak to her,—she's gone off to some meeting or other. Isn't this just the afternoon to be spending indoors?" he commented brusquely. "What a day it would be for the country," he added, sending his ineffectual glance in the direction of Randolph's face.

"We Churchtonians must take what we can get," Randolph replied, with an attempt at indifference. "Our *rus in urbs* isn't everything, but there are times when it must be made to serve."

Foster said nothing. Silent conjecture, seemingly, was offered him as his part.

# 15

## Cope Entertains Several Ladies

COPE'S excuse, involving the expected visit of a relative, may not have been altogether sincere, but it received, within a week or so, the substantial backing of actuality: a relative came. She was an aunt,——his father's sister,——and she came at the suggestion of a concerned landlady. This person, made anxious by a languid young man who had begged off from his classes and who was likely to need more attention than her scanty margin of leisure could grant, had even suggested a hospital while yet it was easy for him to reach one. Though Cope meant to leave her soon, it did not suit him to leave her quite as soon as this; and so Aunt Harriet came in from Freeford to look the situation over and to lend a hand if need be. She spent two nights in a vacant chamber at transient rates; was grudgingly allowed to prepare his "slops," as he called them, in the kitchen; and had time to satisfy herself that, after all, nothing very serious was the matter.

Randolph did not meet this relative, but he heard about her; and her coming, as a sort of family representative, helped him still further in his picture of the *res angusta* of a small-town household: a father held closely to office or warehouse—his own or some one else's; a sister confined to her school-room; a mother who found the demands of the domestic routine too exacting even to allow a three-hour trip to town; and a brother Randolph added this figure quite gratuitously out of an active imagination and a determined desire not to put any of the circle to the test of a personal encounter—and a brother who was perhaps off somewhere "on the road."

The one who met Aunt Harriet was Medora Phillips, and the meeting was brief. Medora had heard from Amy Leffingwell of Cope's absence from his class-room. She herself became concerned; she felt more or less responsible and possibly a bit conscience-stricken. "Next time," she said, "I shall try to have the ventilation right; and I think that, after this, I shall keep to birch beer."

Medora called up Amy at the music-school, one afternoon, at about four. She assumed that the day's work was over, told Amy she was "going around" to see Bertram Cope, and asked her to go with her. "You may act as my chaperon," she said; "for who knows where or how I shall find him?"

As they neared the house a colored man came out, carrying a

small trunk to a mud-bespattered surrey. "What! is he going?" said Medora, with a start. "Well, anyway, we're in time to say good-bye." Then, "What's the matter, Jasper?" she asked, having now recognized the driver and his conveyance.

"Got a lady who's gettin' away on the four forty-three."

"Oh!" said Medora, with a gasp of reassurance.

Cope's aunt said good-bye to him up stairs and was now putting on her gloves in the lower hall, in the company of the landlady. Medora appraised the visitor as a semi-rustic person—one of some substance and standing in her own community; marriage, perhaps, had provided her with means and leisure. She had been willing to subordinate herself to a university town apprehended as a social organism, and she now seemed inclined to accept with docility any observations made by a confident urbanite with a fair degree of verve.

"These young men," said Medora dashingly, "are too careless and proud."

"Proud?" asked the other. She felt clearly enough that her nephew had been careless; but pride is not often acknowledged among the members of an ordinary domestic circle.

"They're all mind," Medora went on, with no lapse of momentum. She knew she must work in brief, broad effects: the surrey was waiting and the train would not delay. "They sometimes forget that their intellectual efforts must rest, after all, on a good sensible physical basis. They mustn't scorn the body."

The departing visitor gave a quick little sigh of relief. The views of this fashionable and forthputting woman were in accord with her own, after all.

"Well, I've told Bert," she said, buttoning her second glove, "that he had better take all his meals in one place and at regular hours. I've told him his health is of just as much account as his students and their studies." She seemed gratified that, on an important point, she had reached unanimity with an influential person who was to remain behind; and she got away without too long delaying the muddy surrey and the ungroomed sorrel.

Medora Phillips looked after her with a grimace. "Think of calling him 'Bert'!"

Cope, when advised, came down in a sort of bathrobe which he made do duty as a dressing-gown. He took the stairs in a rapid run, produced an emphatic smile for the parlor threshold, and put a good measure of energy into his handshakes. "Mighty good of you to call," he said to Mrs. Phillips. "Mighty good of you to call," he said to Amy Leffingwell.

Well, he was on his feet, then. No chance to feel anxiously the brow of a poor boy in bed, or to ask if the window was right or if he wouldn't like a sip of water. Life's little disappointments . . . !

To Amy Leffingwell he seemed pale, and she felt him as glad to sit down at once in the third and last chair the little room offered. She noticed, too, an inkstain on his right forefinger and judged that the daily grind of theme-correction was going on in spite of everything.

"Did you meet my aunt before she got away?" he asked.

"We did," said Medora, "and we are going to add our advice to hers."

"That's very nice of you," he rejoined, flattered. "But within a couple of months," he went on, with a lowered voice and an eye on the parlor door, "I shall be living in a different place and in quite a different way. Until then . . ." He shrugged. His shrug was meant to include the scanty, unpretending furnishings of the room, and also the rough casual fare provided by many houses of entertainment out of present sight.

"I almost feel like taking you in myself," declared Medora boldly.

"That's still nicer of you," he said very promptly and with a reinforcement of his smile. "But I'm on the up-grade, and pretty soon everything will come out as smooth as silk. I shall have ten days at home, for the holidays; then, after that, the new dispensation."

Amy Leffingwell tempered her look of general commiseration with a slight lapse into relief. There was no compelling reason why she should have commiserated; perhaps it all came from a desire to indulge in an abandonment to gentleness and pity.

"Do you know," said Cope, with a sort of embarrassed laugh, "I feel as if I were letting myself become the focus of interest. Oughtn't I to do something to make the talk less personal?"

He glanced about the meagre little room. It gave no cue.

"I'm sure Amy and I are satisfied with the present subject," returned Medora.

But Cope rose, and gathered his bathrobe—or dressing-gown—about him. "Wait a moment. I have some photographs I can show you—several of them came only yesterday. I'll bring them down."

As soon as he had disappeared into the hall, Mrs. Phillips gave a slight smile and said quickly:

"For heaven's sake, Amy, don't look so concerned, and

mournful, and sympathetic! Anybody might think that, instead of your being my chaperon, I was yours!"

"He doesn't look at all well," said Amy defensively.

"He might look better; but we can't pity a young man too openly. Pity is akin to embarrassment, for the pitied."

Cope came down stairs the second time at a lesser pace. He carried a sheaf of photographs. Some were large and were regularly mounted; others were but the informal products of snap-shottery.

He drew up his chair nearer to theirs' and began to spread his pictures over the gray and brown pattern on his lap.

"You know I was teaching, last year, at Winnebago," he said. "Here are some pictures of the place. Science Hall," he began, passing them. "Those fellows on the front steps must be a graduating class.

"The Cathedral," he continued. "And I think that, somewhere or other, I have a group-picture of the choir.

"Sisterhood house," he went on. "Two or three of them standing out in front."

"Sisterhood?" asked Mrs. Phillips, with interest. "What do they do?"

Cope paused. "What do they do, indeed? Well, for one thing, they decorate the altar—Easter, Harvest home, and so on."

"That isn't much. That doesn't take a house."

"Well, I suppose they visit, and teach. Sort of neighborhood centre. Headquarters. Most of them, I believe, live at home."

"Dear me! Is Winnebago large enough to require settlement-work?"

"Don't drive me so! I suppose they want to tone in with the cathedral as a special institution. 'Atmosphere,' you know. Some tracts of our great land are rather drab and vacant, remember. Color, stir,—and distinction, you understand."

"Is Winnebago ritualistic?"

"Not very. While I was there a young 'priest,' an offshoot from the cathedral, started up a new parish in one of the industrial outskirts. He was quite earnest and eloquent and put up a fine service; but nobody except his own father and mother went to hear him preach."

Mrs. Phillips returned to the Sisterhood house.

"Are they nice girls?" she asked acutely.

"Oh, I guess so. I met two or three of them. Nice girls, yes; just trying to be a little different. Here's the boat-house, and some of the fellows in their rowing-clothes. Some sail-boats too."

"Can you sail?" asked Amy. She had the cathedral-choir in one hand and now took the boat-club in the other. She studied both pictures intently, for both were small and crowded.

"Why, I have all the theory and some of the practice. Those small inland lakes are tricky, though."

"Probably no worse than ours," said Mrs. Phillips. "Do help poor Amy," she went on. "*Are* you in either of these groups?"

"No. Didn't I tell you I was trying to get away from the personal? I'm not in any of these pictures." Amy unconsciously let both half-drop, as if they held no particular interest, after all. And the hand into which the next photograph was put gave it but lukewarm welcome.

Mixed in with these general subjects were several of a more

personal nature: groups of twos and threes, and a number of single figures. One face and figure, as Mrs. Phillips presently came to notice, occurred again and again, in various attitudes and costumes. It was a young man of Cope's own age—or perhaps two or three years older. He was of Cope's own height, but slightly heavier, with a possible tendency to plumpness. The best of the photographs made him dark, with black, wavy hair; and in some cases (where sunlight did not distort his expression) he indulged a determined sort of smile. He figured once, all by himself, in choir vestments; again, all by himself, in rowing toggery; a third time, still by himself, in a costume whose vague inaccuracy suggested a character in amateur theatricals.

"Who is this?" inquired Mrs. Phillips, with the last of these in hand.

Cope was prompt, but vague.

"Oh, that's a chum of mine, up there. He belongs to a dramatic club. They give 'The School for Scandal' and 'Caste,' and—well, more modern things. They have to wear all sorts of togs."

"And here he is again? And here? And here?"—shuffling still another picture into view.

"Yes."

"He's fond of costume, isn't he?"

"Very versatile," returned Cope, lightly and briefly. "Clothes to correspond."

Mrs. Phillips began to peer again at the picture of the choir-group. "Isn't he here too?"

"Yes. With the first tenors. There you have him,—third from the left, just behind that row of little devils in surplices."

"You and he sing together?"

"Sometimes—when we *are* together."

"'Larboard Watch' and 'Suona la Tromba' and——?"

"Oh, heavens!" said Cope. He threw up his head quite spiritedly. There was now more color in his cheeks, more sparkle in his eyes, more vibration in his voice. Amy looked at him with a vanishing pity and a growing admiration.

"Let us fellows be of our own day and generation," he added.

"Willingly," said Mrs. Phillips. "But my husband was fond of 'Larboard Watch'; I heard him sing in it before we were married. Shall I ever hear you sing together?" she asked.

"Possibly. He is coming down here early in January. To look after me."

"After you?" Mrs. Phillips reviewed the photographs once more. "I imagine you may sometimes have to look after him."

Cope sobered a little. "Sometimes," he acknowledged. "We shall look after each other," he amended. "We are going to live together."

"Oh, then, he is coming to *stay*? You've been a long time in reaching the point. And why do you say 'possibly' when I ask about your singing together? Aren't you coming to my house 'together'?"

"I withdraw the 'possibly.' Probably."

"And now withdraw the 'probably.' Make it 'certainly.'"

"Certainly."

"'Certainly,'—of course."

"That's better," murmured her companion.

Then Mrs. Phillips must know the newcomer's name, and must have an outline of the proposed plan. And Amy Leffingwell began to look with renewed interest on the counterfeit form and features of the young man who enjoyed Bertram Cope's friendly regard. And so the moments of "entertainment"—Cope's in turn—went on.

"I'm glad he really appears to like *somebody*," declared Mrs. Phillips, on the way home; "it makes him seem quite human." Inwardly, she was resolving to have both the young men to dine at the earliest possible date. It was not always practicable to invite a single young man as often as you wished. Having two to ask simplified the problem considerably.

Cope, flushed and now rather tired, walked up stairs with his photographs, took a perfunctory sip from a medicine-glass, looked at the inkstain on his finger, and sat down at his table. Two or three sheets of a letter were lying on it, and he re read a paragraph or so before dipping his pen.

"You were rather exacting about that week-end excursion. Mr. R. was all right, and a few days of new air and new scenes would have done me a lot of good. Still, I acknowledge your first claim. But remember that I gave up Indian Rock for you, even if you didn't give up Green Bay for me. I hope the fellow who took you hasn't got anything further to propose If he has, I ask for a tip in turn.

"Naturally it wasn't the easiest thing in the world to explain to him, and I haven't seen him since. But I can truly say that a relative *did* come, and that she was needed—or thought she was."

He picked up his pen for a fresh paragraph.

"The new photos—added to those I had—have come in quite nicely. They have just helped me entertain a couple of callers. Women have abounded in these parts to-day: Mrs. Peck, scurrying about more than usual; an aunt from home, getting away with her baggage—more than she needed to bring; and then the two who have just gone. It all makes me feel like wanting to take part in a track-meet or a ball-game—though, as I am now, I might not last two minutes at either. The lady who called was Mrs. Phillips. I thought she might as well know that you were coming. Of course you are already invited, good and plenty, to her house. Look in old music-books and see if you can't find 'Larboard Watch.' If it turns out you can get away *before* the holidays, come down and go out with me to Freeford for Christmas. I have had some rather glum hours and miss you more than ever. I have been within arm's length of one of the University trustees (who can probably place me *now!*)—but I don't know just how much that can be counted upon for, if for anything. Show yourself,—that will help.

"B."

# 16

## *Cope Goes A-Sailing*

COPE was himself in a few days. He set aside his aunt's counsel in regard to a better regimen, as well as her more specific hints, made in view of the near approach of rough weather, that he provide himself with rubbers and an umbrella, even if he would not hear of a rain-coat. "Am I made of money?" he asked. He gave a like treatment to some intimations contributed by Medora Phillips during her call: he met them with the smiling, polite, half-weary patience which a man sometimes employs to inform a woman that she doesn't quite know what she is talking about. He was presently in as active circulation, on the campus and elsewhere, as ever. The few who looked after him at all came to the view that he possessed more mettle than stamina. He had no special fondness for athletics; he was doing little to keep—still less to increase—a young man's natural endowment of strength and vigor. Occasional tennis on the faculty courts, and not much else.

So the vast gymnasium went for little with him, and the wide football field for less, and the great lake, close by, for nothing. This last, however, counted for little more with any one else. Those who knew the lake best were best content to leave it alone. As a source of pleasure it had too many perils: "treacherous" was the common word. Its treachery was reserved, of course, for the smiling period of summer; especially did the great monster lie in wait on summer's Sunday afternoons. Then the sun would shine on its vast placid bosom and the breeze play gently, tempting the swimmer toward its borders and the light pleasure craft toward its depths. And then, in mid-afternoon, a sudden disastrous change; a quick gale from the north, with a wide whipping-up of white caps; and the morrow's newspapers told of bathers drowned in the undertow, of frail canoes dashed to pieces against piers and breakwaters, and of gay, beflagged steam-launches swamped by the newly-risen sea miles from shore: the toll of fickle, superheated August. But in the late autumn the immense, savage creature was more frankly itself: rude, blustery, tyrannical,—no more a smiling, cruel hypocrite. It warned you, often and openly, if warning you would take.

It was on the last Sunday afternoon in October that Cope and Amy Leffingwell were strolling along its edge. They had met casually, in front of the chapel, after a lecture—or a service—by an eminent ethical teacher from abroad,—a bird of passage who must pipe on this Sunday afternoon if he were to pipe at all. Cope, who had lain abed late, made this address a substitute for the forenoon service he had missed. And Amy Leffingwell had gone out somewhat for the sake, perhaps, of walking by the house where Cope lived.

They passed the Science building, with its tower crowned by an ornamental open-work iron pyramid for wireless, and the segregated group of theological dormitories through whose windows earnest ringing young voices were sometimes heard at the practice of sermon-delivery, and the men's club where the billiard tables were doubtless decorously covered with their customary Sunday sheets of black oilcloth, and took intuitively the path which led along the edge of the bluff. Beyond them, further bluffs and a few low headlands; here a lighthouse, there a water-tower; elsewhere (and not so far) the balconied roof of the life-saving station, where the boats, light and heavy, were manned by muscular students: their vigilance and activity, interspersed with long periods of leisure or of absence, helped them to "pay their way." Out toward the horizon a passenger steamer en route to some port farther north, or a long ore-freighter, singularly uneventful between bow and far-distant afterhouse, on its way down from the iron-ranges of Superior.

The path was narrow, but Cope, unexpectedly to himself, had no complaint to make. Really, the girl did better here, somehow, than lots of other girls would have done on a wide sidewalk. Most of them walked too close to you, or too far from you, altering the interval suddenly and arbitrarily, and tending to bump against you when you didn't expect it and didn't want it. They were uncertain at crossings; if it was necessary for them to take your arm, as it sometimes became, in the evening, on a crowded street, why, they were too gingerly or else pressed too close; and if it happened to rain, you sometimes had to take a cab, trafficking with a driver whose tariff and whose disposition you did not know: in fact, a string of minor embarrassments and expenses . . .

But the way, this afternoon, was clear and easy; and there were no annoyances save from other walkers along the same path. The sun shone brightly at intervals. A fresh breeze swept the wide expanse streaked with purple and green and turned an occasional broken wave-crest toward the western light. Some large cumuli were aboard—white, or less white, or even darkling,—the first windy sky of autumn.

Cope and Amy passed the life-saving station, where a few people sat about idly and where one or two visitors pressed noses against glass panes to view the boats within; and they reached presently a sort of little public park which lay along the water. Here a small pier ran out past the shallows, and in front of a shack close by it a man sat resignedly near a group of beached and upturned row-boats. One or two others were still in the water, as was a small sloop. The fellow sat there without expectations: the season was about over; the day was none too promising for such as knew. His attitude expressed, in fact, the accumulated disappointment and resignation of many months. Perhaps he was a new-comer from the interior—some region of ponds and rivers—and had kept through an uneventful summer the notion that so big a spread of water would surely be put to use. The sail of the sloop, half-lowered, flapped in the breeze, and little else stirred.

Our young people overlooked both man and boat.

"It's the same lake," said Amy Leffingwell, rather dreamily, after a common silence of several minutes.

"The same," returned Cope promptly. "It's just what it was a year ago, a century ago; and a millennium ago, I suppose,—if there was anyone here to notice."

She turned on him a rueful, half-protesting smile. "I wasn't thinking of a century ago. I was thinking of a month ago."

"A month ago?"

"Yes; when we were walking along the dunes."

"Oh, I see. Why, yes, it is the same old lake, though it seems hard to realize it. Foreground makes so much difference; and so does—well, population. I mean the human element, or the absence of it."

Amy pondered.

"The one drawback, there, was that we couldn't go out on the water."

"Go out? I should say not. No pier for miles, and the water so shallow that hardly more than a canoe could land. Still, those fishermen out there manage it. But plain summerites, especially if not dressed for it, would have an unpleasant time imitating them."

Amy cast her eye about. Here was a shore, a pier, a boat, a man to let it . . .

"Would you like to go out?" asked the man himself perfunctorily, as from the depths of a settled despair. He pointed a thumb over his shoulder toward the sloop.

The two young people looked at each other. Neither looked at the sky. "Well, I don't know," replied Cope slowly. The sloop was on a pretty small scale; still, it was more to manage than a cat-boat.

"You have the theory, you know," said Amy demurely, "and some practice."

Cope looked at her in doubt. "Can you swim?" he asked.

"Yes," she returned. "I have some practice, if not much theory."

"Could you handle a jib?"

"Under direction."

"Well, then, if you really wish . . ."

The misanthrope, with a twisted smile, helped them get away. The mainsail took a steady set; but the jib, from the first, possessed an active life of its own.

"Not that rope," cried Cope; "the other."

"Very well," returned Amy, scrambling across the cockpit. And so it went.

In six or eight minutes their small catastrophe overtook them. There came a sudden flaw from out one of the racing gray cumuli, and a faint cry or two from the distant shore. Theory had not put itself into practice as quickly as the emergency required,—all the less so in that it had to work through a crew encumbered with a longish skirt and a close jacket. The sloop keeled over; Cope was instantly entangled with the mainsail and some miscellaneous cordage; and Amy, with the water soaking her closely-fitting garments, found herself clutching the cockpit's edge.

She saw Cope's predicament and let go her hold to set him free. He helped shake himself loose with a loud forced laugh and a toss of the head to get his long hair out of his eyes. "We'll leave the wreck," he spluttered, "and make for the shore." The shore, fortunately, was scarcely more than a hundred yards away,—yet never had the great twin towers of the library seemed so distant or the wireless cage on Science hall so futile.

They swam, easily, side by side, he supporting her in her cramped clothes at the start, and she, a bit concerned, somewhat supporting him toward the end. Meanwhile, there was some stir at the life-saving station, a quarter of a mile down the shore.

The last hundred feet meant mere wading, though there was some variability among the sand ridges of the bottom; but the water, at its deepest, never reached their shoulders. Their small accident now began to take on the character of a ceremonial— an immersion incident to some religious rite or observance; and the little Sunday crowd collecting on the water's edge might have been members of some congregation sympathetically welcoming a pair of converts to the faith.

"Let's hold our heads high and walk straight," said Cope, his arm in hers; "heaven knows whom we are likely to meet. And throw your hat away—you'll look better without it. Lord knows where mine is," he added, as he ran a smoothing hand over his long locks.

"Very well," she said, casting away her ruined, ridiculous headgear with her free arm. The other, in his, was giving more support to him, she felt, than he was giving to her.

Just as they were about to reach dry land, amidst the congratulations and the amused smiles of the little group at the foot of the bluff, the belated crew of life-savers swept up in their smallest boat and insisted on capturing them.

"Oh, Mr. Cope," said a familiar voice, "please let us save you. We haven't saved a soul for months."

Cope recognized one of his own students and surrendered, though a kindly house-owner on the bluff had been quick to cry across the intervening yards of water his offer of hospitality. "All right," he said; "take us back to your place, where we can dry and telephone." He hoped, too, that they might have to encounter fewer people at the other spot than at this.

Meanwhile, another boat belonging to the station had set out to aid the owner of the sloop in its recovery. It was soon righted and was brought in. There was no damage done, and there was no charge that Cope could not meet, as he learned next day to his great relief.

The station gave him a dry outfit of clothes, assembled from here and there, and telephoned to Mrs. Phillips to bring fresh garments for Amy. Neither had time to get a chill. A pair of kindly servant-maids, who were loitering on the shore with their young men, insisted on carrying the heroine of the afternoon into retirement, where they expeditiously undressed her, rubbed her, and wrapped her in a quilt snatched from a life-saving bed. Amy was cold indeed, and inclined to shiver. She understood, now, why Cope had not encouraged that bathing party at the dunes.

In a few minutes Medora Phillips tore up in her car, with Helga and a mountain of clothing and wraps. She was inclined to make the most of the occasion, and she did so. With Helga she quickly superseded the pair of sympathetic and ready maids, whom she allowed to fade into the background with too scant recognition of their services; and when she had got Amy thoroughly warmed and rehabilitated she turned her thought toward Cope. Here, certainly, was a young scholastic recluse who had an admirable faculty for getting into the public eye. If one section of Churchton society had talked about his performance at her dinner, all sections of it would now be discussing his new performance on the high seas. Suddenly she was struck with the notion that possibly his first lapse had not left him in condition to stand this second one.

"How are you feeling?" she asked anxiously. "No chill? No shock?"

"I'm all right," he declared. "One of the boys has just given me a drink of—of——" But it was a beverage the use of which was not generally approved in Churchton.

Mrs. Phillips turned round suddenly. "Amy, did you have a drink, too, of—of—of—if 'Of' is what you call it?"

"I did," said Amy firmly; "and I feel the better for it."

"Well, get in, then, and I'll take you home."

Peter grinned from the front seat of the car; Mrs. Phillips placed herself between the two victims on the back one; the life-savers, who had kept the discarded garments to dry, gave them all a few smiles and hand wavings; the two young women and their two young men looked on with some deference; the general crowd gave a little mock-cheer before turning its Sunday leisure to other forms of interest; and the small party whirled away.

Amy leaned a tired, moist head, but a happy one, on Mrs. Phillips' shoulder. "He was so quick," she breathed, "and so brave, and so strong." She professed to believe that he had saved her life. Cope, silent as he looked straight ahead between Peter and Helga, was almost afraid that she had saved his.

# 17

## Cope Among Cross-Currents

Next morning, at breakfast, Amy Leffingwell kept, for the most part, a rapt and meditative eye on her plate. Hortense gave her now and then an impatient, half-angry glare, and had to be cut short in some stinging observations on Cope. "But it *was* foolish," Medora Phillips felt obliged to concede. "What in the world made you do it?"

But Amy continued to smile at the table-cloth. She seemed to be intimating that there was a special folly which transcended mere general folly and approximated wisdom.

After breakfast she spoke a few words to Carolyn. She had had all night to think the matter over; she now saw it from a new angle and in a new light.

"You should have seen how he shook himself free from that sail, and all," she said. "And while we were swimming in he held his hand under my chin—at least part of the time. And when we reached the sandbars he put his arm through mine and helped me over every one." And in this state of mind she went off to her class.

Cope was received by his own class with a subdued hilarity. His young people felt that he had shown poor judgment in going out on the water at all,—for the University, by tacit consent, left the lake pretty well alone. They thought that, once out, he had shown remarkably inept seamanship. And they thought that he had chosen a too near and too well-lighted stage for the exhibition of both. This forenoon the "Eighteenth Century Novelists" involved Smollett, and with every reference to the water looks of understanding traveled from student to student: that the class was of both sexes made the situation no better. Cope was in good enough physical condition,—the unspeakable draught from the unspeakable flask had ensured that,—but he felt what was in the air of the classroom and was correspondingly ill at ease.

He had had, for several days, an understanding with Basil Randolph that they were to go together to the next weekly reception of the president's wife. Randolph wished to push Cope's fortunes wherever he might, and to make him stand out from the general ranks of the young instructors. He had the entrée to the Thursdays at the president's house, and he wanted Cope to meet personally and intimately, under the guidance he could provide, a few of the academic dignitaries and some of the wealthier and more prominent townspeople. Notwithstanding Mrs. Phillips' confident impression, Cope's exploit at her own table had gained no wide currency. The people she had entertained were people who expected and commanded a succession of daily impressions from one quarter or another. With them, a few light words on Cope's achievement were sufficient; they walked straight on toward the sensation the next day was sure to bring. But of course the whole University knew about his second performance. Some of its members had witnessed it, and all of them had read about it, next day, in Churchton's four-page "Index."

The president's wife was a sprightly lady, who believed in keeping up the social end of things. Her Thursdays offered coffee and chocolate at a handsomely appointed table, and a little dancing, now and then, for the livelier of the young professors and the daughters of the town's best-known families; above all, she insisted on "receiving"—even on having a "receiving line." She would summon, for example, the wife of one of the most eminent members of the faculty and the obliging spouse of some educationally-minded banker or manufacturer; and she herself always stood, of course, at the head of her line. When Cope came along with Randolph, she intercepted the flow of material for her several assistants farther on, and carried congestion and impatience into the waiting queue behind by detaining him and "having it out."

She caught his hand with a good, firm, nervous grasp, and flashed on him a broad, meaningful smile.

"Which saved which?" she asked heartily.

Mrs. Ryder, who was farther along in the line, but not too far, beamed delightedly, yet without the slightest trace of malice. An eminent visiting educator, five or six steps behind our hero, frowned in question and had to have the situation explained by the lady in his company.

Cope, a trifle embarrassed, and half-inclined to wish he had not come, did what he could to deprive the episode of both hero and heroine. It was about an even thing, he guessed,—a matter of coöperation.

"Isn't that delightful!" exclaimed the president's wife to the wife of the banker, before passing Cope on. "And so modern! Equality of the sexes . . . Woman doing her share, et cetera! For this," she presently said to the impatient educator from outside, "are we co-educational!" And, "Good teamwork!" she contrived to call after Cope, who was now disappearing in the crowd.

Cope lost himself from Randolph, and presently got away without seeing who was pouring coffee or who was the lightest on foot among the younger professors. The president's wife had asked him, besides, how the young lady had got through it, and had even inquired after her present condition. Well, Amy Leffingwell was enrolled among the University instructors, and doubtless the wife of the institution's head had been well within her rights,—even duly mindful of the proprieties. But "The Index"! That sheet, staid and proper enough on most occasions, had seemed, on this one, to couple their names quite unwarrantably. "Couple!" Cope repeated the word, and felt an injury. If he had known that Amy had carefully cut out and preserved the offending paragraph, his thought would have taken on a new and more disquieting tone.

In the inquiry of the president's wife about the condition of his copartner in adventure he found a second source of dissatisfaction. He had not called up to ask after Amy; but Mrs. Phillips, with a great show of solicitude, had called up early on Monday morning to ask after him. He had then, in turn, made a counterinquiry, of course; but he could take no credit for initiative. Neither had he yet called at the house; nor did he feel greatly prompted to do so. That must doubtless be done; but he might wait until the first fresh impact of the event should somewhat have lost its force.

Mrs. Phillips' voice had kept, over the telephone, all its vibratory quality; its tones expressed the most palpitating interest. It was already clear—and it became even clearer when he finally called at the house—that she was poetizing him into a hero, and that she regarded Amy herself as but a means, an instrument. At this, Cope felt a little more mortified than before. He knew that he had done poorly in the boat, and he was not sure that, in the first moment of the upset, he should have freed himself unaided; and he confessed that he had not been quite in condition to do very well on the way landward. However, all passed. . . . Within a fortnight or less the incident would have dropped back into its proper perspective, and his students would have found some other matter for entertainment. In the circumstances he grasped at the first source of consolation that came. Randolph was now installed in his new apartment and felt that, though not fully settled, he might risk asking Cope to dinner. "You are the first," Randolph had said. Cope could not escape the flattery; it was almost comfort.

His prompt acceptance was most welcome to Randolph. Cope had dwelt, for a moment, on the actual presence of Aunt Harriet and on his need of her. Randolph had made no precise study of recent chronology, taking the reason given over the wire as a valid one and feeling glad that there was no hitch this time.

Randolph gave Cope a rapid view of the apartment before they sat down to dinner. There were fewer pictures on the newly-papered walls than there were to be, and fewer rugs on the freshly-varnished floors. "My standing lamp will be in that corner," said Randolph, in the living-room, "—when it comes." He drew attention to a second bedroom where a man could be put up on occasion: "you, for example, if you ever find yourself shut out late." He saw Sir Galahad's gauntlets on the dresser. He even gave Cope a glimpse of his kitchen, where a self-contained Oriental, slightly smiling but otherwise inexpressive, seemed to be dealing competently with the gas-range. But Cope was impressed, most of all, by the dining-room table and its paraphernalia. At Mrs. Phillips' he had accepted the china, silver and napery as a matter of course—an elaborate entity quite outside his own thoughts and calculations: it was all so immensely far beyond his reach and his needs. Randolph, however, had dealt as a bachelor with a problem which he himself as a bachelor must soon take up, on however different a scale and plane. For everything here was rich and handsome; he should not know how to select such tings—still less how to pay for them. He felt dashed; he felt depressed; once more the wonder of people's "having things." He sipped his soup in the spirit of humility, and did not quite recover with the chops.

Randolph made little talk; he was glad merely to have Cope there. He indulged no slightest reference to the accident; he assumed, willingly enough, that Cope had done well in a sudden emergency, but did not care to dwell on his judgment at the beginning. Still, a young man was properly enough experimental, venturesome . . .

Cope had recovered himself by the time dessert was reached. He accomplished an adjustment to his environment, and Randolph was glad to feel his unaffected response to good food properly cooked and served. "He sha'n't gipsy *all* the time," Randolph said to himself. "I shall try to have him here at least twice a week." Once in a while the evening might be stormy, and then the gauntlets would be laid on the dresser—perhaps after an informal smoke in pajamas among the curios ranged round the small den.

Cope set down his demi-tasse with a slight sigh. "Well," he said, "I suppose that, before long, I shall have to buy a few sticks of furniture myself and a trifle of 'crockery.' And a percolator."

Randolph looked across at him in surprise.

"You are moving, then,— you too?" Not to greatly better quarters, he almost hoped.

"Yes; and we shall need a few small things by way of outfit."

"We." Randolph looked more intently. Housekeeping *à deux*? A roommate? Matrimony? Here was the intrusion of another piece on the board—a piece new and unexpected. Would it turn out to be an added interest for himself, or a plain source of disconcertment?

Cope, having unconsciously set the ball rolling, gave it further impetus. He sketched his absent friend and told of their plans for the winter and spring terms. "I shall try for a large easy chair," he concluded, "unless Arthur can be induced to bring one with him."

Randolph, by this time, had led Cope into the den, established him between padded arms, and given him a cigar. He drew Cope's attention to the jades and swordguards, to the odd assortment of primitive musical instruments (which would doubtless, in time, find a place at the Art Museum in the city), and to his latest acquisition—a volume of Bembo's "Le Prose." It had reached him but a week before from Venice,—"*in Venetia, al segno del Pozzo*, MDLVII," said the title-page, in fact. It was bound in vellum, pierced by bookworms, and was decorated, in quaint seventeenth-century penmanship, with marginal annotations, and also, on the fly leaves, with repeated honorifics due to a study of the forms of address by some young aspirant for favor. Randolph had rather depended on it to take Cope's interest; but now the little *envoi* from the Lagoons seemed lesser in its lustre. Cope indeed took the volume with docility and looked at its classical title-page and at its quaint Biblical colophon; but, "Just who *was* 'Pietro Bembo'?" he asked; and Randolph realized, with a slight shock, that young instructors teach only what they themselves lately have learned, and that, in many cases, they have not learned much.

But in truth neither paid much heed to the tabulated vocables of the Venetian cardinal—nor to any of the other rarities near by. Basil Randolph was wondering how he was to take Arthur

Lemoyne, and was asking himself if his trouble in setting up a new ménage was likely to go for nothing; and Bertram Cope, while he pursued the course of the bookworm through the parchment covers and the yellowed sheets within, was wondering in what definite way his host might aid the fortunes of Arthur Lemoyne and thus make matters a little easier for them both. *"All' ill.^{mo} Sig.^r paron ossevnd.^{mo} . . . All' ill.^{mo} et ecc.^{mo} Sig.^r paron . . . All' ill.^{mo} et R.R.d.^{mo} Sig.^r, Sig.^r Pio. Francesco Bembo, Vesco et Conte di Belluno"*—thus ran the faded brown lines on the flyleaf, in their solicitous currying of favor; but these reiterated forms of address conveyed no meaning to Cope, and offered no opening: now, as once before, he let the matter wait.

Randolph thought over Cope's statement of his plans, and his slight touch of pique did not pass away. Toward the end of the evening, he spoke of the wreck and the rescue, after all.

"Well," he said, "you are not so completely committed as I feared."

"Committed?"

"By your new household arrangements."

"Well, I shall have back my chum."

Randolph put forward the alternative.

"I was afraid, for a moment, that you might be taking a wife."

"A wife?"

"Yes. Such a rescue often leads straight to matrimony—in the story-books, anyhow."

Cope laughed, but with a slight disrelish. "We're in actual life still, I'm glad to think. What I said on one stretch of the shore goes on the other," he declared. "I don't feel any more inclination to wedded life than ever, nor any likelihood"——here he spoke with effort, as if conscious of a possible danger on some remote horizon—"of entering it."

"It *would* have been sudden, wouldn't it?" commented Randolph, with a short laugh. "Well," he went on, "one who inclines to hospitality must work with the material at his disposal. I shall be glad, on some occasion or other," he proceeded, with a slight trace of formality creeping into his tone, "to entertain your friend."

"I shall be more than glad," replied Cope, "to have you meet."

# 18

## *Cope at the Call of Duty*

COPE took his own time in calling upon the Ashburn Avenue circle; but he finally made, in person, the inquiries for which those made by telephone were an inadequate substitute. Yet he waited so long that, only a few hours before the time he had set, he received a sweet but somewhat urgent little note from Amy Leffingwell suggesting his early appearance. He felt obliged to employ the first moments of his call in explaining that he had been upon the point of coming, anyway, and that he had set aside the present hour two or three days before for this particular purpose: an explanation, he acknowledged inwardly, which held no great advantage for him.

"Why am I spinning such stuff?" he asked himself impatiently.

Amy's note of course minimized her aid to him and magnified his aid to her. All this was in accord with established form, but it was in still stronger accord with her determination to idealize his share in the incident. His arm *had* grasped hers firmly—and she felt it yet. But when she went on to say—not for the first time, nor for the second—how kind and sympathetic he had been in supporting her chin against those slapping waves when the shore had seemed so far away, he wondered whether he had really done so. For a moment or two, possibly; but surely not as part of a conscious, reasoned scheme to save.

"She was doing all right enough," he muttered in frowning protest.

Neither did he welcome Mrs. Phillips' tendency to make him a hero. She was as willing as the girl herself to believe that he had kept Amy's chin above water—not for a moment merely, but through most of the transit to shore. He sat there uneasily, pressing his thumbs between his palms and his closed fingers and drawing up his feet crampingly within their shoes; yet it somewhat eased his tension to find that Medora Phillips was disposed to put Amy into a subordinate place: Amy had been but a means to an end—her prime merit consisted in having given him a chance to function. Any other girl would have done as well. A slight relief, but a welcome.

Another mitigation: the house, the room, was full of people. The other young women of the household were present; even the young business-man who had understood the stove and the pump had looked in: no chance for an intense, segregated appreciation. There had been another week-end at the dunes, when this youth had nimbly ranged the forest and the beach to find wood for the great open fireplace; and he had come, now, at the end of the season, to make due acknowledgments for privileges enjoyed. He, for his part, was willing enough to regard Amy as a heroine; but he considered her as a heroine linked with the wrong man and operative in the wrong place. He cared nothing in the world for Cope, and disparaged him as before—when he did not ignore him altogether. If Amy had but been rescued by him, George F. Pearson, instead of by this Bertram Cope, and if she had been snatched from a disorderly set of breakers at the foot of those disheveled sandhills instead of from the prim, prosy, domestic edge of Churchton—well, wouldn't the affair have been better set and better carried off? In such case it might have been picturesque and heroic, instead of slightly silly.

Yes, the room was full. Even Joseph Foster had contrived to get himself brought down by Peter: further practice for the day when he should make a still more ambitious flight and dine at Randolph's new table. He sat in a dark corner of the room and tried to get, as best he might, the essential hang of the situation: the soft, insidious insistence of Amy; the momentum and bravado of his sister-in-law; the veiled disparagement of Cope in which George F. Pearson, seated on a sofa between Carolyn and Hortense, indulged for their benefit, or for his own relief; above all, he listened for tones and undertones from Cope himself. He had never seen Cope before (if indeed it could be said that he really saw him now), and he had never heard his speaking voice save at a remove of two floors. Cope had taken his hand vigorously, as that of the only man (among many women) from whom he had much to expect, and had given him a dozen words in a loud tone which seemed to correspond with his pressure. But Cope's voice, in his hearing, had lapsed from resonance to non-resonance, and from that to tonelessness, and from that to quietude. . . . Was the fellow in process of making a long diminuendo—a possible matter of weeks or of months? As before, when confronted by what had once seemed a paragon of dash and vigor, he scarcely knew whether to be exasperated or appeased.

Through this variety of spoken words and unspoken thoughts Hortense sat silent and watchful. Presently the talk lapsed: with the best will in the world a small knot of people cannot go on elaborately embroidering upon a trivial incident forever. There was a shifting of groups, a change in subjects. Yet Hortense continued to glower and to meditate. What had the incident really amounted to? What did the man himself really amount to? She soon found herself at his side, behind the library-table and its spreading lamp-shade. He was silently handling a paper-cutter, with his eyes cast down.

"See me!" she said, in a tense, vibratory tone. "Speak to me!"—and she glowered upon him. "I am no kitten, like Amy. I am no tame tabby, like Carolyn, sending out written invitations. Throw a few poor words my way."

Cope dropped the paper-cutter. Her address was like a dash of brine in the face, and he welcomed it.

"Tell me; did you look absurd—then?" she dashed ahead.

A return to fresh water, after all! "Why," he rejoined reluctantly, "no man, dressed in all his clothes, looks any the better for being soaked through."

"And Amy,—she must have looked absolutely ridiculous! That wide, flapping hat, and all! I had been telling her for weeks that it was out of style."

"She threw it away," said Cope shortly. "And I suppose her hair looked as well as a woman's ever does, when she's in the water."

"Well," she observed, "it's one thing to be ridiculous and another to go on being ridiculous. I hope you don't mean to do that?"

The pronoun "you" has its equivocal aspects. Her expression, while marked enough, threw no clear light. Cope took the entire onus on himself.

"Of course no man would choose to be ridiculous—still less to stay so. Do, please, let me keep on dry land; I'm beginning to feel water-logged." He shifted his ground. "Why do you try to make it seem that I don't care to talk with you?"

"Because you don't. Haven't I noticed it?"

"I haven't. It seems to me that I———"

"Of course you haven't. Does that make it any better?"

"I'm sure the last thing in the world I should want to do would be to———"

"I know. Would be to show partiality. To fail in treating all alike. Even that small programme isn't much—nor likely to please any girl; but you have failed to carry it out, small as it is. Here in this house, there on the dunes, what have I been—and where? Put into any obscure corner, lost in the woods, left off somewhere on the edge of things. . . ."

Cope stared and tried to stem her protests. She was of the blood,—her aunt's own niece. But whereas Medora Phillips sometimes "scrapped," as he called it, merely to promote social diversion and to keep the conversational ball a-rolling, this young person, a more vigorous organism, and with decided, even exaggerated ideas as to her dues . . . Well, the room was still full, and he was glad enough of it.

"I don't know whether I like you or not," she went on, in a low, rapid tone; "and I don't suppose you very much like me; but I won't go on being ignored . . ."

"Ignored? Why," stammered Cope, "my sense of obligation to this house——"

She shrugged scornfully. His sense of obligation had been made none too apparent. Certainly it had not been brought into line with her desserts and demands.

Cope took up the paper-cutter again and looked out across the room. Amy Leffingwell, questioningly, was looking across at him. He could change feet—if that made the general discomfort of his position any less. He did so.

Amy was standing near the piano and held a sheet or two of new music in her hands. And Medora Phillips, with a word of general explication and direction, made the girl's intention clear. Amy had a new song for baritone, with a violin obbligato and the usual piano accompaniment, and Cope was to sing it. 'Twas an extremely simple thing, quite within his compass; and Carolyn, who could read easy music at sight ("It's awfully easy," declared Amy), would play the piano part; and Amy herself would perform the obbligato (with no statement as to whether it was simple or not).

Carolyn approached the task and the piano in the passive spirit of accommodation. Cope came forward with reluctance:

this was not an evening when he felt like singing; besides, he preferred to choose his own songs. Also, he would have preferred to warm up on something familiar. Amy took her instrument from its case with a suppressed sense of ecstasy; and it is the ecstatic who generally sets the pace.

The thing went none too well. Amy was the only one who had seen the music before, and she was the only one who particularly wanted to make music now. However, the immediate need was not that the song should go well, but that it should go: that it should go on, that it should go on and on, repetitiously, until it should come (or even not come) to go better. She slid her bow across the strings with tasteful passion. She enjoyed still more than her own tones the tones of Cope's voice,—tones which, whether in happy unison with hers or not, were, after all, seldom misplaced, whatever they may have lacked in heartiness and confidence. It was a short piece, and on the third time it went rather well.

"How perfectly lovely!" exclaimed Mrs. Phillips, at the right moment.

Cope smiled deprecatingly. "It might be made to go very nicely," he said.

"It *has* gone very nicely," insisted Amy; "it did, this last time." She waved her bow with some vivacity. She had heaved the whole of her young self into the work; she had been buoyed up by Cope's tones, which, with repetition, had gathered assurance if not expressiveness; and she based her estimate of the general effect on the impression which her own inner nature had experienced. And her impression was heightened when Pearson, forging forward, and ignoring both Cope and Carolyn, thanked her richly and emphatically for her part——a part which, to him, seemed the whole.

Hortense, who had kept her place behind the large lamp-shade, twisted her interlocked fingers and said no word. Foster, who had disposed himself on an inconspicuous couch, kept his own counsel. After all, *omne ignotum*: Cope's singing had sounded better from upstairs. At close range a ringing assertiveness had somehow failed.

Cope had come with no desire to extend his stay beyond the limits of an evening call. He declined to sing on his own account, and soon rose as if to make his general adieux.

"You won't give us one of your own songs, then?" asked Medora Phillips, in a disappointed tone. "And at my dinner——"

No, she could not quite say that, at her dinner, Cope, whatever he had failed to do, had contributed no measure of entertainment for her guests.

"Give us a recitation, then," persisted Medora; "or tell us a story. Or make up"——here she indulged herself in an airily imperious flight——"a story of your own on the spot."

A trifling request, truly. But——

"Heavens!" said Cope. "I am not an author——still less an *improvvisatore*."

"I am sure you could be," returned Medora fondly. "Just try."

Cope sat down again and began to run his eye uncomfortably about the room, as if dredging the air for an idea. Behind one corner of a mirror was a large bunch of drying leaves. They had been brought in from the sand dunes as a decorative souvenir of the autumn, and had kept their place through mere inertia: an oak bough, once crimson and russet; a convoluted length of bittersweet, to which a few split berries still clung; and a branch of sassafras, with its intriguing variety of leaves—a branch selected, in fact, because it gave, within narrow compass, the plant's entire scope and repertoire as to foliage.

Cope caught at the sassafras as a falling balloonist catches at his parachute.

"Well," he said, still reluctant and fumbling, "perhaps I can devise a legend: the Legend, let us say, of the Sassafras Bush."

"Good!" cried Medora heartily.

Pearson, whispering to Amy Leffingwell, gave little heed to Cope and his strained endeavor to please Mrs. Phillips. Foster, quite passive, listened with curiosity for what might come.

"Or perhaps you would prefer folk-lore," Cope went on. "Why the Sassafras has Three Kinds of Leaves, or something like that."

"Better yet!" exclaimed Medora. "Listen, everybody. Why the Sassafras has Three Kinds of Leaves."

Pearson stopped his buzzings, and Cope began. "The Wood-nymphs," he said slowly, "were a nice enough lot of girls, but they labored under one great disadvantage: they had no thumbs."

Hortense pricked up her ears. Did he mean to be personal? If so, he should find that one of the nymphs had a whole hand as surely as he himself had a cheek.

Cope paused. "Of course you've got to postulate *something*," he submitted apologetically.

"Of course," Medora agreed.

"So when they bought their gloves, or mittens, or whatever their handgear might be called, they usually patronized the hickory or the beech or some other tree with leaves that were——"

"Ovate!" cried Medora delightedly.

"Ovate, yes; or whatever just the right word may be. But a good many of them traded at the Sign of the Sassafras, where they found leaves that were similar, but rather more delicate."

"I believe he's going to do it," thought Foster.

"Yet the nymphs knew that they lacked thumbs and kept on wanting them. So, during the long, dull winter, they put their minds to it, and finally thumbs came."

"Will-power!" said Medora.

"And early in April they went to the Sassafras and said: 'We have thumbs! we have thumbs! So we need a different sort of mitten.'

"The Sassafras was only half awake. 'Thumbs?' he repeated. 'How many?'

" 'Two!' cried the nymphs. 'Two!'

"A passing breeze roused the Sassafras. He became at least three-quarters awake."

"I doubt it," muttered Hortense.

" 'That's interesting,' he said. 'I aim to supply all new needs. Come back in a month or so, and meanwhile I'll see what I can do for you.'

"In May the nymphs returned with their thumbs and asked, 'How about our new mittens?' "

The story was really under way now, and Cope went on with more confidence and with greater animation.

" 'Look and see,' said the Sassafras.

"They looked and saw. Among its simple ordinary leaves were several with two lobes—one on each side. 'Will these do?'

"'Do?' said the nymphs. 'We said we had two thumbs, but we meant one on each hand, stupid. Do? We should say not!'

"The Sassafras was mortified. 'Well,' he said, 'that's all I can manage this season. I'm sorry not to have understood you young ladies and your needs. Come back again next spring.'

"It was a long time to wait, but they waited. Next May——"

Amy, now unworried by George Pearson, began to get the thread of the thing. Foster was sure the thread would run through. Hortense was still alert for ulterior meanings. Poor Cope, however, had no ambition to spin a double thread,—a single one was all he was equal to.

"Next May the nymphs, after nursing their thumbs for a year——"

Hortense frowned.

"——came back again; and there, among the plain leaves and the double-lobed leaves, were several fresh bright, smooth ones with a single lobe well to one side,—the very thing for mittens. And——"

"Yes, he has done it," Foster acknowledged.

"And that," ended Cope rather stridently, as he rose to go on the flood of a sudden yet unexpected success, "is Why the Sassafras——"

"Why the Sassafras has Three Kinds of Leaves!" cried Medora in triumph. Mittens for midsummer made no difficulty.

Cope gave Carolyn careful thanks for her support at the piano, and did not see that she felt he too could be a poet if he only would. He went out of his way to shake hands with Hortense, and did not realize how nearly a new quarrel had opened. He stepped over to do the like with Amy; but she went out with him into the hall,—the only one of the party who did,—and even accompanied him to the front door.

"Thank you so much," she said, looking up into his face smilingly and holding his hand with a long, clinging touch. "It went beautifully; and there are others that will go even better."

"Others?" He thought, for an instant, that she was thanking him for his Legend and was even threatening to regard him as a flowing fount of invention; but he soon realized that her mind was fixed exclusively on their duet—if such it was to be called.

"The deuce!" he thought. "Enough is enough."

Despite his success with the Sassafras, he went home discomforted and even flustered. That hand was too much like the hand of possession. The girl was stealing over him like a light, intangible vapor. He struck ahead with a quicker gait, as if trying to outwalk a creeping fog. One consolation, however: Hortense had come like a puff of wind. Even a second squall from the same quarter would not be altogether amiss.

And had there not been one further fleeting source of reassurance? Had he not, on leaving, caught through the open door of the drawing room an elevation of Medora Phillips' eyebrows which seemed to say fondly, indulgently, yet a bit ironically, "Oh, you foolish girl!"? Yet if a girl is foolish, and is going to persist in her folly, a lightly lifted pair of eyebrows will not always stay her course. Her gathering momentum is hardly to be checked by such slender means.

# 19

## Cope Finds Himself Committed

AMY LEFFINGWELL, having written once, found it easier to write again. And having strolled along the edge of the bluff with Cope on that fateful Sunday, she found it natural to intercept him on other parts of the campus (where their paths might easily cross), or to stroll with him, after casual encounters carefully planned, through sheets of fallen leaves under the wide avenues of elms just outside. Her third note almost summoned him to a rendezvous. It annoyed him; but he might have been more than annoyed had he known of her writing, rather simply, to a rather simple mother in Fort Lodge, Iowa, about her hopes—and her expectations. Her mother had, of course, heard in detail of the rescue; and afterward had heard in still greater detail, as the roseate lime-light of idealization had come to focus more exactly on the scene. She had had also an unaffected appreciation—or several—of Cope's personal graces and accomplishments. She had heard, lastly, of Cope's song to her daughter's obbligato: a duet *in vacuo*, since Carolyn had been suppressed and the surrounding company had been banished to a remote circumference. What wonder that she began to see her daughter and Bertram Cope in an. admirable isolation and to intimate that she hoped, very soon, for definite news?

Well, not a few of us have met an Amy Leffingwell: some plump-faced, pink-cheeked child, with a delicate little concave nose not at all "strong," and a fine little chin none too vigorously moulded, and a pair of timid candid blue eyes shadowed by a wisp or so of fluffy hair—and have not always taken her for what she was. She "wouldn't hurt a kitten," we say; and we assume that her "striking out a line for herself" is the last thing she would try to do. Yet such an unimpressive and disarming façade may mask large chambers of stubbornness and tenacity.

Amy knew how long and hard she had thought of Cope, and she asked for some evidence that he had been thinking long and hard of her. She desired a "response." But, in fact, he had been thinking of her only when he must. He thought of her whenever he saw himself caught in that flapping sail, and he thought of her whenever he recalled that she had taken it on herself to select his songs. But he did not want her to make out-and-out demands on his time and attention. Still less did he want her to talk about "happiness." This had come to be her favorite topic, and she discoursed on it profusely: he was almost ungracious enough to say that she did so glibly. "Happiness"—that conventional bliss toward which she was turning her mind as they strolled together on these late November afternoons—was for him a long way ahead. How furnish a house, how clothe and feed a wife?—at least until his thesis should be written and a place, with a real salary, found in the academic world. How, even, buy an engagement ring—that costly superfluity? How even contrive to pay for all the small gifts and attentions which an engagement involved? Yet why ask himself such questions? For he was conscious of a fundamental repugnance to any such scheme of life and was acutely aware that—for awhile, at least, and perhaps for always—he wanted to live in quite a different mode.

Amy's confident assumptions began to fill the house, to alter its atmosphere. Medora Phillips, who had begun by raising her eyebrows in light criticism, now lowered them in frowning protest. She had found Cope "charming"; but this charm of his was to add to the attractiveness of her house and to give her a high degree of personal gratification. It was not to be frittered away; still less was it to be absorbed elsewhere. Hortense, who had been secretly at work on a portrait-sketch of Cope in oil, and rather despising herself for it, now began to make another bold picture in her own mind. She saw herself handing out the sketch to Cope in person, with an air of high bravado; she might say, if bad came to worse, that she had found some professional interest in his color or in his "planes." On one occasion Medora hardily requisitioned Cope for an evening at the theatre, in the city; miles in and miles back she had him in her car all to herself; and if Amy, next day, appeared to feel that wealth and organization had taken an unfair advantage of simple, honest love, Medora herself was troubled by no stirrings of conscience.

The new atmosphere reached even Foster on the top floor; and when, one evening in mid-December, he finally carried out his long-meditated plan to dine with Randolph, the household situation was uppermost in his mind. That he had not the clearest understanding of the situation did not diminish his interest in it. Though he sat in the dark, and far apart, some sense all his own, cultivated through years of deprivation, came to his aid. Peter brought him down the street and round the corner; and Randolph's Chinaman, fascinated by his green shade and his tortuous method of locomotion (once out of his wheeled-chair), did the rest. "You had better stay all night," Randolph had suggested; and he was glad to avoid a second awkward trip on the same evening.

Foster had wondered whether Cope would be present. He had not asked to meet him—for he hardly knew whether he wished to or not. Though this was an "occasion,"—and his,— he had left Randolph to act quite as he might choose. There was a third chair at table and Randolph delayed dinner ten minutes while waiting for it to be filled.

"Well, let's go in and sit down," he said presently, with a slight twist of the mouth. He spoke lightly, as if it were as easy for Foster to sit down as for himself. But Foster got into his place after a moment and contrived to spread his napkin over his legs.

"I expected Bertram Cope," Randolph went on; "but he isn't here, and I have no word from him and do not know whether——"

He paused, obviously at a loss.

"Not here?" repeated Foster. "Is there, then, one place where he is not?"

"Why, Joe————!"

"Our house is full of him!" Foster burst out raucously. He had removed the green *abat-jour*, for the candle-shades (as they sometimes will) were performing their office. In the low but clear light his face seemed distorted.

"He rises to my floor like incense. The very halls and stairways reek with his charms and perfections."

"Well, you escape him here," said Randolph ruefully.

"The whole miserable place is steaming with expectation,—with the deadly aroma of a courtship going stale. I can't stand it! I can't stand it!"

"Courtship?"

"You may think it takes two, but it doesn't. That foolish girl has thrown the whole place into discomfort and confusion; and I don't know who's for or who's against————"

"What foolish girl?" asked Randolph quickly. Sing Lo was at his elbow, changing plates: it was assumed, justly enough, that he would not be able to follow the intricacies of a situation purely occidental.

"Our Amy," replied Foster, with a dash of bitterness.

"Amy Leffingwell?" asked Randolph, still more quickly.

Foster had blind eyes, but alert ears. He felt that Randolph was surprised and displeased. And indeed his host was both. That boy fallen maladroitly in love? thought Randolph. It was a second check. He had exerted himself to show a friendliness for Cope, had expected to enjoy him while he stayed on for his months in town, and had hoped to help push his fortunes in whatever other field he might enter. He had even taken his present quarters—no light task, all the details considered—to make Cope's winter agreeable, no less than his own. And now? First the uncounted-upon friend from Wisconsin with whom Cope was arranging to live; next, this sudden, unexpected affair with that girl at Medora's. Did the fellow not know his own mind? Could he formulate no hard-and-fast plan? Here Randolph, in his disappointment, inconsistently forgot that a hard-and-fast plan was largely his real annoyance and grievance. Then he remembered. He looked at the vacant place, and tried for composure and justice.

"I shall probably hear some good reason, in due time," he said.

"I hope so," rejoined Foster; "but it takes these young fellows to be careless—and ungrateful." He made no pretense of ignoring the fact that Randolph had moved into this apartment more on account of Cope than for any other reason.

"H'm, yes," responded Randolph thoughtfully. "I suppose it is the tendency of a young fellow who has never quite stood on his own legs financially to accept about everything that comes his way, and to accept it as a matter of course."

"It is," said Foster.

"I know that *I* was that way," continued Randolph, looking studiously at the nearest candle-shade. "I was beyond the middle twenties before I quite launched out for myself, and any kindness received was taken without much question and without much thanks. I presume that he still has some assistance from home . . ."

He dropped youthful insouciance over favors received to consider the change that marriage makes in a young man's status. "I wouldn't go so far as to assert that a young man married is a man that's marred——"

"This *is* stiff doctrine," Foster acknowledged.

"But somehow he does seem done for. He is placed; he is cut off from wide ranges of interesting possibilities; he offers himself less invitingly to the roving imagination . . ."

Meanwhile Cope, with Randolph's invitation driven altogether from his mind by more urgent matters, was pacing the streets, through the first snow-flurries of the winter, and was wondering, rather distractedly, just where he stood. Precisely what words, at a very brief yet critical juncture, had he said, or not said? Exactly how had he phrased or failed to phrase—the syllables which constituted, perhaps, a turning-point in his life?

Amy Leffingwell had demanded his attendance for one more walk, that afternoon, and he had not been dextrous enough, face to face with her, to refuse. She had expressed herself still more insistently on "happiness"—(on hers, his, theirs; the two were one, in her view)—and on a future shared together. In just what inadequate way had he tried to fend her off? Had he said, "I shall have to wait?" Or had his blundering tongue said, instead, "We should have to wait?"—or even worse, "We shall have to wait?" In any event, he had used that cowardly, temporizing word "wait"—for she had instantly seized upon it. Why, yes, indeed; she was willing to wait; she had expected to wait . . .

He turned out from an avenue lighted with electric globes, past which the snowflakes were drifting, and entered a quieter and darker side-street. In the dusk she had put up her face, expecting to be kissed; and he, partly out of pity for the expression that came when he hesitated, and partly out of pure embarrassment and inexpertness, had lightly touched her lips. That had sealed it, possibly. He saw her sitting in rapt fancy in her bedroom—if not more vocal in the rooms below. He saw her writing to an unseen mother in a tone of joyful complacency, and looking at her finger for a ring which he could not place there. He saw the distaste of his own home circle, to which this event had come at least a year too soon. He saw the amazement, and worse, of Arthur Lemoyne, whose plans for coming to town were now all made and to whom this turn would prove a psychological shock which might deter him from coming at all. But, most of all, he saw—and felt to the depths of his being—his own essential repugnance to the life toward which he now seemed headed. What an outlook for Christmas! What an unpleasant surprise for his parents! What opportunity in Amy Leffingwell's holiday vacation at Fort Lodge to reinforce the written page by the spoken word! Still forgetful of his engagement with Randolph, he continued to walk the streets. He turned in at midnight, hoping he might sleep, and trusting that morning would throw a less sinister light on his misadventure.

Long before this, Joseph Foster had been put to bed, by Sing-Lo, in this spare room. It was Foster's crutch, rather than a knightly sword, which leaned against the door-jamb; and it was Foster's crooked members, rather than the straight young limbs of Cope, which first found place among the sheets and blankets of that shining new brass bedstead.

# 20

## Cope Has a Distressful Christmas

COPE awakened at seven. After an early interval of happy lightness, there came suddenly and heavily the crushing sense of his predicament. How monstrous it was that one instant of time, one ill-considered action, one poorly-chosen word could clamp a repellent burden on a man for the rest of his life!

Well, he must expect telephone messages and letters. They came. That afternoon Mrs. Peck had "a lady's voice" to report: "It sounded like a *young* lady's voice," she added. And she looked at Cope with some curiosity: a "young lady" asking for him over the wire was the rarest thing in the world.

Next day came the first note. The handwriting was utterly

new to him; but his intuition, applied instantly to the envelope, told him of the source. The nail, driven, was now to be clinched. She had the right to ask him to come; and she did ask him to come—"soon."

Cope's troubled eyes sought the calendar above his table. How many days to Christmas? How much time might he spend in Freeford? How long before Christmas might he arrange to leave Churchton? The holidays at home loomed as a harbor of refuge. By shortening as far as possible the interval here and by lengthening as far as possible the stay with his family, he might cut down, in some measure, the imminent threatenings of awkwardness and constraint; then, beyond the range of anything but letters, he might study the unpleasant situation at his leisure and determine a future course.

He set himself to answer Amy's note. He hoped, he said, to see her in a few days, but he was immensely busy in closing the term-work before the holidays; he also suggested that their affair—"their" affair!—be kept quiet for the present. Yet he had all too facile a vision of beatific meditations that were like enough to give the situation away to all the household; and he was nervously aware of Amy Leffingwell as continually on the verge of bubbling confidences.

He also wrote to Lemoyne. His letter was less an announcement than a confession.

"I like this!" began Lemoyne's reply, with abrupt, impetuous sarcasm. "You have claimed, more than once," he went on, "to have steadied me and kept me out of harm's way; but I've never yet made any such demands on you as you are making on me. This thing can't go on, and you know it as well as I do. Nip it. Nip it now. Don't think that our intimacy is to end in any such fashion as this, for it isn't—especially at this particular time." . . .

Lemoyne proceeded to practical matters. "If that room is still free, engage it from the first of January. I will have a few things sent down. Father is weakening a little. Anyhow, I've got enough money for a couple of months. I will join you in Freeford between Christmas and New Year's (nearer the latter, probably), and we will go back together." . . .

Cope rather took heart from these rough, outspoken lines. Lemoyne was commonly neither rough nor outspoken; but here was an emergency, involving his own interests, which must be dealt with decisively. Cope seemed to feel salvation on the way. Perhaps that was why he still did so little to save himself. He took the new room; he had one meeting with Amy; and he left for home at least two days before he was strictly entitled to do so.

The meeting took place in Mrs. Phillips' drawing-room; he would trust himself to no more strolls on the campus, to no more confabs in college halls. There was protection in numbers, and numbers seldom failed beneath Medora Phillips' roof. They failed this time, however. Mrs. Phillips and Hortense were away at a reading; only Amy and Carolyn were at home. Cope seized on Carolyn as at a straw. He thanked her warmly again for her halting offices in the matter of that last song, and he begged that he might hear some of her recent verse. His appeal was vehement, almost boisterous: Carolyn, surprised, felt that he was ready at last to grant her a definite personality.

Amy tried in vain to remove Carolyn from the board. But Carolyn, like Hortense, had finally joined the ranks of the "recognized"; she was determined (being still ignorant, Cope was glad to see, regarding Amy's claims) to make this recognition so marked as to last beyond the moment. She played a little—not well. She read. She even accompanied Amy to the door at the close of Cope's short stay. He shook hands with them both. He had decided that he would do no more than this with Amy, in any event, and Carolyn's presence made his predetermined course easy, even obligatory. Yet he went out into the night feeling, somehow, that he had acted solely on his resolution and that he might consider himself a man of some decisiveness, after all. Amy had looked disappointed, but had contrived to whisper that she would write from Iowa. That, of course, was to be looked for, and would represent the combined efforts of herself and her home circle; yet he had a fortnight for consideration and counsel.

Cope, during his first few days at home, was moody and ab-stracted: his parents found him adding little to the Christmas cheer. His mother, always busy over domestic cares and now busier than ever, thought that he must have been working too hard. She would stand in the kitchen door with a half-trimmed pie on one hand and ponder him as he sat in the dining-room, staring absorbedly at the Franklin stove. His father, who saw him chiefly in the evening, by the gas-light of the old-fashioned house, found his face slightly pinched: was his pocket pinched too, and would he be likely, before leaving, to ask help toward making up a deficit? His sister Rosalys, who lived a life of dry routine, figured him as deep in love. He let several days pass without hinting what the real situation was.

There was interest all round when, the day before Christmas, the postman came along the bleak and flimsy street and left a letter for him. Cope was away from the house, and Rosalys, studying the envelope's penmanship and even its postmark, found vague confirmation of her theory: some college girl—one of his own students, probably—was home on vacation just as he was. If so, a "small town" person of caste and character like themselves; not brilliant, but safe. She set up the letter edgewise on the back parlor mantelpiece.

When Cope came in at noon and saw the letter, his face fell. He put it in his pocket, sat silent at table, and disappeared as soon as the meal was over. Rosalys, whose pupils were off her mind for a few days and who had thought to spare, began to shade her theory.

Cope read the letter in the low-cciled back bedroom (the ceiling sloped away on one side) which had been his for so many years. Those years of happy boyhood—how far away they seemed now, and how completely past! Surely he had never thought to come back to these familiar walls to such effect as this. . . . Well, what did it say?

It said, in its four pages (yes, Amy had really limited herself thus), how joyous she was that the dear Christmas season had brought her such a beautiful love-gift; it said that mother was so pleased and happy—and even mentioned a sudden aunt; it said how willingly she would wait on until . . .

That evening Cope made his announcement. They were all seated round the reading-lamp in the back parlor, where the old Brussels carpet looked dim and where only venerated age kept the ornate French clock from seeming tawdry. Cope looked down at the carpet and up at the clock, and spoke.

Yes, they must have it.

His mother took the shock first and absorbed most of it. She led a humdrum life and she was ready to welcome romance. To help adjust herself she laid her hands, with a soft, sweeping motion, on the two brown waves that drew smoothly across her temples, and then she transferred them to his, held his head, and gave him a kiss. Rosalys took his two hands warmly and smiled, and he tried to smile back. His father twisted the tip of his short gray beard, watched his son's mien, and said little. Day after tomorrow, with the major part of their small Christmas festivities over, he would ask how this unexpected and unwarranted situation had come about, and how, in heaven's name, the thing was to be carried through: by what means, with whose help? . . . In his complex of thought the word "thesis" came to his tongue, but he kept from speaking it. He had been advised that his son had at last struck out definitely into some bookish bypath—just what bypath mattered little, he gathered, if it were but followed to the end. Yet the end was still far—and the boy evidently realized this. He was glad that Bertram was sober over the prospect and over his present plan—which was a serious undertaking, just now, in truth.

Cope had to adjust himself to all this, and to endure, besides, the congratulations—or the comments—of a number of tiresome relatives; and it was a relief when, on the twenty-ninth, Arthur Lemoyne finally arrived.

Lemoyne had been heralded as a young man of parts, and as the son of a family which enjoyed, in Winnebago, some significant share of worldly prosperity, and, therefore, of social consideration. The simpler Copes, putting him in the other back bedroom, the ceiling of which sloped the opposite way, wondered if they were quite giving him his just dues. When Rosalys came to set away his handbag and to rearrange, next morning, his brushes on the top of the dresser, she gathered from various indications supplied by his outfit that the front chamber, at whatever inconvenience to whomever, would have been more suitable. But, "Never mind," said her mother; "they'll do very well as they are—side by side, with the door conveniently between. Then Bert can look after him a little more and we a little less."

Lemoyne presented himself to the combined family gaze as a young man of twenty-seven or so, with dark, limpid eyes, a good deal of dark, wavy hair, and limbs almost too plumply well-turned. In his hands the flesh minimized the prominence of joints and knuckles, and the fingers (especially the little fingers) displayed certain graceful, slightly affected movements of the kind which may cause a person to be credited—or taxed—with possessing the "artistic temperament." To end with, he carried two inches of short black stubble under his nose. He was a type which one may admire—or not. Rosalys Cope found in him a sort of picturesque allure. Rather liking him herself, she found a different reason for her brother's liking. "If Bert cares for him," she remarked, "I suppose it's largely by contrast—he's so spare and light-colored himself."

It was evident that, on this first meeting, Lemoyne meant to ingratiate himself—to make himself attractive and entertaining. He had determined to say a thing or two before he went away, and it would be advantageous to consolidate his position.

He had had five or six hours of cross-country travel, with some tedious waits at junctions, and at about ten o'clock, after some showy converse, he acknowledged himself tired enough for bed. Cope saw him up, and did not come down again. The two talked till past eleven; and even much later, when light sleepers in other parts of the house were awake for a few minutes, muffled sounds from the same two voices reached their ears.

But Cope's words, many as they were, told Lemoyne nothing that he did not know, little that he had not divined. The sum of all was this: Cope did not quite know how he had got into it; but he knew that he was miserable and wanted to get out of it.

Lemoyne had asked, first of all, to see the letter from Iowa. "Oh, come," Cope had replied, half-bashful, half-chivalrous, "you know it wasn't written for anybody but me."

"The substance of it, then," Lemoyne had demanded; and Cope, reluctant and shame-faced, had given it. "You've never been in anything of this sort, you know," he submitted.

"I should say not!" Lemoyne retorted. "Nor you, either. You're not in it now,—or, if you are, you're soon going to be out of it. You would help me through a thing like this, and I'm going to help you."

The talk went on. Lemoyne presented the case for a broken engagement. Engagements, as it was well known to human experience, might, if quickly made, be as quickly unmade: no novelty in that. "I had never expected to double up with an engaged man," Lemoyne declared further. "Nothing especially jolly about that—least of all when the poor wretch is held dead against his will." As he went on, he made Cope feel that he had violated an *entente* of long standing, and had almost brought a trusting friend down from home under false pretenses.

But phrases from Amy's letter continued to plague Cope. There was a confiding trust, a tender who-could-say-just-what? . . .

"Well," said Lemoyne, at about two o'clock, "let's put it off till morning. Turn over and go to sleep."

But before he fell asleep himself he resolved that he would make the true situation clear next day. He would address that sympathetic mother and that romantic sister in suitably cogent terms; the father, he felt sure, would require no effort and would even welcome his aid with a strong sense of relief.

So next day, Lemoyne, deploying his natural graces and his dramatic dexterities, drew away the curtain. He did not go so far as to say that Bertram had been tricked; he did not even go so far as to say that he had been inexpert: he contented himself with saying that his friend had been over-chivalrous and that his fine nature had rather been played upon. The mother took it all with a silent, inexpressive thoughtfulness, though it was felt that she did not want her boy to be unhappy. Rosalys, if she admired Lemoyne a little more, now liked him rather less. Her father, when the declaration reached him by secondary impact, did feel the sense of relief which Lemoyne had anticipated, and came to look upon him as an able, if somewhat fantastic, young fellow.

Cope himself, when his father questioned him, said with frank disconsolateness, "I'm miserable!" And, "I wish to heaven I were out of it!" he added.

"*Get* out of it," his father counselled; and when Cope's own feelings were clearly known through the household there was no voice of dissent. "And then buckle down for your degree," the elder added, to finish.

"If I only could!" exclaimed Cope, with a wan face,—convinced, youthfully, that the trouble through which he was now striving must last indefinitely. "I should be glad enough to get my mind on it, I'm sure."

He walked away to reconstruct a devastated privacy. "Arthur, I'm not quite sure that I thank you," he said, later.

"H'm!" replied Lemoyne non-committally. "I hope," he added, more definitely articulate, "that we're going to have a pleasanter life in our new quarters. I'm getting mighty little pleasure—if you'll just understand me—here!"

# 21

## *Cope, Safeguarded, Calls Again*

IF Cope came back from Freeford with the moral support of one family, Amy Leffingwell came back from Fort Lodge with the moral support of another. Hers was a fragmental family, true; but its sentiment was unanimous; she had the combined support of a pleased mother and of an enthusiastic maiden aunt.

Amy reached Churchton first, and it soon transpired through the house in which she lived that she was engaged to Bertram Cope. Cope, returning two days later, with Lemoyne, found his new status an open book to the world—or to such a small corner of the world as cared to read.

Cope had written from Freeford, explaining to Randolph the

broken dinner-engagement: at least he had said that immediate concerns of importance had driven the date from his mind, and that he was sorry. Randolph, only too willing to accept any fair excuse, good-naturedly made this one serve: the boy was not so negligent and ungrateful, after all. He got the rest of the story a few days later, in a message from Foster. What *was* the boy, then? he asked himself. He recalled their talk as they had walked past the sand-hills on that October Sunday. Cope had disclaimed all inclination for matrimony. He had confessed a certain inability to safeguard himself. Was he a victim, after all? A victim to his own ineptitude? A victim to his own highmindedness? Well, whatever the alternative, a field for the work of the salvage-corps had opened.

At the big house on Ashburn Avenue a like feeling had come to prevail. Medora Phillips herself had passed from the indulgently satirical to the impatient, and almost to the indignant. Her niece thought the new relation clearly superfluous. She put away the portrait in oil, but she rather hoped to resume work on it, some time. Meanwhile, she was far from kind to Amy.

Cope soon made an obligatory appearance at the house. He was glad enough to have the presence and the support of Arthur Lemoyne. The call came on a rigorous evening at the beginning of the second week in January. The two young men had about brought their new quarters to shape and subjection. They had spent two or three evenings in shifting and rearranging things— trifling purchases in person and larger things sent by express. They had reached a good degree of snugness and comfort; but——

"We've got to go to-night!" said Cope firmly.

"To-night?" repeated Lemoyne. "Unless I'm mistaken, we're in for a deuce of a time." He snuggled again into the big easy chair that had just arrived from Winnebago.

"We are!" returned Cope, with unhappy mien. "But it's got to be gone through with."

"I'm talking about the weather," rejoined Lemoyne plumply. He was versed in the reading of signs as they presented themselves a hundred and fifty miles to the north, and he thought he could accurately apply his experience to a locale somewhat beyond his earlier ken. The vast open welter of water to the east would but give the roaring north wind a greater impetus. "We're going to have to-night the storm of the season."

"Storm or no storm, I can't put it off any longer. I've got to go."

As they started out the wind was keen, and a few fine flakes, driven from the north, flew athwart their faces. When they reached Mrs. Phillips' house, Peter, wrapped in furs, was sitting in the limousine by the curb, and two or three people were seen in the open door of the vestibule.

"Well, the best of luck, *cher Professeur*," Cope heard the voice of Mrs. Phillips saying, in a quick expulsion of syllables. "This is going to be a bad night, I'm afraid; but I hope your audience will get to the hall to hear you, and that our Pierre will be able to get you back to us."

"Oh, Madame," returned the plump little man, "what a climate!" And he ran down the walk to the car.

Yes, Mrs. Phillips had another celebrity on her hands. It was an eminent French historian who was going across to the campus to deliver the second lecture of his course. "How lucky," she had said to Hortense, just after dinner, "that we went to hear him *last* night!" Their visitor was handsomely accommodated—and suitably, too, she felt—in the Louis Quinze chamber, and he was expected back in it a little after ten.

"Why, Bertram Cope!" she exclaimed, as the two young men came up the walk while the great historian ran down; "come in, come in; don't let me stand here freezing!"

It turned out to be a young man's night. Mrs. Phillips had invited a few "types" to entertain and instruct her Frenchman. They had come to dinner, and they had stayed on afterward.

Among them was the autumn undergraduate whom Cope, at an earlier day, had disdainfully called "Phaon," a youth of twenty. "You know," said Medora Phillips to Randolph, a few days later, when reviewing the stay of her newest guest, "Those sophisticated, world-worn people so appreciate our fresh, innocent, ingenuous boys. M. Pelouse told me, on leaving, that Roddy quite met his ideal of the young American. So open-faced, so inexperienced, so out of the great world . . ."

"Good heavens!" said Randolph impatiently. "Do they constitute the world? You might think so,—going about giving us awards, and hanging medals on us, and certifying how well we speak French! Fudge! The world is changing. It would be better," he added, "if more of us—college students included—learned how to speak a decenter English. I went to their dramatic club the other evening. Such pronunciation! Such delivery! I almost longed for the films."

A second "young American" was present—George F. Pearson. Pearson lived with his parents in another big house a block down the street. Mrs. Phillips had summoned him as a type that was purely indigenous—the "young American business man." Pearson had just made a "kill," as he called it—a coup executed quite without the aid of his father, and he was too full of his success to keep still; he was more typical than ever. The Professor had looked at him in staring wonder. So had Amy Leffingwell—in the absence of another target for her large, intent eyes.

But Medora Phillips knew all about George and Roddy. The novelty was Lemoyne, and she must learn about him. She readily seized the points that composed his personal aspect, which she found good: his general darkness and richness made him a fine foil for Cope. She quickly credited him with a pretty complete battery of artistic aptitudes and apprehensions. She felt certain that he would appreciate her ball-room and picture-gallery, and would figure well within it. The company was young, the night was wild, and cheer was the word. She presently led the way upstairs. Foster, as soon as he heard the first voices in the hall and the first footfalls on the bare treads of the upper stairs, shut his door.

Lemoyne felt the big bare room—bare save for a piano and a fringe of chairs and settles, large and small—as a stage; and he surmised that he, the newcomer, was expected to exhibit himself on it. He became consciously the actor. He tried now the assertive note, and now the quiet note; somehow the quiet was the louder of the two. Pearson, who was in a conquering mood tonight, scented a rival in the general attention, and one not wholly unworthy. Pearson was the only one of the four in evening dress, and he felt that to be an advantage. He, at least, had been properly attired to meet the elegant visitor from abroad. As for poor Roddy, he had come in an ordinary sack: perhaps it was partly this which had prompted M. Pelouse (who was of course dressed for the platform) to find the boy such a paragon of simple innocence.

All costumes were alike to Lemoyne; he had appeared in dozens. If he lacked costume now, he made it up in manner. He had bestowed an immensity of manner on Amy Leffingwell, downstairs: his cue had been a high, delicate, remote gravity. "I know, I know," he seemed to say; "and I make no comment." Upstairs he kept close by Cope: he was proprietary; he was protective. If Cope settled down in a large chair, Lemoyne would drape himself over the arm of it; and his hand would fall, as like as not, on the back of the chair, or even on Cope's shoulder. And when he came to occupy the piano-stool, Cope, standing alongside, would lay a hand on his. Mrs. Phillips noticed these minor familiarities and remarked on them to Foster, who had lately wheeled his chair in. Foster, a few days later, passed the comment on to Randolph, with an astringent comment of his own.—At all events, Amy Leffingwell remained in the distance, and George Pearson shared the distance with her.

Foster had broken from his retirement on hearing the voices of Cope and Lemoyne combined in song. The song was "Larboard Watch," and he remembered how his half-brother had sung in it during courtship, with the young fellow who had acted, later, as his best man. Lemoyne, at the first word of invitation, had seated himself at the instrument—a lesser than the "grand" downstairs, but not unworthy; then, with but a measure or so of prelude, the two voices had begun to ring out in the old nautical ballad. Lemoyne felt the composition to be primitive, antiquated and of slight value; but he had received his cue, and both his throat and his hands wrought with an elaborate expressiveness. He sang and played, if not with sincerity, at least with effect. His voice was a high, ringing tenor; not too ringing for Cope's resonant baritone, but almost too sweet: a voice which might cloy (if used alone) within a few moments. Cope was a perfect second, and the two went at it with a complete unity of understanding and of sentiment. Together they viewed—in thirds—"the gath'ring clouds"; together—still in thirds—they roused themselves "at the welcome call" of "Larboard watch, ahoy!" Disregarding the mere words, they attained, at the finish, to something like feeling—or even like a touch of passion. Medora Phillips had never heard Cope sing like that before; had never seen so much animation in his singing face. By the fourth bar there had been tears in her eyes, and there was a catch in her breath when she exclaimed softly, "You dear boys!" It was too soon, of course, to make Lemoyne "dear"—the one boy was Cope. It was really his voice which she had heard through the soaring, insinuating tones of the other. Foster, sitting beside her, suddenly raised his shade and peered out questioningly, both at the singers and at his sister-in-law. He seemed surprised—and more.

Pearson was surprised too, but kept his applause within limits. However, he praised Lemoyne for his accompaniment. Then he begged Amy for an air on the violin; and while they were determining who should play her accompaniment, the wind raged more wildly round the gables and the thickening snow drove with a fiercer impetus against the windows.

Lemoyne (who was a perfectly good sight-reader) begged that he might not be condemned to spoil another's performance. This was the result of an understanding between Cope and himself that neither was to contribute further. Presently a simple piece was selected through which the unskilled Carolyn might be trusted to pick her way. Cope listened with a decorous attention which was designed to indicate the highest degree of sympathetic interest; but his attitude, so finely composed within, yet so ineffectively displayed without, was as nothing to the loud promptness of Pearson's praise. Amy glanced at Cope with questioning surprise; but she met Pearson's excesses of commendation with a gratified smile.

Shortly before ten o'clock there was a stir at the front door. Mrs. Phillips rose hastily. "It is M. Pelouse; let me go down and get him."

Yes, it was M. Pelouse. "Oh, Madame!" he said, as before, but with an expressiveness doubly charged, "what a climate!" He was panting and was covered with fine snow. Behind him was Peter, looking very grave and dour.

"Shall I be wanted further?" asked Peter in a tense tone, and with no trace of his usual good-natured smile.

"What! Again?" cried Mrs. Phillips, while Helga, farther up the hall, was undoing the Professor; "three times on a night like this? No, indeed! Get back into the garage as fast as you can."

"Oh, Madame!" said the Professor, now out of his wrappings and in better control of his voice. "They were so faithful to our beautiful France! The *salle* was almost full!"

"Well," said Mrs. Phillips to herself, "they got there all right, then. I hope most of them will get back home alive!"

"What a climate!" M. Pelouse was still saying, as he entered the ball-room. He had not been there before. He ran an appraising eye over the pictures and said little. But as soon as he learned that some of them were the work of the late M. Phillips he found words. He led the company through a tasteful jungle of verbosity, and left the ultimate impression that Monsieur had been a remarkable man, whether as artist or as collector.

Yet he did not forget to say once more, "What a climate!"

"Is it really bad outside?" asked Pearson. M. Pelouse shrugged his shoulders. It was *affreux*.

"It is indeed," corroborated Mrs. Phillips: she had spent her moment at the front door. "Nobody that I can find room for leaves my house tonight." This meant that Cope and Lemoyne were to occupy the chintz chamber.

M. Pelouse gradually regained himself. Cope interested him. Cope was, in type, the more "American" of the two new arrivals. He was also, as M. Pelouse had heard, the *prétendant*,— yes, the *fiancé*. Well, he was calm and inexpressive enough: no close and eager attendance; cool, cool. "How interesting," said the observer to himself. "And Mademoiselle, quite across the room, and quite taken up" happily, too, it seemed—"with another man: with the other man, perhaps? . . ."

At half past ten Pearson rose to leave; Cope and Lemoyne rose at the same time. "No," said Mrs. Phillips, stopping them both; "you mustn't think of trying to go. I can't ask Peter to take you, and you could never get across on foot in the world. I can find a place for you."

"And about poor Roddy?" asked Hortense.

"Roddy may stay with me," declared Pearson. "I can put him up. Come on, Aldridge," he said; "you're good for a hundred yard dash." And down they started.

"I don't want to stay," muttered Cope to Lemoyne, under cover of the others' departure. "Devil take it; it's the last thing in the world I want to do!"

"It's awkward," returned Lemoyne, "but we're in for it. After all, it isn't *her* house, nor her family's. Besides, you've got me."

Mrs. Phillips summoned Helga and another maid, who were just on the point of going to bed, and directed their efforts toward the chintz chamber. "Ah, well," thought M. Pelouse, "the *fiancé*, then, is going to remain over night in the house of his *fiancée!*" It was droll; yet there were extenuating circumstances. But—such a singular climate, such curious temperaments, such a general chill! And M. Pelouse was presently lost to view among the welcome trappings of Louis Quinze.

# 22

## Cope Shall Be Rescued

Next morning Cope left the house before breakfast. He had had the forethought to plead an exceptionally early engagement, and thus he avoided meeting, after the strain of the evening before, any of the various units of the household. He and Lemoyne, draping their parti-colored pajamas over the foot of the bedstead, left the chintz chamber at seven and walked out into the new day. The air was cold and tingling; the ground was white as a sheet; the sky was a strident, implacable blue. The glitter and the glare assaulted their sleepy eyes. They turned up their collars, thrust their hands deep into their pockets, and took briskly the half mile which led to their own percolator and electric toaster.

Cope threw himself down on the bed and let Lemoyne get the breakfast. Well, he had called; he had done the just and expected thing; he had held his face through it all; but he was tired after a night of much thought and little sleep. Possibly he might not have to call again for a full week. If 'phone messages or letters came, he would take them as best he could.

Nor was Lemoyne very alert. He was less prompt than usual in gaining his early morning loquacity. His coffee was lacking in spirit, and much of his toast was burnt. But the two revived, in fair measure, after their taxing walk.

They had talked through much of the dead middle of the night. Foster, wakeful and restless, had become exasperated beyond all power of a return to sleep. Concerns of youth and love kept them murmuring, murmuring in the acute if distant ears of one whom youth had left and for whom love was impossible. Beyond his foolish, figured wall were two contrasted types of young vigor, and they babbled, babbled on, in the sensitized hearing of one from whom vigor was gone and for whom hope was set.

"What do you think of her?" Cope had asked. Then he had thrown his face into his pillow and left one ear for the reply.

"She is a clinger," returned Lemoyne. "She will cling until she is loosened by something or somebody. Then she will cling to the second somebody as hard as she did to the first. I'm not so sure that it's you as an individual especially."

Cope had now no self-love to consider, no self-esteem to guard. He did not raise his face from out the pillow to reply.

But he found Lemoyne rather drastic. Arthur had shown himself much in earnest, of course; he had the right, doubtless, to be reproachful; and he was fertile in suggestions looking toward his friend's freedom. Yet his expedients were not always delicate or fair: Cope would have welcomed a lighter hand on his exacerbated spirit, a more disinterested, more impartial touch. He was glad when, one afternoon at five, a few days later, he met Randolph on the steps of the library. Randolph, by his estimate, was disinterested and impartial.

The weather still held cold: it was no day for spending time, conversationally, outside; and they stepped back for a little into a recess of the vestibule. Cope found an opening by bolstering up his previous written excuses. He was still very general.

"That's all right," replied Randolph, in friendly fashion. "Some time, soon, we must try again. And this time we must have your friend." His glance was kind, yet keen; nor was it brief.

Randolph had already the outlines of the situation as Foster understood them. He sometimes slipped in, on Sunday forenoon, to read the newspapers to Foster, instead of going to church. Hortense and Carolyn came up now and then: indeed, this reading was, theoretically, a part of Carolyn's duties, but she was coming less and less frequently, and often never got beyond the headlines. So that, every other Sunday at least, Randolph set aside prayer-book and hymnal for dramatic criticisms, editorials, sports and "society."

This time Foster was full of the events of Friday night. "As I make it out, he kept away from her the whole evening, and that new man helped him do it. Our friend down the street,

Hortense says, showed every disposition to cut in, and the girl showed at least some disposition to let him. I don't wonder: when you come right down to it, he's twice the man the other is."

"Young Pearson?"

"Yes."

"Clever lad. Confident. But brash. Just what his father used to be."

"He praised her playing. Cope sat dumb. And next morning he hurried away before breakfast. You know what kind of a morning it was. Anything very pressing at the University on a Saturday morning at eight?"

"I hardly know."

"How about this sudden new friend?" Foster twitched in his chair. "Medora," he went on, "seems to have no special fancy for him. She even objects to his calling Cope 'Bert.' Of course he sings. And he seems to be self-possessed and clever. But 'self-possessed'—that doesn't express it. He was so awfully, so publicly, at home; at least that's as I gather it. Always hanging over the other man's chair; always finding a reason to put his hand on his shoulder . . ."

"Body-guard? No wonder Pearson came to the fore."

"I don't know. What I've heard makes me think of———"

And here, Foster, speaking with a keen and complicated acerbity, recalled how, during earlier years of travel, he had had opportunity to observe a young married couple at a Saratoga hotel. They had made their partiality too public, and an elderly lady not far away in the vast "parlor" had audibly complained that they brought the manners of the bed-chamber into the drawing-room.

"They talked half through the night, too," Foster added bitterly.

"Young men's problems," said Randolph. "Possibly they were considering Pearson."

"Possibly," repeated Foster; and neither followed further, for a moment, the pathway of surmise.

Presently Randolph rose and scuffled through the ruck of newspapers, with which no great progress had been made. "Is Medora at home?" he asked.

"I think she's off at church," said Foster discontentedly. "And Hortense went with her."

"I'll call her up later. If I can get her for Wednesday—and Pearson too . . ."

Foster, accustomed to piecing loose ends as well as he could, did not ask him to finish. Randolph picked up a crumpled sheet from the floor, reseated himself, and read out the account of yesterday's double performance at the opera.

When Randolph, then, met Cope in the vestibule of the library, on Monday, he felt that he had ground under his feet. Just how solid, just how extensive, he was not quite sure; but he could safely take a few steps experimentally. Cope was a picture of uncertainty and woe; his face was an open bid for sympathy and aid.

"You are unhappy," said Randolph; "and I think I know why." He meant to advance toward the problem as if it were a case of jealousy—a matter of Pearson's intrusion and of Amy's seemingly willing acceptance of it.

Cope soon caught Randolph's idea, and he stared. He did not at all resent Randolph's advances; misapprehension, in fact, might serve as fairly, in the end, as the clearest understanding.

Randolph placed his hand on Cope's shoulder. "You have only to assert yourself," he said. "The other man is an intruder; it would be easy to warn him off before he starts in to win her."

"George Pearson?" said Cope. "Win her? In heaven's name," he blurted out, "let him!"

It was a cry of distaste and despair, in which no rival was concerned. Randolph now had the situation in its real lines.

"Well, this is no place for a talk," he said. "If you should care to happen in on me some evening before long . . ."

"I have Wednesday," returned Cope, with eagerness.

"Not Wednesday. I have an engagement for that evening. But any evening a little later."

"Friday? The worst of my week's work is over by then."

"Friday will do." And they parted.

Randolph had secured for his Wednesday evening Medora Phillips and Hortense. Hortense was the young person to pair with Pearson, who had thrown over an evening at his club for the dinner with Randolph. The talk was to be—in sections and installments—of Amy Leffingwell, and of Cope in so far as he might enter. Medora would speak; Hortense would speak; Randolph himself should speak. To complete the party he had asked his relations from the far side of the big city. His sister would preside for him; and his brother-in-law might justify his expenditure of time and trouble by stopping off in advance for a brief confab, as trustee, at the administration building, with the president. A compatriot had been secured by Sing-Lo to help in dining-room and kitchen.

Randolph had planned a short dinner. His sister, facing the long return-drive, would doubtless be willing to leave by nine-thirty. Then, with two extraneous pieces removed from the board, the real matter in hand might be got under way.

Mrs. Phillips was most lively from the start. She praised the house, which she was seeing for the first time. She extolled Sing-Lo's department, and Sing-Lo, who delighted in entertainments, was one broad smile. She had a word of encouragement for his less smiling helper, whom she informally christened Sing-Hi; and she chatted endlessly with Mrs. Brackett—perhaps even helped tire her out. Yes, George Pearson was to be urged forward for the rescue of Bertram Cope.

Pearson spoke up loud and clear among the males. He was a business-man among business-men, and during the very few moments formally allowed for the cigars he made himself, as he felt, tell. And after the Bracketts left—at nine twenty-five— he was easily content to stay on for three-quarters of an hour longer.

At nine-forty Pearson was saying, amidst the cigarette-smoke of the den:

"Does she expect to teach the violin all her life?"

He was both ironical and impatient. Clearly a charming, delicate creature like Amy Leffingwell might better decorate the domestic scene of some gentleman who enjoyed position and prosperity.

"I hope not, indeed," said Hortense, in a deep contralto.

Pearson cast on Hortense a look which rewarded such discernment.

"Of course he has nothing, now," said Randolph, with deliberation. "And he may be nothing but a poor, underpaid professor all his life."

"No ring—yet," said Hortense, further. Her "yet" meant "not even yet." Her deep tone was plausibly indignant.

"I'm rather glad of that," remarked Mrs. Phillips, with an eye pretendedly fixed on the Mexican dolls. "I can't feel that they are altogether suited to each other."

"He doesn't care for her," pursued Hortense.

"Does she really care for him?" asked Pearson.

No answer. One pair of eyes sought the floor; another searched the ceiling; a third became altogether subordinate to questioning, high-held brows.

Pearson glanced from one face to another. The doubt as to her "caring" seemed universal. The doubt that she cared deeply, essentially, was one that he had brought away from the ball-room. And he went home, at ten twenty-three, pretty well determined that he would very soon try to change doubt to certainty.

"Thank you so much," said Mrs. Phillips to Randolph, as he went out with her and Hortense to put them in the car. "I'm sure we don't want him to be burdened and miserable; and I'm sure we all do want her to be happy. George is a lovely, capable chap,—and, really, he has quite a way."

# 23

## *Cope Regains His Freedom*

ON Friday evening Randolph, at home, was glancing now and then at the clock (as on a previous occasion), while waiting for Cope. At eight-fifteen the telephone rang; it was Cope, with excuses, as before. He was afraid he should be unable to come; some unexpected work . . . It was that autumn excursion all over again.

Randolph hung up the receiver, with some impatience. Still, never mind; if Cope would make no effort to save himself, others were making the effort for him. He had considerable confidence in George Pearson's state of mind, as well as in George's egoism and drive.

Foster heard of Cope's new delinquency, through Randolph's own reluctant admission. "He is an ingrate, after all," said Foster savagely, and gave his wheels an exceptionally violent jerk. And Randolph made little effort, this time, toward Cope's defense.

"You've done so much for him," Foster went on; "and you're willing to do so much more."

"I *could* do a great deal, of course. There may be a good reason this time, too," said Randolph soberly.

"Humph!" returned Foster.

Cope had hung up the receiver to turn toward Lemoyne and to say:

"I really ought to have gone."

"Wait until I can go with you," Lemoyne insisted, as he had been insisting just before. The still unseen man of Indian Rock was again the subject of his calculations.

"You've been asked," Cope submitted. "He has been very friendly to me, and I am sure he would be the same to you."

"I think that, personally, I can get along without him," the other muttered ungraciously to himself.

Aloud he said: "As I've told you, I've got the president of the dramatic club to see tonight, and it's high time that I was leaving." He looked with intention at the desk which had superseded that old table, with ink-stained cover, at which Cope had once worked. "You can use a little time to advantage over those themes. I'll be back within an hour."

Lemoyne had entered for Psychology, and was hoping that he now enjoyed the status necessary for participation in the college theatricals. But he was relying still more on a sudden defection or lapse which had left the dramatic club without a necessary actor at a critical time. "It's me, or postponement," he said; "and I think it's me." The new opportunity—or bare chance— loomed before him with immensity. Cope's affair might wait. He would even risk Cope's running over to Randolph's place alone.

Cope seated himself at his desk with loyalty, or at least with docility; and Lemoyne, putting on his hat and coat, started out for the fraternity house where the president of the club was in residence.

Five minutes after Lemoyne's departure Cope heard the telephone ringing downstairs, and presently a patient, middle-aged man knocked at the door and told him the call was for him.

Cope sighed apprehensively and went down. Of course it was Amy. Would he not come over for an hour? Everybody was away, and they could have a quiet talk together.

Cope, conscious of others in the house, replied cautiously. Lemoyne, he said, had gone out and left him with a deskful of themes: tiresome routine work, but necessary, and immensely absorptive of time. He was afraid that he could scarcely come this evening . . .

Amy's voice took on a new tone. Why, she seemed to be feeling, must Arthur Lemoyne be mentioned, and mentioned so early? Yet Bertram had put him—instinctively, unconsciously—at the head of the little verbal procession just begun.

Cope's response was dry and meagre; free speech was impossible over a lodging-house telephone set in the public hall. Amy, who knew little of Cope's immediate surroundings at the moment, went on in accents of protest and of grievance, and Cope went on replying in a half-hushed voice as non-committally as he was able. He dwelt more and more on the trying details of his work in words which conveyed no additional information to any fellow-dwellers who might overhear.

"You haven't been to see me for a week," came Amy's voice petulantly, indignantly.

"I'm very sorry, I'm sure," returned Cope in a carefully generalized tone of suavity. It was successful with the spinster in the side room above, but it was no tone to use with a protesting *fiancée.*

"Why do you neglect me so?" Amy's voice proceeded, with no shade of appeasement.

"There is no intention of that," replied Cope; "——so far as I know," he added, for ears about or above.

Again Amy's tone changed. It took on a tang of anger, and also a curious ring of finality—as if, suddenly, a last resolution had been reached. "Good night," she said abruptly, and the interview was over.

Cope forgot Randolph, and Lemoyne, and his themes. Lemoyne, returning within the hour, found him seated at his desk in self-absorbed depression, his work untouched.

"Well, they've taken me," he began; "and I shall have a fairly good part." Cope made no effort to respond to the other's glowing self-satisfaction, but sat with thoughtful, downcast eyes at his desk before the untouched themes. "What's the matter?" asked Lemoyne. "Has she been calling up again?"

Cope raised his head and gave him a look. Lemoyne saw that his very first guess had been correct.

"This is a gay life!" he broke out; "just the life I have come down here to lead. You're making yourself miserable, and you're making me miserable. It's got to end."

Cope gave him a second woeful glance.

"Write to her, breaking it off," prompted Lemoyne. "Draft a letter tonight."

His mind was full of *clichés* from his reading and his "scripts." He had heard all the necessary things said: in fact, had said them himself—now in evening dress, now in hunting costume, now in the loose habiliments of Pierrot—time and time again. The dissatisfied *fiancé* need but say that he could not feel, after all, that they were as well suited to each other as they ought to be, that he could not bring himself to believe that his feeling for her was what love really should be, and that———

Thus, with a multiplicity of "that's," they accomplished a rough draft which might be restudied and used on the morrow. "There!" said Lemoyne to the weary Cope at eleven o'clock; "it ought to have been written a month ago."

Cope languidly slipped the oft-amended sheet under his pile of themes and in a spent voice suggested bed.

Over night and through the following forenoon the draft lay on his desk. When he returned to his room at three o'clock a note, which had been delivered by hand, awaited him. It was from Amy Leffingwell.

Cope read it, folded his arms on his desk, bowed his head on his arms, and, being alone, gave a half-sob. Then he lifted his head, with face illumined and soul refreshed. Amy had asked for an end to their engagement.

"What does she say?" asked Lemoyne, an hour later.

"She says what you say!" exclaimed Cope with shining eyes and a trace of half-hysteric bravado. "She does not feel that we are quite so well suited to each other as we ought to be, nor that her feeling toward me is what love really . . . Can she have been in dramatics too!"

"Your letter," returned Lemoyne, with dignity, "would have been understood."

"Quite so," Cope acknowledged, in a kind of exultant excitation. He caught the rough draft from his desk—it was all seared with new emendations—tore it up, and threw the fragments into the waste-basket. "Thank Heaven, I haven't had to send it!" In a moment, "What am I to write now?" he asked with irony.

"The next will be easier," returned Lemoyne, still with dignity.

"It will," replied Cope.

It was,—so much easier that it became but an elegant literary exercise. A few touches of nobility, a few more of elegiac regret, and it was ready at nine that night for the letter-box. Cope dropped it in with an iron clang and walked back to his quarters a free man.

A few days later Lemoyne, working for his new play, met Amy Leffingwell in the music-alcove of the University library. She had removed her gloves with their furry wristlets, and he saw that she had a ring on the third finger of her left hand. Its scintillations made a stirring address to his eye.

Cope heard about the ring that evening, and about Amy Leffingwell's engagement to George Pearson the next day.

He had no desire to dramatize the scene of Pearson's advance, assault and victory, nor to visualize the setting up of the monument by which that victory was commemorated. Lemoyne did it for him.

Pearson had probably indulged in some disparagement of Cope—a phase on which Lemoyne, as a faithful friend, did not dwell. But he clearly saw George taking Amy's hand, on which there was still no ring, and declaring that she should be wearing one before to-morrow night. He figured both George and Amy as rather glad that Cope had not given one, and as more and more inclining, with the passage of the days, to the comfortable feeling that there had never been any real engagement at all.

Lemoyne attempted to put some of his visualizings before Cope, but Cope cut him short. "Now I will settle down to work on my thesis," he said, "and get my degree at the June convocation."

"Good," said Lemoyne; "and now I can get my mind on the club." He went to the window and looked out on the night. The stars were a-glitter. "Let's take a turn round the block before we turn in."

They spent ten minutes in the clear winter air. As Cope, on their return, stooped to put his latch-key to use, Lemoyne impulsively threw an arm across his shoulder. "Everything is all right, now," he said, in a tone of high gratification; and Urania, through the whole width of her starry firmament, looked down kindly upon a happier household.

# 24

## Cope in Danger Anew

A SIMILAR satisfaction came to prevail in University circles, and in the lesser circle which Cope had formed outside. His own classroom, after a week, became a different place. There had been some disposition to take a facetious view of Cope's adventure. His class had felt him as cool and rather stiff, and comment would not be stayed. One bright girl thought he had spoiled a good suit of clothes for nothing. The boys, who knew how much clothes cost, and how much every suit counted, put their comment on a different basis. The more serious among them went no further, indeed, than to say that if a man had found himself making a mistake, the sooner he got out of it the better. For weeks this affair of Cope's had hung over the blackboard like a dim tapestry. Now it was gone; and when he tabulated in chalk the Elizabethan dramatists or the Victorian novelists there was nothing to prevent his students from seeing them.

Medora Phillips became sympathetic and tender. She let him understand that she thought he had been unfairly treated. This did not prevent her from being much kinder to Amy Leffingwell. Amy, earlier, had been so affected by the general change of tone that, more than once, she had felt prompted to take herself and her belongings out of the house. But she still lingered on, as she was likely to do, during a short engagement; and Mrs. Phillips was now amiability itself to George and Amy both.

Her method of soothing Cope was to take him to the theatre and the opera in town: he could scarcely come to the house. It was now late in January and the opera season was near its end. People were tiring of their boxes, or had started South: it had become almost a work of merit to fill a friend's box for her. During the last week of the season, Mrs. Phillips was put in position to do this. She invited Cope, and took along Hortense, and found in the city itself a married pair who could get to the place and home again without her help. Lemoyne would have made six, and the third man; but he was not bidden. Why pack the box? A better effect was made by presenting, negligently, one empty seat. Lemoyne dressed Cope, however. He had brought to Churchton the outgrown evening clothes; and Cope, in his exuberance, bought a new pair of light shoes and white gloves. He looked well as he sat on the back seat of the limousine with Medora Phillips, during the long drive in; and he looked well—strikingly, handsomely well—in the box itself. Indeed, thought

Medora, he made other young men in nearby boxes—young men of "means" and "position"—look almost plebian. "He is charming," she said to herself, over and over again.

What about him "took" her? Was it his slenderness, his grace? Was it his youthfulness, intact to this moment and promising an extension of agreeable possibilities into an entertaining future? Or was it more largely his fundamental coolness of tone? Again he was an icicle on the temple—this time the temple of song. "He *is* glittering," said Medora, intent on his blazing blue eyes, his beautiful teeth ever ready for a public smile, and the luminous backward sweep of his hair; "and he is *not* soft." She thought suddenly of Arthur Lemoyne; he, by comparison, seemed like a dark, yielding plum-pudding.

On the way into town Medora had had Hortense sit in front with Peter. This arrangement had enabled her to lay her hand more than once on Cope's, and to tell him again that he had been rather badly treated, and that Amy, when you came to it, was a poor slight child who scarcely knew her own mind. "I hope she had not made a mistake, after all," breathed Medora.

All this soothed Cope. The easy motion of the luxurious car half-hypnotized him; a scene of unaccustomed splendor and brilliancy lay just ahead . . . What wonder that Medora found him scenically gratifying in her box (the dear creature's titillation made it seem "hers" indeed), and gave his name with great gusto to the young woman of the notebook and pencil? And the box was not at the back, but well along to one side, where people could better see him. Its number, too, was lower; so that, next morning, he was well up in the list, instead of at the extreme bottom, where two or three of the young men of means and position found themselves. Some of the girls in his class read his name, and had no more to say about wet clothes.

Hortense, on the front seat of the car, had had the good sense to say little and the acumen to listen much. She knew that Cope must "call" soon, and she knew it would be on some evening when he had been advised that Amy was not at home. There came, before long, an evening when Amy and George Pearson went into town for a musical comedy, and Cope walked across once more to the familiar house.

Hortense was in the drawing-room. She was brilliantly dressed, and her dark aggressive face wore a look of bravado. In her rich contralto she welcomed Cope with an initiative which all but crowded her aunt into second place. Under the very nose of Medora Phillips, whom she breezily seemed to regard as a chaperon, she brought forward the sketch of Cope in oils, which she had done partly from observation and partly from memory. She may have had, too, some slight aid from a photograph,—one which her aunt had wheedled out of Cope and had missed, on one occasion at least, from her desk in the library. Hortense now boldly asked his coöperation for finishing her small canvas.

Though the "wood-nymphs" of last autumn's legend might indeed be, as he had broadly said, "a nice enough lot of girls," they really were not all alike and indistinguishable: one of them at least, as he should learn, had thumbs.

Hortense wheeled into action.

"The composition is good," she observed, looking at the canvas as it stood propped against the back of a Chippendale chair; "and, in general, the values are all right. But——" She glanced from the sketch back to the subject of it.

Cope started. He recognized himself readily enough. However, he had had no idea that self-recognition was to be one of the pleasures of his evening.

"——but I shall need you yourself for the final touches—the ones that will make all the difference."

"It's pretty good as it is," declared Mrs. Phillips, who, privately, was almost as much surprised as Cope. "When did you get to do it?"

This inquiry, simple as it was, put the canvas in a new light—that of an icon long cherished as the object of private devotion. Hortense stepped forward to the chair and made an adjustment of the picture's position: she had a flush and a frown to conceal. "But never mind," she thought, as she turned the canvas toward a slightly different light; "if Aunt Medora wants to help, let her."

She did not reply to her aunt's question. "Retouched from life, and then framed—who knows?" she asked. Of course it would look immensely better; would look, in fact, as it was meant to look, as she could make it look.

She told Cope that she had set up a studio near the town square, not far from the fountain-basin and the elms——

"Which won't count for much at this time of year," interjected her aunt.

"Well, the light is good," returned Hortense, "and the place is quiet; and if Mr. Cope will drop in two or three times, I think he will end by feeling that I have done him justice."

"This is a most kind attention," said Cope, slightly at sea. "I ought to be able to find time some afternoon . . ."

"Not too late in the afternoon," Hortense cautioned. "The light in February goes early."

When Lemoyne heard of this new project he gave Cope a *look*. He had no concern as to Mrs. Phillips, who was, for him, but a rather dumpy, over-brisk, little woman of forty-five. If she must run off with Bert every so often in a motor-car, he could manage to stand it. Besides, he had no desire to shut Cope—and himself—out of a good house. But the niece, scarcely twenty-three, was a more serious matter.

"Look out!" he said to Cope. "Look out!"

"I can take care of myself," the other replied, rather tartly.

"I wish you could!" retorted Lemoyne, with poignant brevity. "I'll go with you."

"You won't!"

"I'd rather save you near the start, than have to try at the very end."

Cope flung himself out; and he looked in at Hortense's studio—which she had taken (or borrowed) for a month—before the week was half over.

Hortense had stepped into the shoes of a young gentlewoman who had been trying photography, and who had rather tired of it. At any rate, she had had a chance to go to Florida for a month and had seized it. Hortense had succeeded to her little north skylight, and had rearranged the rest to her own taste; it was a mingling of order and disorder, of calculation and of careless chance. She had a Victory of Samothrace and a green-and-gold dalmatic from some Tuscan town—— But why go on?

Cope had not been in this new milieu fifteen minutes before Randolph happened along.

Randolph, as a friend of the family, could scarcely be other than persona grata. Hortense, however, gave him no great welcome. She stopped in the work that had but been begun. The winter day was none too bright, and the best of the light would soon be past, she said. The engagement could stand over. In any event, he was there ("he," of course, meaning Cope), and a present delay would only add to the total number of his calls. Hortense began to wipe her brushes and to talk of tea.

"I'll go, I'll go," said Randolph obligingly. "I heard about the new shop only yesterday, and I wanted to see it. I don't exact that I shall witness the mysteries in active operation."

Cope's glance asked Randolph to remain.

"There are no mysteries," returned Hortense. "It's just putting on a few dabs of paint in the right places."

She continued to take a few dabs from her brushes and to talk tea. "Stay for a sip," she said.

"Very well; thank you," replied Randolph, and wondered how long "a sip" might mean.

In the end it meant no longer for him than for Cope; they came away together. Hortense held Cope for a moment to make a second engagement at an earlier hour.

Randolph had not met Cope for several days, except at the opera, where he had left his regular Monday evening seat in the parquet to spend a few moments in Mrs. Phillips' friend's box. He had never seen Cope in evening dress before; but he found him handsome and distinguished, and some of the glamour of that high occasion still lingered about the young man as he now walked through High Street, in his rather shabby tweeds, at Randolph's side.

Randolph looked back upon his dinner as a complete success: Pearson was engaged, and Cope was free. He now said to Cope:

"Of course you must know I feel you were none too handsomely treated. George is a pleasant, enterprising fellow, but somewhat sudden and rapacious. If he is happy, I hope you are no less happy yourself. . . ." Thus he resumed the subject which had been dropped at the Library door.

Cope shrank a little, and Randolph felt him shrinking. He fell silent; he understood. Pain sometimes took its own time to travel, and reached its goal by a slow, circuitous route. He thought suddenly of his bullfight in Seville, twenty-five years before. He had sat out his six bulls with entire composure; yet, back in America, some time later, he had encountered a bullfight in an early film and had not been able to follow it through. Cope, perhaps, was beginning to feel the edge of the sword and the drag at his vitals. The thing was over, and his, the elder man's, own part in it successfully accomplished; so why had he, conventional commentator, felt the need of further words?

He let the unhappy matter drop. When he spoke again he reminded Cope that the invitation for himself and Lemoyne still held good. Amy had been swept from the stage; but Lemoyne, a figure of doubt, was yet in its background. "I must have a 'close-up'," Randolph declared to himself, "and find out what he comes to." Cope had shown some reluctance to meet his advances—a reluctance which, he felt, was not altogether Cope's own.

"I know we shall be glad to come sometime," replied Cope, with seeming heartiness. This heartiness may have had its element of the genuine; at any rate, here was another "good house," from which no one need shut himself out without good cause. If Lemoyne developed too extreme a reluctance, he would be reminded that he was cherishing the hope of a position in the registrar's office, for at least half of the day; also, that Randolph enjoyed some standing in University circles, and that his brother-in-law was one of the trustees.

"Yes, indeed," continued Cope, in a further corroboration which might better have been dispensed with.

"You will be welcome," replied Randolph quietly. He would have preferred a single assurance to a double one.

# 25

## Cope in Double Danger

MEANWHILE Cope and Lemoyne refined daily on the details of their new ménage and applied themselves with new single-mindedness to their respective interests. Cope had found a subject for his thesis in the great field of English literature,—or, rather, in a narrow bypath which traversed one of its corners. The important thing, as he frequently reminded Lemoyne, was not the thesis itself, but the aid which it might give his future. "It will make a difference, in salary, of three or four hundred dollars," he declared.

Lemoyne himself gave a few hours a week to Psychology in its humbler ranges. There were ways to hold the attention of children, and there were forms of advertising calculated to affect favorably the man who had money to spend. In addition, the University had found out that he could sing as well as act, and something had been said about a place for him in a musical play.

Between-times they brought their quarters into better order; and this despite numerous minor disputes. The last new picture did not always find at once its proper place on the wall; and sometimes there were discussions as to whether it should be toast or rolls, and whether there should be eggs or not. Occasionally sharp tones and quivering nostrils, but commonly amity and peace.

They were seen, or heard of, as going about a great deal together: to lectures, to restaurants, to entertainments in the city. But they went no longer, for the present, to Ashburn Avenue; they took their time to remember Randolph's repeated invitation; and there was, as yet, no further attendance at the studio in the Square,—for any reference to the unfinished portrait was likely to produce sharp tones and quivering nostrils indeed.

Other invitations began to come to Cope,—some of them from people he knew but slightly. He wondered whether his swoon and his shipwreck really could have done so much to make him known. Sometimes when these cards seemed to imply but a simple form of entertainment, at a convenient hour of the late afternoon, he would attend. It did not occur to him to note that commonly Medora Phillips was present: she was always in "active circulation," as he put it; and there he let things lie.

One of these entertainments was an afternoon reception of ordinary type, and the woman giving it had thrown a smallish library into closer communication with her drawing-room without troubling to reduce the library to order: books, pamphlets, magazines lay about in profuse carelessness. And it was in this library that Cope and Medora Phillips met.

"You've been neglecting me," she said.

"But how can I———?" he began.

"Yes, I know," she returned generously. "But after the first of May— Well, he is a young man of decisiveness and believes in quick action." She made a whiff, accompanied by an outward and forward motion of the hands. She was wafting Amy Leffingwell out of her own house into the new home which George Pearson was preparing for her. "After that—— -"

"Yes, after that, of course."

Mrs. Phillips was handling unconsciously a small pamphlet which lay on the library table. It was a magazine of verse—a monthly which did not scorn poets because they happened to live in the county in which it was published. The table of contents was printed on the cover, and the names of contributors were arranged in order down the right-hand side. Mrs. Phillips, carelessly running her eye over it while thinking of other things, was suddenly aware of the name of Carolyn Thorpe.

"What's this?" she asked. She ran her eye across to the other edge of the cover, and read, "Two Sonnets."

"Well, well," she observed, and turned to the indicated page. And, "When in the world———?" she asked, and turned back to the cover. It was the latest issue of the magazine, and but a day or two old.

"Carolyn in print, at last!" she exclaimed. "Why, isn't this splendid!"

Then she returned to the text of the two sonnets and read the first of them—part of it aloud.

"Well," she gasped; "this is ardent, this is outspoken!"

"That's the fashion among woman poets to-day," returned Cope, in a matter-of-fact tone. "They've gone farther and farther, until they hardly realize how far they *have* gone. Don't let them disturb you."

Mrs. Phillips reread the closing lines of the first sonnet, and then ran over the second. "Good heavens!" she exclaimed; "when *I* was a girl———!"

"Times change."

"I should say so." She looked from the magazine to Cope. "I wonder who 'the only begetter' may be."

"Is that quite fair? So many writers think it unjust—and even obtuse and offensive—if the thing is put on too personal a basis. It's all just an imagined situation, manipulated artistically . . ."

Mrs. Phillips looked straight at him. "Bertram Cope, it's *you*!" She spoke with elation. These sonnets constituted a tribute. Cope, she knew, had never looked three times, all told, at Carolyn Thorpe; yet here was Carolyn saying that she . . .

Cope dropped his eyes and slightly flushed.

"I wonder if she knows it's out?" Mrs. Phillips went on swiftly. "Did you?"

"I?" cried Cope, in dismay.

"You were taking it all so calmly."

"'Calmly'? I don't take it at all! Why should I? And why should you think there is any ref———?"

"Because I'm so 'obtuse' and 'offensive,' I suppose. Oh, if *I* could only write, or paint, or play, or something!"

Cope put his hand wearily to his forehead. The arts were a curse. So were gifted girls. So were over-appreciative women. He wished he were back home, smoking a quiet cigarette with Arthur Lemoyne.

Mrs. Ryder came bustling up—Mrs. Ryder, the mathematical lady who had given the first tea of all.

"I have just heard about Carolyn's poems. What it must be to live in the midst of talents! And I hear that Hortense has finally taken a studio for her portraits."

"Yes," replied Mrs. Phillips. "And she"—with a slight emphasis—"is doing Mr. Cope's picture,"—with another slight emphasis at the end.

Cope felt a half-angry tremor run through him. He was none the less perturbed because Medora Phillips meant obviously no offense. Hortense and Carolyn were viewed as but her delegates; they were doing for her what she would have been glad to be able to do for herself. Clearly, in her mind, there was not to be another Amy.

Well, that was something, he thought. He laughed uneasily, and gave the enthusiastic Mrs. Ryder a few details of the art-world (as she called it),—details which she would not be denied.

"I must call on dear Hortense, some afternoon," she said.

"Do," returned Hortense's aunt. "And mention the place. Let's keep the dear girl as busy as possible."

"If it were only photographs . . ." submitted Mrs. Ryder.

"That's a career too," Mrs. Phillips acknowledged.

They all drifted out into the larger room. Mrs. Ryder left them,—perhaps to distribute her small change of art and literature through the crowd.

"You're not forgetting Hortense?" Mrs. Phillips herself said, before leaving him.

"By no means," Cope replied.

"I hear you didn't make much of a start."

"We had tea," returned Cope, with satirical intention.

This left Medora Phillips unscathed. "Tea puts on no paint," she observed, and was lost in the press.

It need not be assumed that knowledge of Carolyn Thorpe's verse gained wide currency through University circles, but there was a copy of the magazine in the University library. Lemoyne saw it there. He scarcely knew whether to be pleased or vexed. Finally he decided that there was safety in numbers. If Cope really intended to go to that studio, it was just as well that there should be an impassioned poetess in the background. And it was just as well that Cope should know she was there. Lemoyne took a line not unlike Mrs. Phillips' own.

"I only wish there were more of them," he declared, looking up from his desk. "I'd like a lady barber for your head, a lady shoemaker for your feet, a lady psychologist for your soul———"

"Stop it!" cried Cope. "I've had about all I can stand. If you want to live in peace, as you sometimes say, do your share to keep the peace."

"You *are* going to have another sitting?"

"I am. How can I get out of it?"

"You don't want to get out of it."

"Well, after all the attentions they've shown us———"

"Us? You."

"Me, then. Shall I be so uncivil as to hold back?"

"It might not displease her if you did."

"Her?"

"Your Mrs. Phillips. If I may risk a guess———"

"You may not. Your precious 'psychology' can wait. Don't be in such a damned hurry to use it."

"It had better be used in time."

"It had better not be used at all. Drop it. Think about your new play, or something."

"Oh, the devil!" sighed Lemoyne. "Winnebago seems mighty far off. We got on there, at least." He bent again over his desk.

Cope put down his book and came across. There were tears, perhaps, in his eyes—the moisture of vexation, or of contrition, or of both. "We can get along here, too," he said, with an arm around Lemoyne's shoulder.

"Let's hope so," returned Lemoyne, softening, with his hand pressed on Cope's own.

# 26

## Cope as a Go-Between

THIS brief exchange might have passed for a quarrel and a reconciliation; and the reconciliation seemed to call for a seal. That was soon set by another of Randolph's patient invitations to dinner.

"Let's go," said Cope; "I've got to go again—sometime."

"I don't care about it, very much," replied Lemoyne.

"If you want any help of his toward a position . . . Time's passing. And a man can't be expected to bestir himself much for another man he's never even seen."

"All right. I'll go with you."

Randolph was glad to see Cope again, whom he had not met

since the half hour in Hortense Dunton's studio. He was also glad to secure, finally, a close and leisurely look at Lemoyne. Lemoyne took the same occasion for a close and leisurely look at Randolph. Each viewed the other with dislike and distrust. Each spoke, so far as might be, to Cope—or through him. Sing-Lo, who was prepared to smile, saw few smiles elsewhere, and became sedate, even glum.

Randolph felt a physical distaste for Lemoyne. His dark eyes were too liquid; his person was too plump; the bit of black bristle beneath his nose was an offense; his aura—— Yet who can say anything definite about so indefinite a thing as an aura, save that one feels it and is attracted or repelled by it? Lemoyne, on his side, developed an equal distaste (or repugnance) for the "little gray man"—as he called Randolph to himself and, later, even to Cope; though Randolph, speaking justly, was exactly neither gray nor little. Lemoyne noted, too, the early banishment of Randolph's eyeglasses, which disappeared as they had disappeared once or twice before. He felt that Randolph was trying to stay young rather late, and was showing himself inclined to "go" with younger men longer than they would welcome him. Why didn't he consort with people of his own age and kind? He was old; so why couldn't he *be* old?

The talk led—through Cope—to reminiscences of life in Winnebago. Randolph presently began to feel Lemoyne as a variously yet equivocally gifted young fellow—one so curiously endowed as to be of no use to his own people, and of no avail for any career they were able to offer him. A bundle of minor talents; a possible delight to casual acquaintances, but an exasperation to his own household; an ornamental skimmer over life's surfaces, when not a false fire for other young voyagers along life's coasts. Yet Bertram Cope admired him and had become absorbed in him. Their life in that northern town, with its fringe of interests—educational, ecclesiastical, artistic and aquatic— had been intimate, fused to a degree. Randolph began to realize, for the first time, the difficulties in the way of "cultivating" Cope. Cope was a field already occupied, a niche already filled.

While Randolph was gathering (through Cope) details of the life in Winnebago, Lemoyne was gathering (through Cope) details of the life in Churchton during the past autumn. He began to reconstruct that season: the long range of social entertainments, the proposed fall excursions, the sudden shifting of domicile. Randolph, it was clear, had tried to appropriate Cope and to supplant (knowingly or unknowingly) Cope's closest friend. Lemoyne became impatient over the fact that he was now sitting at Randolph's table. However, if Randolph could help him to a place and a salary, that would make some amends.

Presently Cope, having served as an intermediary, became the open centre of interest. His thesis was brought forward as a suitable subject of inquiry and comment. It was a relief to have come to a final decision; but no relief was in sight for a long time from the slavery of close reading. Every moment that could be spared from his classroom was given up to books—authors in whom he might be interested or not interested, but who must be gone through.

"A sort of academic convention," said Cope, rather wanly; "but a necessary one."

His eyes had begun to show excessive application; at least they looked tired and dim. His color, too, was paler. He had come to suggest again the young man who had been picked up from Medora Phillips' dining-room floor and laid out on the couch in her library, and who had shown a good deal of pallor during the few days that followed. "Take a little more air and exercise," Randolph counselled.

"A good rule always, for everybody," said Lemoyne, with a withholding of all tone and expression.

"I believe," Randolph continued, "that you are losing in both weight and color. That would be no advantage to yourself—and it might complicate Miss Dunton's problem. It's perplexing to an artist when one's subject changes under one's very eye."

"There won't be much time for sitting, from now on," observed Lemoyne concisely.

"I might try to go round once more," said Cope, " —in fairness. If there are to be higher lights on my cheekbones and lower lights for my eyes, an hour or so should serve to settle it."

"I wouldn't introduce many changes into my eyes and cheekbones, if I were you," said Randolph. Lemoyne was displeased; he thought that Randolph was taking advantage of his position as host to make an observation of unwarranted saliency, and he frowned at his plate.

Cope flushed, and looked at his.

The talk drifted toward dramatics, with Winnebago once more the background; but the foreground was occupied by a new musical comedy which one of the clubs might try in another month, and the tone became more cheery. Sing-Lo, who had come in with a maple mousse of his own making, smiled at last; and he smiled still more widely when, at the end of the course, his chief occidental masterpiece was praised. Sing-Lo also provided coffee and cigars in the den; and it was here that Cope felt the atmosphere right for venturing a word in behalf of Lemoyne.

There had been few signs of relenting in Winnebago; and some modest source of income would be welcome—in fact, was almost necessary.

"Of course work *is* increasing in the offices," said Randolph, looking from one young man to the other; "and of course I *have*, directly or indirectly, some slight 'influence.'"

He felt no promptings to lend Lemoyne a hand; yet Cope himself, even if out of reach, might at least remain an object of continuing kindness.

"But if you are to interest yourself in some new undertaking by 'The Grayfriars,'" he said to Lemoyne, "will you have much time and attention to give to office-work?"

"Oh, I have time," replied Lemoyne jauntily, "and not many studies. Half a day of routine work, I thought . . . Of course I'm not a manager, or director, or anything like that. I should just have a part of moderate importance, and should have only to give good heed to rehearsals . . ."

"Well," said Randolph thoughtfully.

"I hope you can do something," put in Cope, with fervor.

"Well," said Randolph again.

This uncomfortable and unsatisfactory dinner of three presently drew to its end. "I'd have made it four," said Randolph to Foster, a day or two later, "if I'd only thought of it in time."

"*I* don't want to meet them again," returned Foster quickly.

"Well," said Randolph, "I've no fondness for the new fellow, myself; but——"

"And I don't care about the other, either."

Randolph sighed. This was plainly one of Foster's off days. The only wonder was he had not more of them. He sat in darkness, with few diversions, occupations, ameliorations. His mind churned mightily on the scanty materials that came his way. He founded big guesses on nothings; he raised vast speculative edifices on the slightest of premises. To dislike a man he could not even see! Well, the blind—and the half-blind—had their own intuitions and followed their own procedures.

"Then you wouldn't advise me to speak a word for him?—for them?"

"Certainly not!" rejoined Foster, with all promptness. "They've treated you badly. They've put you off; and they came, finally, only because they counted on getting something out of you."

"Oh, I wouldn't say that of Cope."

"I would. And I do. They're completely wrapped up in their own interests, and in each other; and they're coupled to get anything they can out of Number Three. Or out of Number Four. Or Five. Or out of X,—the world, that is to say."

Randolph shrugged. This was one of Foster's bad days indeed.

"And what's this I hear about Hortense?" asked Foster, with bitterness.

"That won't amount to much."

"It won't? She's out in the open, finally. She took that place for a month with one express object—to get him there, paint or no paint. She's fretful and cantankerous over every day of delay, and soon she'll be in an undisguised rage."

"What does her aunt say to it?"

"She's beginning to be vexed. She's losing patience. She thinks it's a mistake—and an immodest one. She wants to send her away for a visit. To think of it!—as soon as one girl lets go another takes hold,—and a third person holds on through all!"

"Joe! Joe!"

But Foster was not to be stayed.

"And that poetry of Carolyn's! Medora herself came up and read it to me. It was a 'tribute,' she thought!"

"That won't amount to anything at all."

"It won't? With Hortense scornfully ridiculing it, and Carolyn bursting into tears before she can make her bolt from the room, and Amy wondering whether, after all . . . ! If things are as bad as they are for me up here, how much worse must they be for the rest of them below! And that confounded engagement has made it still worse all round!"

Randolph ran his palms over his perplexed temples. "Whose?"

"Whose? No wonder you ask! Engagements, then."

"When are they going to be married?"

"The first week in May, I hear. But Pearson is trying for the middle of April. His flat is taken." Foster writhed in his chair.

"Why do they care for him?" he burst out. "He's nothing in himself. And he cares nothing for them. And he cares nothing for you," Foster added boldly. "All he has thought for is that fellow from up north."

"Don't ask me why they care," replied Randolph, with studied sobriety. "Why does anybody care? And for what? For the thing that is just out of reach. He's cool; he's selfish; he's indifferent. Yet, somehow, frost and fire join end to end and make the circle complete." He fell into reflection. "It's all like children straining upward for an icicle, and presently slipping, with cracked pates, on the ice below."

"Well, *my* pate isn't cracked."

"Unless it's the worst cracked of all."

Foster tore off his shade and threw it on the floor. "Mine?" he cried. "Look to your own!"

"Joe!" said Randolph, rising. "That won't quite do!"

"Be a fool along with the others, if you will!" retorted Foster. "Oh!" he went on, "Haven't I seen it all? Haven't I felt it all? You, Basil Randolph, mind your own ways too!"

Randolph thought of words, but held his tongue. Words led to other words, and he might soon find himself involved in what would seem like a defense—an attitude which he did not relish, a course of which he did not acknowledge the need. "Poor Joe!" he thought; "sitting too much by himself and following overclosely the art of putting things together—anyhow!" Joe Foster must have more company and different things to consider. What large standard work—what history, biography, or bulky mass of memoirs in from four to eight volumes—would be the best to begin on before the winter should be too far spent?

Four or five days later, Randolph wrote to Cope that there was a good prospect for a small position in the administration offices of the University, and a week later Lemoyne was in that position. Cope, who recognized Randolph's handling of the matter as a personal favor, replied in a tone of some warmth. "He's really a very decent fellow, after all,—of course he is," pronounced Randolph. Lemoyne himself wrote more tardily and more coolly. He was taking time from his Psychology and from "The Antics of Annabella," it appeared, to acquaint himself with the routine of his new position. Randolph shrugged: he must wait to see which of the three interests would be held the most important.

# 27

## *Cope Escapes a Snare*

LEMOYNE'S first week in his new berth held him rather close, and Cope was able to move about with less need of accounting for his every hour. One of his first concerns was to get over his sitting with Hortense Dunton. His "sitting," he said: it was to be the first, the only and the last.

He came into her place with a show of confidence, a kind of blustery bonhomie. "I give you an hour from my treadmill," he declared brightly. "So many books, and such dry ones!"

Hortense, who had been moping, brightened too. "I thought you had forgotten me," she said chidingly. Yet her tone had less acerbity than that which she had employed, but a few moments before, to address him in his absence. For she often had in mind, at intervals longer or shorter, Cope's improvisation about the Sassafras—too truly that dense-minded shrub had failed to understand the "young ladies" and their "needs."

"My thesis," he said. "From now on, it must take a lot of my thought and every moment of my spare time." He looked at the waiting canvas. "Clinch it to-day. Hurry it through."

He spoke with a factitious vivacity which almost gave a sense of chill. She looked at him with a shade of dissatisfaction and discomfort.

"What! must it all be done in a drive?" she asked.

"By no means. Watch me relax. Is that my chair? See me drop into complete physical and mental passivity—the *kef* of the Arabs."

He mounted the model-throne, sank into the wide chair, and placed his hands luxuriously on its arms. His general pose mattered little: she had not gone beyond his head and shoulders.

Hortense stared. Would he push her on the moment into the right mood? Would he have her call into instant readiness her colors and brushes? Why, even a modest amateur must be allowed her minutes of preparation and approach.

"Passivity?" she repeated, beginning to get under way. "Shall I find you very entertaining in that condition?"

"Entertaining? Me, the sitter? Why, I've always heard it was an important part of a portrait-painter's work to keep the subject interested and amused."

He smiled in his cold, distant way. The north light cut across the forehead, nose and chin which made his priceless profile. The canvas itself, done on theory in a lesser light, looked dull and lifeless.

Hortense felt this herself. She did not see how she was going to key it up in a single hour. As she considered among her brushes and tubes, she began to feel nervous, and her temper stirred.

"You have a great capacity for being interested and amused," she said. "Most men are like you. Especially young ones. They are amused, diverted, entertained—and there it ends."

Cope felt the prick. "Well, we are bidden," he said; "and we come. Too many of us have little to offer in return, except appreciation and goodwill. How better appreciate such kindness as Mrs. Phillips' than by gratefully accepting more of it?" (Stilted copy-book talk; and he knew it.)

"You haven't been accepting much of it lately," she returned, feeling the point of a new brush. She spoke with the consciousness of empty evenings that might have been full.

"Hardly," he replied. And he felt that this one word sufficed.

"Well, the coast will be clear after the twentieth of April."

"That is the date, then, is it?" The more he thought of the impending ceremony, the more grateful he was for his escape. Thankfulness had salved the earlier wound; no pain now came from his touching it.

"Yes; on that day the house will see the last of them."

"The wedding, then, will——?"

"Yes. Aunt Medora says, 'Why go to Iowa?—you're at home here.' Why, indeed, drag George away out to Fort Lodge? Let her own people, who are not many, come to us. Aunt will do everything, and do it handsomely."

She slanted her palette and looked toward the skylight. Cope's own glance swept non-committally the green burlap walls. Both of them were seeing pictures of the wedding preparations. Hortense saw delivery-boys at the front door, with things that must be held to the light or draped over chairs. She saw George haling Amy to the furniture-shops and to the dealers in wall-paper. She saw them in cosy shaded confab evening after evening, in her aunt's library. It was a period of joy, of self-absorption, of unsettlement, of longing, of irritation, of exasperation—oh, would it never end! Cope saw a long string of gifts and entertainments, a diamond engagement-ring, a lavishly-furnished apartment . . . How in the world could he himself have compassed all this? And how blessed was he among men that he had not been obliged to try!

Hortense went through some motions with her brush, yet seemed to be looking beyond him rather than at him.

"There will be a bridal trip of a week or so," she concluded; "and they will be in their new home on the first of May."

"Very good," said Cope. He thought he was thinking to himself, but he spoke aloud. "And that ends it." This last he really did say to himself.

He sank more comfortably into his chair, kept his face properly immobile, and spoke no further word. Hortense brought back her gaze to focus and worked on for a little time in silence. The light was good, her palette was full, her brushes were well-chosen, her eyes were intent on his face. It was a handsome face, displayed to the best advantage. She might look as long as she liked, and a long look preceded every stroke.

Presently she paused, opening her eyes wider and holding aloft her brush. "There will be a bride's-maid," she said.

"The deuce!" he thought. "That didn't end it!" But he said nothing aloud.

"Guess who!"

"Why, how should *I*——?"

"Guess!" she cried peremptorily, in a tone of bitter derision. "You won't? Well, it's Carolyn—our poor, silly Carolyn! And what do you suppose she has started in to do? She is writing an epitha—an epithal——"

"——amium," contributed Cope. "An epithala-mium."

"Yes, an epithala-mium!" repeated Hortense, with an outburst of jarring laughter. "Isn't she absurd! Isn't she ridiculous!"

"Is she? Why, it seems to me a delicate attention, a very sweet thought." If Carolyn could make anything out of Amy—and of George—why, let her do it.

"You *like* her poetry!" cried Hortense in a high, strained voice. "You enjoy her epithalamiums, and her—sonnets . . ."

Cope flushed and began to grow impatient. "She is a sweet girl," he said; "and if she wishes to write verse she is quite within her rights."

" 'Sweet'! There you go again! 'Sweet'—twice. She ought to know!"

"Perhaps she does know. Everybody else knows."

"And perhaps she doesn't!" cried Hortense. "Tell her! Tell her!"

Cope stared. "She is a sweet girl," he repeated; "and she has been filling very discreetly a somewhat difficult position———"

He knew something of the suppressed bitterness which, in subordinate places, was often the lot of the pen. He found himself preferring, just here, "pen" to "typewriter": he would give Carolyn a touch of idealization—though she had afflicted him with a heavy stroke of embarrassment.

"'Difficult position'?" shrilled Hortense. "With Aunt Medora the very soul of kindness? I like that! Well, if you want to rescue her from her difficult position, do it. If you admire her— and love her—tell her so! *She'll* be grateful—just read those sonnets over again!"

Hortense dropped her palette and brushes and burst into outrageous tears.

Cope sat bolt upright in that spacious chair. "Tell her? I have nothing to tell her. I have nothing to tell anyone!"

His resonant words cut the air. They uttered decision. He did not mean to make the same mistake twice.

Hortense drew across her eyes an apron redolent of turpentine and stepped toward the throne.

"Nothing? Why this sudden refuge in silence?" she asked, almost truculently, even if tremulously. "You usually find enough words—even though they mean little."

"I'm afraid I do," he admitted cautiously.

"You have nothing to tell anyone? Nothing to tell—me?"

Cope rose. "Nothing to tell anyone," he repeated. "Nothing."

"Then let me tell you something." There was an angry thrill in her voice. "For I am not so selfish and cold-hearted as you are. I have seen nobody but you all these months. I have never tried harder to please anybody. You have scarcely noticed me—you have never given me a glance or a thought. You could interest yourself in that silly Amy and in our foolish Carolyn; but for me—me— Nothing!"

Cope came down from the throne. If she had lavished her maiden thoughts on him, by day or evening or at night, he had not known and could hardly be supposed to know. Indeed, she had begun by treating him with a cursory roughness; nor had he noticed any great softening later on.

"Listen," he said. Under the stress of embarrassment and alarm his cold blue eyes grew colder and his delicate nostrils quivered with an effect a little too like disdain. "I like you as well as another; no more, no less. I am in no position to think of love and marriage, and I have no inclination that way. I am willing to be friends with everybody, and nothing more with anybody." The sentences came with the cruel detachment of bullets; but, "Not again, not twice," was his uppermost thought. Any bluntness, any ruggedness, rather than another month like that of the past holiday season.

He took a step away and looked to one side, toward the couch where his hat and coat were lying.

"Go, if you will," she said. "And go as soon as you like. You are a contemptible, cold-hearted ingrate. You have grudged me every minute of your company, everywhere—and every second you have given me here. If I have been foolish it is over now, and there shall be nothing to record my folly." She stepped to the easel and hurled the canvas to the floor, where it lay with palette and brushes.

Cope stood with his hat in his hand and his coat over his arm.

He seemed to see the open volume of some "printed play." After all, there was a type which, even under emotional stress, gave a measure of instinctive heed to structure and cadence. Well, if there was relief for her in words, he could stand to hear her speak for a moment or two more, not longer.

"One word yet," she said in a panting voice. "Your Arthur Lemoyne. That preposterous friendship cannot go on for long. You will tire of him; or more likely he will tire of you. Something different, something better will be needed,—and you will live to learn so. I should be glad if I never saw either one of you again!"

She turned her stormy face away, and Cope slipped out with a blended sense of mortification, pain and relief.

# 28

## *Cope Absent from a Wedding*

COPE went out on the square with his being a-tingle. If Hortense, on another occasion, had thrown a dash of brine, on this occasion she had rubbed in the salt itself. And he had struck a harsh blow in turn; the flat of his mind was still stinging, as if half the shock of the blow had remained behind. "But it was no time for half-measures," he muttered to himself. "Not again; not twice!" he repeated.

Hortense remained for several days in a condition of sullen anger—she was a cloud lit up by occasional unaccountable flashes of temper. "Whatever in the world is the matter with her?" asked her aunt in more directions than one. And Amy

Leffingwell, blissfully busy over her little trousseau and her selection of china-patterns, protested and wide-open, inquiring blue eyes against the intrusion of such a spirit at such a joyous time.

But Hortense, though better days intervened now and then, did not improve essentially; and she contrived at the climacteric moment of Amy's career to make herself felt—unduly felt—after all.

The wedding took place during the latter half of April, as demanded by the enterprising wooer. Then there would be a rapid ten-day wedding-journey, followed by a prompt, business-like occupancy of the new apartment on the first of May exactly.

Pearson's parents prepared to welcome Amy handsomely; and her own people—some of them—came on from Iowa to attend the ceremony. There was her mother, who had been rather disconcerted by the sudden shift, but who was satisfied with George Pearson the moment she saw him, and who found him even more vivid and agreeable than Amy's photograph of him had led her to expect. There was the aunt, who had lived a bare, starved life, and who luxuriated, along with her sister, in the splendor of the Louis Quinze chamber. And there was a friendly, wide-awake brother of fourteen who was tucked away in the chintz room up stairs, whence he issued to fraternize in the ball-room with Joe Foster, whose exacerbated spirit he did much to soothe.

This young brother was alert, cheery, chatty. He was not at all put out by Foster's wheeled chair and eyeshade, nor by the strange contortions which Foster went through when, on occasion, he left the chair for a couch or for some chair of ordinary type. He got behind the wheels, and together they made the tour of the landscapes, marines, and genre-pieces which covered the walls. The boy was sympathetic, without being obtrusively so, and his comments on the paintings were confident and unconventional. "So different from *ce cher* Pelouse," said Foster, with a grimace. He enjoyed immensely the fragmental half-hours given him through those two days. His young companion was lavish in his reports on life's vast vicissitudes at Fort Lodge, and was always ready with comparisons between things as observed in his home town and in Churchton itself. He came as a tonic breeze; and the evening after he departed, Foster, left moping alone in the let-down which followed the festivities, said to himself more than once, "If I had had a boy, I should have wanted him just like Dick."

Dick's mother and aunt stood up as well as they could against the bustling, emphatic geniality of Medora Phillips; and they were able, after a little, to adjust themselves to the prosperity of the Pearsons. These, they came to feel, were essentially of the same origin and traditions as themselves: just plain people who, however, had settled on the edge of the Big Town to make money and had made it. Pearson the elder was hardly more prepotent than Mr. Lusk, the banker at home. George himself was a dashing go-ahead: if he turned into a tired business-man his wife would know how to divert him.

Medora Phillips provided rice. Also she satisfied herself as to where, if the newer taste were not too delicate, she could put her hand on an old shoe. She was happy to have married off Amy; she would be still happier once Amy got away. More room would be left for other young people. By "other young people" she meant, of course, certain young men. By "certain young men" she thought she meant Cope and Lemoyne. Of course she meant Cope only.

"If Carolyn keeps amiable and if Hortense contrives to regain her good-nature, we may have some pleasant days yet," she mused.

But Hortense did not regain her good-nature; she did not even maintain her self-control. In the end, the ceremony was too much for her. George and Amy had plighted their troth in a floral bower, which ordinarily was a baywindow, before a minister of a denomination which did not countenance robes nor a ritual lifted beyond the chances of wayward improvisation; and after a brief reception the new couple prepared for the motor-car dash which was to take them to a late train. In the big wide hallway, after Amy had kissed Carolyn and thanked her for her poem and was preparing for the shower of rice which she had every reason to think she must face, there was a burst of hysterical laughter from somewhere behind, and Hortense Dunton, to the sufficing words, "O Bertram, Bertram!" emitted with sufficing clearness, fainted away.

Her words, if not heard by all the company, were heard by a few to whom they mattered; and while Hortense, immediately after the departure of the happy pair, was being revived and led away, they left occasion for thought. Carolyn Thorpe cast a startled glance. The aunt from Iowa, who knew that Bertrams did not grow on every bush, and whose senses the function had preternaturally sharpened for any address from Romance, seized and shook her sister's arm; and, later on, in a Louis Quinze *causeuse*, up stairs, they agreed that if young Cope really had had another claimant on his attention, it was all the better that their Amy had ended by taking George. And Medora Phillips, in the front hall itself——

Well, to Medora Phillips, in the front hall, much was revealed as in a lightning-flash, and the revelation was far from agreeable. What advantage in Amy's departure if Hortense continued to cumber the ground? Hortense must go off somewhere, for a sojourn of a month or more, to recover her health and spirits and to let the house recover its accustomed tone of cheer.

Medora forced these considerations to the back of her mind and saw most of her guests out of the house. Toward the end of it all she found herself relaxing in the library, with Basil Randolph in the opposite chair. Randolph himself had figured in the ceremony. This had been a crude imitation of a time-hallowed form and had allowed for an extemporaneous prayer and for a brief address to the young couple; but it had retained the familiar inquiry, "Who giveth——?" "Who *can* give?" asked Medora of Amy. Poor Joe was rather out of the question, and Brother Dick was four or five years too young. Was there, then, anyone really available except that kind Mr. Randolph? So Basil Randolph, after remembering Amy with a rich and handsome present, had taken on a paternal air, had stepped forward at the right moment, and was now recovering from his novel experience.

The two, as they sat there, said little, though they looked at each other with half-veiled, questioning glances. Medora, indeed, improvised a little stretch of silent dialogue, and it made him take his share. She felt dislocated, almost defeated. Hortense's performance had set her to thinking of Bertram Cope, and she figured the same topic as uppermost in the mind of Basil Randolph.

"Well, you have about beaten me," she said.

"How so?" she made him ask, with an affectation of simplicity.

"You know well enough," she returned. "You have played off the whole University against my poor house, and you have won. Your influence with the president, your brother on the board of trustees . . . If Bertram Cope has any gratitude in his composition . . ."

"Oh, well," she let him say, "I don't feel that I did much; and I'm not sure I'm glad for what I did do."

"You may regret it, of course. That other man is an uncertain quantity."

"Oh, come," he said; "you've had the inside track from the very start: this house and everything in it . . ."

"You have a house of your own, now."

"Your dinners and entertainments . . ."

"You have your own dinner-table."

"Your limousine, your chauffeur,—running to the opera and heaven knows where else . . ."

"Taxis can always be had. Yes," she went on, "you have held the advantage over a poor woman cooped up in her own house. While I have had to stick here, attending to my housekeeping, you have been careering about everywhere,—you with a lot of partners and clerks in your office, and no compulsion to look in more than two or three times a week. Of *course* you can run to theatres and clubs. I wonder they don't dispense with you altogether!"

"There's the advantage of a business arranged to run itself— so far as *I* am concerned."

"Yes, you have had the world to range through: shows and

restaurants; the whole big city; strolls and excursions, and who knows what beside . . ."

Thus Medora Phillips continued silently, and with no exact sense of justice, to work up her grievance. Presently she surprised Randolph with a positive frown. She had made a quick, darting return to Hortense.

"I shall send her away," she said aloud. The girl might join her studio friend, who had stopped at Asheville on her way North, and stay with her for a few weeks. Yes, Hortense might go and meet the spring—or even the summer, if that must be. The spring here in town she herself would take as it came. "I shall welcome a few free, easy breaths after this past fortnight," she finished audibly.

Randolph squared himself with her mood as best he could. "You are tired and nervous," he said with banality. "Get the last of us out and go to bed. I'll lead the way, and will give these loiterers as marked an example as possible."

Medora Phillips hushed down her house finally and went thoughtfully up stairs to her room. Amy had gone off, and Hortense was sentenced to go. There remained only Carolyn. Was there any threat in her and her sonnets?

# 29

## Cope Again in the Country

MEDORA treated Hortense to a few cautious soundings, decided that another locale was the thing to do her good, and sent her South forthwith.

"It's a low latitude," she said to herself; "but it's a high altitude. The season is late, but she won't suffer."

Hortense, who had been sullen and fractious, met her aunt half-way, and agreed passively when Medora said:

"It will benefit you to see the spring come on in a new scene and in a new fashion. You will find the mountains more interesting than the dunes." So Hortense packed her things and joined her friend for a brief sojourn in sight of the Great Smokies.

Thus, when Medora herself went forth to meet the spring among the sand-hills, she had only Carolyn and the other members of her domestic staff. Yet no simplest week-end without a guest or so, and she asked Cope to accompany them.

"You need it," she told him bluntly; "—you need a change, however slight and brief. You are positively thin. You make me wish that thesises——"

"Theses," Cope corrected her, rather spiritlessly.

"——that theses, then, had never been invented. To speak familiarly, you are almost 'peakèd.'"

Cope, with the first warm days, had gone back to the blue serge suit of the past autumn, and he filled it even less well than before. And his face was thin to correspond.

"Besides," she went on, "we need you. It will be a kind of camping-out for a day or two—merely that. We must have your help to pitch the tent, so to speak, and to pick up firewood, and to fry the bacon. . . . And this time," she added, "you shall not have that long tiresome trip by train. There will be room in the car."

She did not attempt to make room for Lemoyne. She was glad to have no need to do so; Lemoyne was deeply engrossed otherwise— "Annabella" and her "antics" were almost ready for the public eye. The first of May would see the performance, and the numerous rehearsals were exacting, whether as regarded the effort demanded or the time. Every spare hour was going into them, as well as many an hour that could hardly be spared. Lemoyne, who had been cast originally for a minor female part, now found himself transferred, through the failure of a principal, to a more important one. For him, then, rehearsals were more exigent than ever. He cut his Psychology once or twice, nor could he succeed, during office hours, in keeping his mind on office-routine. His superiors became impatient and then protestant. The annual spring dislocation of ordered student life was indeed a regular feature of the year's last term; yet to push indulgence as far as Arthur Lemoyne was pushing it——!

Cope was concerned; then worried. "Arthur," he said, "be reasonable about this. You've got real work to do, remember."

But Lemoyne's real work was in the musical comedy. "This is the biggest chance I've ever had in my life," he declared, "and I don't want to lose out on it."

So Cope rolled away to the dunes and left Lemoyne behind for one Saturday night rehearsal the more.

Duneland gave him a tonic welcome. Under a breezy sky the far edge of the lake stood out clear. Along its nearer edge the vivacious waves tumbled noisily. The steady pines were welcoming the fresh early foliage of such companions as dressed and undressed in accord with the calendar; the wrecked trunks which had given up life and its leafy pomps seemed somehow less sombre and stark; and in the threatened woodlands behind the hills a multiplicity of small new greeneries stirred the autumn's dead leaves and brightened up the thickets of shrubbery. The arbutus had companioned the hepatica, and the squads of the lupines were busily preparing their panoply of lavender-blue racemes. Nature was breaking bounds. On the inland horizon rose the vast bulk of the prison. As on other excursions, nobody tried too hard to see it.

"It's all too lovely," exclaimed Medora Phillips. "And what is quite as good," she was able to declare, "the house itself is all right." Winter had not weakened its roof nor wrenched away its storm-windows; no irresponsible wayfarer had used it for a lodging, nor had any casual marauder entered to despoil. Medora directed the disposition of the hamper of food with a relieved air and sent Cope down with Peter for an armful or two of driftwood from the assertive shore.

"And you, Carolyn," she said, "see if the oil-stove will really go."

Down on the beach itself, where the past winter's waste was still profusely spread, Cope rose to the greening hills, to the fresh sweep of the wind, and to the sun-shot green and purple streakings over the water. The wind, in particular, took its own way: dry light sand, blown from higher shelvings, striped the dark wet edges of the shore; and every bending blade of sand-grass drew a circle about itself with its own revolving tip.

Cope let the robust and willing Peter pick up most of the firewood and himself luxuriated in the spacious world round about him. Yes, a winter had flown—or, at any rate, had passed —and here he was again. There had been annoyances, but now he felt a wide and liberal relief. Here, for example, was the special stretch of shore on which Amy Leffingwell had praised his singing and had hinted her desire to accompany him,—but never mind that. Farther on was the particular tract where Hortense Dunton had pottered with her water-colors and had harried him with the heroines of eighteenth century fiction,—but never mind that, either. All those things were past, and he was free. Nobody remained save Carolyn Thorpe, an unaggressive girl with whom one could really trust oneself and with whom one could walk, if required, in comfort and content. Cope threw up his head to the hills and threw out his chest to the winds, and laid quick hands on a short length of weather-beaten hemlock plank. "Afraid I'm not holding up my end," he said to Peter.

At the house again, he found that Carolyn had brought the oil-stove back into service, and, with Helga, had cast the cloth over the table and had set some necessary dishes on it. He fetched a pail or two of water from the pump, and each time placed a fresh young half-grown sassafras leaf on the surface. "The trade-mark of our bottling-works," he said facetiously; "to show that our products are pure." And Carolyn, despite his facetiousness, felt more than ever that he might easily become a poet. Medora viewed the floating leaves with indulgent appreciation. "But don't let's cumber ourselves with many cares," she suggested; "we are here to make the best of the afternoon. Let's out and away,—the sooner the better."

The three soon set forth for a stroll through spring's reviving domain. Cope walked between Medora and Carolyn, or ahead of them, impartially sweeping away twigs and flowering branches from before their faces. The young junipers were putting forth tender new tips; the bright leaves of the sassafras shone forth against the pines. Above the newly-rounded tops of the oaks and maples in the valley below them the Three Witches rose gauntly; and off on their far hill the two companion pines— (how had he named them? Romeo and Juliet? Pelleas and Melisande?)—still lay their dark heads together in mysterious confidences under the heightening glow of the late afternoon sun. Carolyn looked from them back to Cope and gave him a shy smile.

He did not quite smile back. Carolyn was well enough, however. She was suitably dressed for a walk. Her shoes were sensible, and so was her hair. Amy had run to fluffiness. Hortense had often favored heavy waves and emphatic bandeaux. But Carolyn's hair was drawn back plainly from her forehead, and was gathered in a small, low-set knot. "Still, it's no concern of mine," he reminded himself, and walked on ahead.

Carolyn's sensible shoes brought her back, with the others, at twilight. The three took up rather ornamentally (with aid from Peter and Helga) the lighter details of housekeeping. Toward the end of the stroll, Cope and Carolyn,—perhaps upon the mere unconscious basis of youth,—had rather fallen in together, and Medora Phillips, once or twice, had had to safeguard for herself her face and eyesight from the young trees that bordered their path. But that evening, as they sat on a settle before the driftwood fire, Medora took pains to place herself in the middle. Carolyn was a sweet young flower, doubtless—humbler, possibly, than Amy or Hortense; yet she too perhaps must be extirpated, gently but firmly, from the garden of desire.

"You look better already," Medora said to Cope. "You'll go back to-morrow a new man."

Her elbow was on the back of the settle and close to his shoulder. His face caught the glow from the fire.

"Oh, I'm all right, I assure you," he said.

"You *do* look better," observed Carolyn on her own account. "This air is everything. Only a few hours of it——"

"Another bit of wood on the fire, if you please, Carolyn," said her patroness.

"Let me do it," said Cope. He rose quickly and laid on a stick or two. He remained standing on the edge of the glow. He hoped nobody would say again that he was looking rather thin and pale.

"And what is Mr. Lemoyne doing this evening?" presently asked Mrs. Phillips in a dreamy undertone. Her manner was casual and negligent; her voice was low and leisurely. She seemed to place Lemoyne at a distance of many, many leagues. "Rehearsing, I suppose?"

"Yes," replied Cope. "This new play has absorbed him completely."

"He will do well?"

"He always does. He always has."

"Men in girls' parts are so amusing," said Carolyn. "Their walk is so heavy and clumsy, even if their dancing isn't. And when they speak up in those big deep bass and baritone voices . . . !"

"Arthur will speak in a light tenor."

"Will his walk be heavy and clumsy?" asked Mrs. Phillips.

"He is an artist," replied Cope.

"Not too much of one, I trust," she returned. "I confess I like boys best in such parts when they frankly and honestly seem to be boys. That's half the fun—and nine-tenths of the taste."

"Taste?"

"Yes, taste. Short for good taste. There's a great deal of room for bad. A thing may be done too thoroughly. Once or twice I've seen it done that way, by—artists."

Cope, in the half-light, seemed rather unhappy.

"He finds time for—for all this—this technique?" Mrs. Phillips asked.

"He's very clever," replied Cope, rather unhappy still. "It does take time, of course. I'm concerned," he added.

"About his other work?"

"Yes." He stepped aside a little into the shadow.

"Come back to your place," said Medora Phillips. "You look quite spectral."

Cope, with a light sigh, returned to his post on the settle and to his share in the firelight. Silence fell. From far below were heard the active waves, moaning themselves to rest. And a featureless evening moved on slowly.

# 30

## *Cope as a Hero*

AT TEN o'clock Cope found himself tucked away in a small room on the ground floor. It had been left quite as planned and constructed by the original builder of the house. It was cramped and narrow, with low ceiling and one small window. It gave on a short side-porch which was almost too narrow to sit on and which was apropos of no special prospect. Doubtless more than one stalwart youth had slept there before him,—a succession of farmers' sons who fed all day on the airs and spaces of the great out-of-doors, and who needed little of either through a short night's rest. It was more comfortable at the end of April than other guests had found it in mid-August.

A little before eleven he awoke the house with a loud, ringing cry. Some one outside had passed his narrow window; feet were heard on the back porch and hands at the kitchen door. Peter was out as quickly as Cope himself; and the women, in differing stages of dress and half-dress, followed at once.

While Mrs. Phillips and Carolyn were clinging to Cope, who had rushed out in undershirt and trousers, Peter had a short tussle on the porch with the intruder. He came in showing a scratch or two on his face, and he reported the pantry window broken open.

"Some tramp along the beach saw our lights," suggested Carolyn.

"What was he like, Peter?" asked Mrs. Phillips.

"I couldn't make out in the dark," Peter replied. "But he fought hard for what he took, and he got away with it." He felt the marks on his face. "Must have been a pretty hungry man."

"It was some refugee hiding in my woods," said Medora Phillips. She made her real thought no plainer. She never liked to see, in her walks, that distant prison, and she never spoke of it to her guests; but the fancy of some escaped convict lurking below among her thickets was often present in her mind.

Her fancy was now busy with some burglar, or even some murderer, who had made his bolt for liberty; and she clung informally to the clarion-voiced Cope as to a savior. She saw, with displeasure, that Carolyn was disposed to cling too. She asked Carolyn to control herself and told her the danger was over; she even requested her to return to her room. But Carolyn lingered.

Medora herself stood with Cope in the light of the dying fire. She was dressed almost as inadequately as he, but she felt that she must cling tremblingly to him and thank him for something or other.

"I don't know what you've saved us from," she panted. "We may owe our very lives to you!"

Peter, in the background, again thoughtfully felt his face and became conscious of a growing ache in the muscles of his arms. He retired, with a smile, to a still more distant plane. The regular did the work and the volunteer got the praise.

Mrs. Phillips presently gave up her drooping hold on the reluctant Cope and called Peter forward. "Is anything missing?" she asked.

"Only part of the breakfast, I expect," said Peter, with a grin. "And maybe some of the lunch. He surely was a hungry man!"

"Well, we sha'n't starve. See to all the doors and windows before you go back to bed."

But going back to bed was the one thing that she herself felt unable to do. She asked Carolyn to bring her a wrap of some kind or other, and sat down on the settle to talk it over. Cope had modestly slipped on a coat. The fire was dying—that was the only difference between twelve o'clock and ten.

"If I had known what was going to happen," declared Medora volubly, "I never could have gone to bed at all! And to think"— here she left Carolyn's end of the settle and drew nearer to Cope's—"that I should ever have even thought of coming out here without a man!"

She now rated her midnight intruder as a murderer, and believed more devoutly than ever that Cope had saved all their lives. Cope, who knew that he had contributed nothing but a loud pair of lungs, began to feel rather foolish.

Nor did the anomalous situation commend itself in any degree to his taste. But it hit Medora Phillips' taste precisely, and she continued to sit there, pressing an emotional enjoyment from it. An hour passed before her excitement—an excitement kept up, perhaps, rather factitiously—was calmed, and she trusted herself back in her own room.

Breakfast was a scanty affair,—it must be that if anything was to be left over for lunch. While they were busy with toast and coffee voices were heard in the woods—loud cries in call and answer.

"There!" said Medora, setting down her cup; "I knew it!"

Presently two men came climbing up to the house, while the voices of others were still audible in the humpy thickets below.

The men were part of a search-party, of course,—a posse; and they wanted to know whether . . .

"He tried to break in," said Medora Phillips eagerly; "but this gentleman . . ."

She turned appreciatively to Cope. Carolyn, really impressed by her well-sustained seriousness and ardor, almost began to believe that they owed their lives to Bertram Cope alone.

"Was he a—murderer?" asked Medora.

The men looked serious, but made no categorical reply. They glanced at the wrecked pantry window, and they looked with more intentness at the long sliding footprints which led away, down the half-bare sand-slope. Then they slid down themselves.

Medora asked Carolyn to do what she could toward constructing a lunch and then walked down to the shore with Cope to compose her nerves. No stroll today along the ridged amphitheatre of the hills, whence the long, low range of buildings, under that tall chimney, was so plainly in view. Still less relishing the idea of a tramp through the woods themselves, the certain haunt—somewhere—of some skulking desperado. No, they would take the shore itself—open to the wide firmament, clear of all snares, and free from every disconcerting sight.

"Poor Carolyn!" said Medora presently. "How fluttered and inefficient she was! A good secretary—in a routine way—but so lacking in initiative and self-possession!"

Cope's look tended to become a stare. He thought that Carolyn had been in pretty fair control of herself,—had been less fluttery and excited, indeed, than her employer.

But Medora had been piqued, the night before, by Carolyn's tendency to linger on the scene and to help skim the emotional cream from the situation.

"And in such dishabille, too! I hope you don't think she seemed immodest?"

But Cope had given small heed to their dress, or to their lack of it. In fact, he had noticed little if any difference between them. He only knew that he had felt a degree more comfortable after getting his own coat on.

"Carolyn understands her place pretty well," mused Medora. "Yet . . ."

"Anybody might be excused for looking anyhow, at such a time," observed Cope, fending off the intrusion of a new set of considerations; "and in such a sudden stir. I hope nobody noticed how I looked!"

"Well, you were noticeable," declared Medora, with some

archness. She had been conscious enough of his spare waist, his sinewy arms, his swelling chest. "It was easy enough to see where the noise came from," she said, looking him over.

"Yes, I supplied the noise—and that only. It was Peter, please remember, who supplied the muscle."

She declined to let her mind dwell on Peter. Peter possessed no charm. Besides, he was prosaically on the payroll.

They continued to saunter along the sand. Yesterday's sparse clouds had vanished, along with much of yesterday's wind. The waters that had tumbled and vociferated now merely murmured. The lake stood calmly blue, and the new green was thickening on the hills. Confident birds flitted busily among the trees and shrubs. Spring was disclosed in its most alluring mood.

Suddenly three or four figures appeared on the beach, a quarter of a mile away. They had descended through one of the sandy and ravaged channelings which broke at intervals the regulated rim of the hills, and they came on toward our two strollers. Medora closed her eyes to peer at them. "Are they marching a prisoner?" she asked.

"They all appear to be walking free."

"Are they carrying knapsacks?"

"Khaki, puttees,—and knapsacks, I think."

"Some university men said they might happen along to-day. If they really have knapsacks, and anything to eat in them, they're welcome. Otherwise, we had better hide quick—and hope they'll lose the place and pass us by."

One of the advancing figures lifted a semaphoric arm. "Too late," said Cope; "They recognize you."

"Then we'll walk on and meet them," declared Medora.

The newcomers were young professors and graduate students. They were soon in possession of the thrilling facts of the past night, and one of them offered to be a prisoner, if a prisoner was desired. When they heard how Bertram Cope had saved the lives of defenseless women in a lonely land, they inclined to smile. Two of them had been present on another shore when Cope had "saved" Amy Leffingwell from a watery death, and they knew how far heroics might be pushed by women who were willing to idealize. Cope saw their smiles and felt that he had fumbled an opportunity: when he might have been a truncheon, he had been only a megaphone.

The new arrivals, after climbing the sandy rise to the house, were shown the devastated kitchen and were asked to declare what provisions they carried. They had enough food for their own needs and a trifle to spare. Lunch might be managed, but any thought of a later meal was out of the question. "We'll start back at four-thirty," said Medora to Peter. "Meanwhile"—to the college men—"the world is ours."

After lunch the enlarged party walked forth again. Mrs. Phillips had old things to show to fresh eyes: she formed the new visitors into a compact little group and let them see how good a guide she could be. Cope and Carolyn strolled negligently— even unsystematically—behind. Once or twice the personally conducted looked back.

"I hope she won't tell them again how I came to the rescue," said Cope. "It makes a man feel too flat for words. Anybody might think, to hear her go on, that I had saved you all from robbery and murder . . ."

"Why, but didn't you?" inquired Carolyn seriously.

# 3 1

## *Cope Gets New Light on His Chum*

COPE had the luck to get back to Churchton with little further in the way of homage. He was careful with Carolyn; she had perhaps addressed him in a sonnet, and she might go on and address him in an ode. He thought he had done nothing to deserve the one, and he would do almost anything to escape the other. She was a nice pleasant quiet girl; but nice pleasant quiet girls were beginning to do such equivocal things in poetical print!

Having returned to town by a method that put the minimum tax on his powers, Cope was in shape, next day, for an hour on the faculty tennis-courts. He played with no special skill or vigor, but he made a pleasing picture in his flannels; and Carolyn, who happened to pass—who passed by at about five in the afternoon, lingered for the spectacle and thought of two or three lines to start a poem with.

Cope, unconscious of this, presently turned his attention to Lemoyne, who was on the eve of his first dress rehearsal and who was a good deal occupied with wigs and lingerie. Here one detail leads to another, and anyone who goes in wholeheartedly may go in dreadfully deep. Their room came to be strown with all the disconcerting items of a theatrical wardrobe. Cope soon reached the point where he was not quite sure that he liked it all, and he began to develop a distaste for Lemoyne's preoccupation with it. He came home one afternoon to find on the corner of his desk a long pair of silk stockings and a too dainty pair of ladies' shoes. "Oh, Art!" he protested. And then,—not speaking his essential thought,— "Aren't these pretty expensive?"

"The thing has got to be done right," returned Lemoyne. "Feet are about the first thing they notice."

At the actual performance Lemoyne's feet were noticed, certainly; though perhaps not more than his head. His wig, as is usually the case with dark people, was of a sunny blond hue. Its curls, as palpably artificial as they were voluminous, made his eyes look darker and somehow more liquid than ever. The contrast was piquant, almost sensational. Of course he had sacrificed, for the time, his small moustache. Lemoyne was not "Annabella" herself, but only her chief chum; yet shorter skirts and shorter sleeves and a deliberately assumed feminine air helped distinguish him from the hearty young lads who manœuvred in the chorus.

Just who are those who enjoy the epicene on the stage? Not

many women, one prefers to think; and surely it arouses the impatience, if not worse, of many men. Most amateur drama is based, perhaps, on the attempted "escape": one likes to bolt from his own day, his own usual costume, his own range of ideas, and even from his own sex. Endeavors toward this last are most enjoyable—or least offensive—when they show frank and patent inadequacy. It was Arthur Lemoyne's fortune—or misfortune—to do his work all too well.

Mrs. Phillips found his performance as little to her taste as she had anticipated. Carolyn Thorpe got as much enjoyment out of the gauche carriage and rough voices of the "chorus girls" as she had expected, but was not observed to warm toward "Annabella's" closest friend. The Pearsons, back from their wedding trip, had seats near the big crimson velvet curtain. Pearson himself openly luxuriated in the amusing ineptitude of two or three beskirted acquaintances among the upper classmen, but frowned at Lemoyne's light tenor tones and mincing ways. Of course the right sort of fellow, even if he had to sing his solo in the lightest of light tenors, would still, on lapsing into dialogue, reinstate himself apologetically by using as rough and gruff a voice as he could summon. Not so Lemoyne: he was doing a consistent piece of "characterization," and he was feminine, even overfeminine, throughout.

"I never liked him, anyway," said George to Amy.

Amy gave a nod of agreement. Yet why this critical zeal? There was but one man to like, after all.

"That make-up! That low-cut gown!" said George, in further condemnation. "There's such a thing as going too far."

Basil Randolph met Cope in the back lobby at the close of the performance. The dramatic season in the city itself had begun to languish; besides that, Randolph, in order to maintain his place on the edge of the life academical, always made it a point to remember the Grayfriars each spring.

"A very thorough, consistent piece of work—your friend's," said Randolph. He spoke in a firm, *net*, withholding tone, looking Cope full in the face, meanwhile. What he said was little, perhaps, of what was in his mind; yet Cope caught a note of criticism and of condemnation.

"Yes," he almost felt constrained to say in reply, "yes, I know what you did for him—for me, rather; and possibly this is not the outcome foreseen. I hope you won't regret your aid."

Randolph went past him placidly. He seemed to have little to regret. On the contrary, he almost appeared to be pleased. He may have felt that Lemoyne had shown himself in a tolerably clear light, and that it was for Cope, should he choose, to take heed.

Two days later, Randolph gave his impression of the performance to Foster. "It's just what I should have expected," declared the cripple acrimoniously. "I'm glad you never had any taste for the fellow; and I should have been quite as well pleased if I hadn't found you caring for the other."

Randolph took refuge in a bland inexpressiveness. There was no need to school his face: he had only to discipline his voice.

"Oh, well," he said smoothly, "it's only a passing *amitié*— something soon to be over, perhaps." He used an alien word because he could not select, on the instant, from his stock of English, the word he needed, and because he was not quite sure what idea he wanted to express. "I only wish," he went on, in the same even tone, "that this chap had been doing better by his work. At one early stage of the rehearsals there was a lot of registration and fee-paying for the new term. Well, if he hasn't been satisfactory, they needn't blame me. Let them blame the system that diverts so much time and attention to interests quite outside the regular curriculum."

"You talk like a book!" said Foster, with blunt disdain.

"Language————" began Randolph.

"————was made to conceal thought," completed the other. "Stop talking. Stop thinking. Or, if you must think, just get your thoughts back on your business."

Foster might have expressed himself still more pungently if he had been aware, as Cope was, of an episode which took place, behind the scenes, at the close of the performance. Lemoyne's singing and dancing in the last act had had a marked success: after all, people had come to enjoy and to applaud. Following two or three recalls, a large sheaf of roses had been passed over the footlights; for a close imitation of professional procedure was held to give the advantage of strict vraisemblance. This "tribute" Lemoyne took in character, with certain graces, pirouettes and smiles. His success so mounted to his head (for he was the one person in the case who approximated a professional effect) that after he had retired he could not quiet down and leave his part. He continued to act off-stage; and in his general state of ebulliency he endeavored to bestow a measure of upwelling femininity upon another performer who was in the dress of his own sex. This downright fellow, in cutaway and silk hat, did not understand,—or at least had no patience with a rôle carried too far. He brusquely cleared himself of Lemoyne's arm with a good vigorous push. This effort not only propelled Lemoyne against some scenery and left him, despite the voluminous blond wig, with a bruise on his forehead; it immediately pushed him out of his part, and it ended by pushing him out of the organization and even out of the University.

"Keep off, will you!" said the young *élégant* crudely.

Lemoyne's "atmosphere" dissipated suddenly. His art-structure collapsed. As he looked about he saw plainly that the other man's act was approved. He had carried things too far. Well, such are the risks run by the sincere, self-revealing artist.

When all this reached Cope, he felt a personal chagrin. Truly, the art of human intercourse was an art that called for some care. Lemoyne's slight wound left no trace after forty-eight hours—perhaps his "notices" in "The Index" and "The Campus" had acted as a salve; but certain sections of opinion remained unfriendly, and there was arising a new atmosphere of distaste and disapproval.

The college authorities had not been satisfied, for some time, with his clerical labors, and some of them thought that his stage performance—an "exhibition" one of them termed it—called for reproof, or more. They laid their heads together and Lemoyne and Cope were not long in learning their decision. Lemoyne was pronounced a useless element in one field, a discrepant element in another, a detriment in both. His essentially slight connection with the real life of the University came to be more fully recognized. Alma Mater, in fine, could do without him, and meant to. Censure was the lot of the indignant boys who officered the society, and who asked Lemoyne to withdraw; and complete scission from the nourishing vine of Knowledge was his final fate.

No occupation; no source of income. Winnebago was cold; nor was it to be warmed into ardor by press-notices. It had seen too many already and was tired of them.

The two young men conferred. Again Basil Randolph was their hope.

"He ought to be able to do something for me in the city," said Lemoyne. "He's acquainted in business circles, isn't he?"

Cope bent over him—paler, thinner, more solicitous. "I'll try it," he said.

Cope once more approached Randolph, but Randolph shook his head. He had no faith in Lemoyne, and he had done enough already against his own interests and desires.

Lemoyne fluttered about to little effect for a few weeks, while Cope was finishing up his thesis. Beyond an accustomed and desired companionship, Lemoyne contributed nothing—was a drag, in truth. He returned to Winnebago a fortnight before the convocation and the conferring of degrees; and it was the understanding that, somehow, he and Cope should share together a summer divided between Winnebago and Freeford. Randolph was left to claim Cope's interest, if he could.

# 32

## *Cope Takes His Degree*

LEMOYNE'S departure but a fortnight before Cope's small share in the convocation seemed to hint at mutual dissatisfaction; it might even stand for a disagreement, or possibly a quarrel. "It's just as well that he went," said Randolph to himself. "His presence here was no advantage to Bertram —nor to anybody else." And with another fortnight Cope himself would be gone; and who knew in what distant quarter he might take up his autumn work? His ambitions, as Randolph knew, pointed to some important university in the East. Meanwhile, make the most of the flying days.

Medora Phillips took the same view. She let Carolyn Thorpe

loose for a week's spring vacation, and sent Cope word that she was alone in a darkened, depopulated home. Amy married. Hortense banished. Carolyn waved aside. With all such varying devotions removed, why should he not look in on her loneliness, during these final days, for dinner or tea? He was still "charming"—however difficult, however recalcitrant. And he was soon to depart. And who could believe that the fall term would bring his equal or his like?

Randolph, still taking his business easily, had suggestions for walks and lunches; he had also free time to make his suggestions operative. But Cope, though frequently seen in active movement on the campus and through the town, gave little heed to either of his elderly friends. He met them both, in High Street, on different occasions, and thanked and smiled and promised—and kept away. He was doubtless absorbed in his special work, in the details of the closing year. He may have thought (as young men have been known to think) that, in accepting their invitations, he had done enough for them already. He had shown his good will on several occasions; let that suffice. Or he may have thought (as young men have been found capable of thinking) not at all: other concerns, more pressing and more contemporaneous, may have crowded them out of his mind altogether.

"I wonder if it's sensitiveness?" asked Randolph of Foster. "His chum didn't go away in the best of good odor. . . ."

"Settle it for yourself," returned Foster brusquely. "And recall that you have an office—and might have office-hours. Still, if you insist on asking me———"

"I don't. But you may speak, if you like."

"And if you will consent to be fobbed off with a short-measure answer——"

"That's right. Don't say all you think."

"Then I would put it somewhere between indifference and ingratitude. Nearer the latter. We know the young."

"I don't feel that I've done so very much for him," said Randolph, rather colorlessly.

"You were inclined to."

"H'm, yes. I could have opened up avenues that would have made his year here a very different thing. Perhaps he didn't realize what I could do. And perhaps he found me too old."

"Shall you attend the convocation?"

"I go usually. I'll push him off from shore and waft him good-bye."

"Good-bye? Good riddance!"

"You never liked him."

"I never did. If he leaves town without showing up here, no loss."

"Medora expects him here?"

"I think so."

Randolph descended to the lower floor. Mrs. Phillips was alone, seated behind a tea-service that steamed with expectation.

"Going?" she asked.

"Going. Joe is grouchy and violent today. And he keeps on reminding me that I have an office."

Medora glanced at the clock. Expectation seemed to be simmering down.

"Stay a few moments if you like. Forget the office a little longer. I'll make some fresh."

"Not all these preparations for me?"

"Well, they're here. Take advantage."

"You're all alone?"

"Alone. The house is empty."

Medora tried to look as if at the heart of a tremendous vacuum.

"I can't fill it."

"You can fill fifteen minutes."

"Oh, if you're going to confound time and space . . . !"

He sat down receptively.

Medora rang a bell and harried Helga a little.

She glanced at Randolph. He sat there as if less to fill than to be filled.

"Say something," she said.

"Are you going to the convocation?"

"No."

He sat silent.

"Does that exhaust the subjects of interest?" she asked.

"Pretty nearly. Doesn't it?"

Medora fell silent in turn,—let the light clatter of the tea things speak for her.

"Are you going to the convocation?" he presently asked again.

"Such variety!" she mocked.

"Are you?"

She hesitated.

"Yes," she said.

"That's better. Let's go together——as friends."

"Who would imagine us going as enemies?"

"Who, indeed?" Yet if they went together they went as reconciled competitors,——they went as the result of a truce.

"I should like to see Bertram Cope in cap and gown," he said.

"He has worn them before, he tells me."

"As a——?"

"As a member of the choir, during his undergraduate days."

"I see."

"I never noticed him especially, then," she acknowledged.

"We can notice him now."

Medora made a slight grimace. "Yes, we can notice." He the actor; they the audience. "A farewell performance."

"A final view."

Convocation day came clear, fair, mild. The professors walked in colorful solemnity beneath the elms and up the middle aisle of the chapel, lending both to outdoors and indoors the enlivenment of hoods red, yellow, purple. The marshals led strings of candidates —long strings and short—to the platform where the president sat, and the deans presented in due order their bachelors, masters and doctors. The rapid handing out of the diplomas brought frequent applause—bits, spatters, volleys, as the case might be. There was recognition for a Chinaman, for a negro law-student, for a pair of Filipinos; there was a marked outburst for a husky young man who was assumed by the uninformed to have been a star in the university's athletic life; there was a respectful but emphatic acknowledgment for a determined-looking middle-aged woman with gray hair, who was led on with four men as a little string of five; there was a salvo for a thoughtful, dignified man of thirty-odd, who went up as a group in himself, attended by marshals before and behind; and there was a slight spatter of applause for Bertram Cope (one of a small procession of six), yet rather more for a smiling young man who followed him. . . .

Cope looked somewhat spare, despite his voluminous gown. The trying lights added little color to his face, and brought his cheek-bones into undue prominence. But he took his sheepskin with a bow and a gesture that extinguished several of his companions; and he faced the audience, on descending from the stage, with a composed effect gained by experience in the choir. The lustre in the ceiling lit up his yellow hair and his blue eyes: "He is as charming as ever!" thought Medora Phillips.

"He's had a hard pull of it," commented Randolph.

"I hope his own people will feed him up this summer," said Medora. Her emphasis was wayward; "He wouldn't let *me* do it," she seemed to mean.

"Nor me," she almost made Randolph say.

There was a recessional, and then the crowds of students flooded the corridors and circulated under the fresh foliage of the campus. Randolph and Medora Phillips passed out with the rest of the assemblage. In the midst of one of the avenues of elms they noticed Cope as the center of a little group: two plain, elderly people (his parents, doubtless) and—and——

Medora Phillips looked twice. Yes, the other figure was Carolyn Thorpe, offering congratulations. Carolyn had returned to her post and her work the day before. "H'm," thought Medora, disposed to be miffed. Still, Carolyn had, after all, the same right to attend as anyone else.

Medora and Basil Randolph added their congratulations to Carolyn's. Cope, still in academic garb, performed the necessary introductions. His air was eager, but cursory; smiling and ready, yet impersonal and cool; above all, expeditious. If his parents passed on with the impression that Medora Phillips and Basil Randolph were but casual acquaintances, worthy of nothing beyond brief formalities, the blame was his own.

"I'm showing father and mother over the campus," he said, with an open smile and a wave with his diploma, as he edged away.

The elders docilely took their cue, and moved away with him.

"Well," said Randolph, "there *are* buildings, of course; and fountains, and sun-dials, and memorial benches; but . . ."

"They add nothing to him," pronounced Medora, as she looked back on the retiring party.

"Did you expect them to?" he asked. "Charm, like guilt, is personal. Anyhow, there seems to be no brother," he added.

"Well, come, Carolyn," said Medora, to her returned secretary, who was looking after the party too; "let's start for home. Good afternoon, Basil."

"What nice, good, pleasant, friendly people they are!" breathed Carolyn.

Randolph had strolled away, and Medora Phillips turned a studious glance on her companion. Carolyn was conceivably in a state of mind—keyed up to an all-inclusive appreciation. Did that foreshadow further verse?—a rustic rhapsody, a provincial pantoum? But Medora withheld question. Much as she would have enjoyed a well-consolidated impression of the visitors, she did not intend to secure it by interrogating Carolyn Thorpe.

# 33

*Cope in a Final View*

C O P E , after a few days, followed his parents back to Freeford.
He may have said good-bye to his landlady and to some of his associates in his department; but he contrived no set adieux for the
friends who had done so much for him—or had tried to—
through the past year. Basil Randolph and Medora Phillips had
their last view of him when, diploma in hand, he led his parents
away, over the campus.

"Oh, well," said Randolph resignedly, "we were less important to him than we thought. Only a couple of negligible items
among many. Entered in his ledger—if we *were* entered—and
now faded away to a dim, rusty, illegible scrawl . . ."

"Stop it, Basil! You make me feel old, antique, antediluvian. I don't want to. I shan't let myself be pushed back and ignored. I'm going to give Amy and George a rousing big dinner before long; and when the fall term opens I shall entertain as never before. And if that young man from the South turns up here during the summer to see Hortense, I shall do a lot for them."

Hortense Dunton had long since returned, of course, from the Tennessee and North Carolina mountains; but she ignored the convocation. One drop of bitterness, if tasted again—even reminiscently— would have turned everything to gall. Instead, she found a measure of sweetness in the letters which followed on her return from that region. They were addressed in a bold, dashing young hand, and bore the postmark "Nashville." Hortense was inclined to let them lie conspicuously on the front hall table, for half an hour or so, before she took them up. Little might be absolutely known about her passage with Cope; but there the letters lay, for her aunt's eye and for Carolyn Thorpe's.

Carolyn prattled a little, not indiscreetly, about her meeting with the Freeford family on the campus. As Basil Randolph himself had done months before, she endeavored to construct a general environment for them and to determine their place in the general social fabric. She had, however, the advantage of having seen them; she was not called to make an exiguous evocation from the void. She still held that they were nice, good, pleasant, friendly people: if they had subordinated themselves, docilely and automatically, to the prepotent social and academic figures of the society about them, that in no wise detracted from the favorable impression they had made on her.

"Just the right parents for Bertram," she said fondly, to herself. She made, almost unconsciously, the allowance that is still generally made, among Americans, for the difference between two generations: the elder, of course, continues to provide a staid, sober, and somewhat primitive background for the brilliancy of the younger. Her own people, if they appeared in Churchton, might seem a bit simple and provincial too.

Hortense took Carolyn's slight and fond observations with a silent scorn. When she spoke at all, she was likely to say something about "family"; and it was gathered that the dashing correspondent at Nashville was conspicuously "well-connected." Also, that he belonged to the stirring New South and had put money in his purse. Hortense's contempt for the semi-rustic and impecunious Cope became boundless.

About the middle of July a letter lay on the front-hall table for Carolyn. It was from Cope.

"Only think!" said Carolyn to herself, in a small private ecstasy within her locked bedchamber; "he wrote on his own account and of his own accord. Not a line from me; not a suggestion!"

The letter was an affair of two small pages. "Yours very sincerely, Bertram L. Cope" simply told "My dear Miss Thorpe" that he had been spending three or four days in Winnebago, Wisconsin, and that he had now returned home for a month of further study, having obtained a post in an important university in the East, at a satisfactory stipend. A supplementary line conveyed regards to Mrs. Phillips. And that was all.

Was it a handful of husks, or was it a banquet? Carolyn took it for the latter and lived on it for days. Little it mattered what or how much he had written: he had written, and of his own accord—as Carolyn made a point of from the first. There is an algebraic formula expressive of the truth that "1" is an infinitely greater number of times than "0." And a single small taper is infinitely greater in point of light and cheer than none at all. Carolyn's little world underwent illumination, and she with it. She promptly soared to a shining infinity.

Medora Phillips could not overlook Carolyn's general glow, nor the sense of elevation she conveyed. Things became clearer still when Carolyn passed on the scanty message which Cope had added at the end. "Best regards to Mrs. Phillips"—there it was, so far as it went. And Medora felt, along with Carolyn, that a slight mention was an immensity of times greater than no mention at all. "Very kind, very thoughtful of him, I'm sure," she said without irony.

Carolyn let her read the letter for herself. It was a brief, cool, succinct thing, and not at all unsuited for general circulation. "Best regards to Mrs. Phillips. Yours very sincerely, Bertram L. Cope," she read again; then, like Carolyn, she retired for meditation.

Well, from its dozen or fifteen lines several things might fairly be inferred. "Three or four days in Winnebago"—a scanty pattern for a visit. Had three or four been enough? Had Lemoyne been found glum and unpleasant? Had those months of close companionship brought about a mutually diminished interest? Not a word as to Lemoyne's accompanying him to Freeford, or joining him there later. On the contrary, a strong implication that there would be sufficient to occupy him without the company of Lemoyne or anybody else: evidences of an eye set solely on the new opportunity in the East.

"Well, if he is going to get along without him," said Medora to herself, "it will be all the better for him. He was never any advantage to him," she added, with an informal and irresponsible use of her pronouns. But she knew what she meant and had no auditor to satisfy.

When, however, she touched on the matter with Basil Randolph she showed more exactitude. Randolph had lingered late upstairs with Foster, and he had been intercepted, on his way out, with an invitation to remain to dinner. "Very well," he said. "Sing-Lo is not invariably inspired on Monday evening. I shall be glad to stay."

He felt, in fact, the need of a little soothing. Foster had been taking a farewell shot at Cope and had been rough and vindictive. He had heard something of the antics of "Annabella's" partner and had magnified characteristically the seriousness of the offense. "What hope for him"—meaning Cope—"so long as he goes on liking and admiring that fellow?"

"Well," returned Randolph, in an effortless platitude, "liking is the great mystery—whether you take its coming or its going."

"The sooner this one goes, the better," snapped Foster. "Have you heard from that fellow at all?" he inquired.

"'That fellow'? What fellow—this time?"

"The other one, of course. Cope."

"No."

Foster wiped out Cope with one question.

"Likely to 'cultivate' some other young chap, next year?"

Randolph had a moment of sober thoughtfulness.

"No."

"Good! Get back into harness; have 'hours' and all the rest of it. Best thing in the world for you. The young care so much for us—the devil they do!"

Foster gave a savage, dragging clutch at his shade and twisted rebelliously in his chair.

Randolph left him to himself and went below.

Downstairs dinner proceeded cautiously. There was no chance for an interchange of thought until the two young women should have been got out of the way. Hortense had her own affair at the back of her head, and Carolyn hers. Neither could sympathize with the other. Hortense's manner to Carolyn was one of half-suppressed insolence. Carolyn, buoyed up interiorly, seemed able to endure it,——perhaps was not fully conscious of it. There was relief when, after dessert, each arose and went her respective way.

Medora and Randolph settled down on a causeuse in the drawing-room. The place was half-lighted, but Randolph made out that his companion was taking on a conscious air of pseudo-melancholy. Her eyes roved the dim, cluttered room with studied mournfulness, and she said, presently:

"Dear old house! Undergoing depopulation, and soon to be a waste."

"Depopulation?"

"Yes; they're leaving it one by one. First, Amy. You remember Amy?"

"I believe so."

"She married George and went away. You recall the occasion?"

"I think I was present."

"And now it's Hortense."

"Is it, indeed?"

She told him about the gallant young Southerner in Tennessee, and gave a forecast of a probable pairing.

"And next it will be Carolyn."

"Carolyn? Who has cast his eye on her?"

Medora shot it out.

"Bertram Cope!"

"Cope!" Randolph gave himself another twist in that well-twisted sofa.

"Cope," she repeated. If the boy were indeed beyond her own reach, she would report his imminent capture by another with as much effect as she could command.

And she told of Carolyn's fateful letter.

"So that's how it stands?" he said thoughtfully.

"I don't say 'how' it stands. I don't say that it 'stands' at all. But he has prospects and she has hopes."

"Prospects and hopes,—a strong working combination."

Medora took the leap. "She will marry him, of course," she said decidedly. "After his having jilted Amy——"

"'Jilted' her? Do you understand it that way?"

"And trampled on Hortense——"

"'Trampled'? Surely you exaggerate."

"And ignored me—— You will let me use that mild word, 'ignored'?"

"Its use is granted. He has ignored others too."

"After all that, who is there left in the house *but* Carolyn? Listen; I'll tell you how it will be. She has answered his letter, of course,—imagine whether or not she was prompt about it!—and he will answer hers——"

"*Will* answer it?"

"Not at once, perhaps; but soon: in the course of two or three weeks. Then she will reply,—and there you have a correspondence in full swing. Then, in the fall he will write her from his new post in the East, and say: 'Dear Girl,—At last I can——,' and so on."

"You mean that you destine poor Carolyn for a man who is so apt at jilting and trampling and ignoring?"

"Who else is there?" Medora continued to demand sturdily. "In October they will be married——"

"Heaven forbid!" ejaculated Randolph.

"You have something better to suggest?"

"Nothing better. Something different. Listen, as you yourself say. Next October I shall call on you, put my hand in my inside pocket, bring out a letter and read it to you. It will run like this: 'My dear Mr. Randolph,—You will be pleased, I am sure, to hear that I now have a good position at the university in this pleasant town. Arthur Lemoyne, whom you recall, is studying psychology here, and we are keeping house together. He wishes to be remembered. I thank you for your many kindnesses,' — that is put in as a mere possibility,—'and also send best regards to Mrs. Phillips and the members of her household. Sincerely yours, Bertram L. Cope.'"

"I won't accept that!" cried Medora. "He will marry Carolyn, and I shall do as much for her as I did for Amy, and as much as I expect to do for Hortense."

"I see. The three matches made and the desolation of the house complete."

"Complete, yes; leaving me alone among the ruins."

"And nothing would rescue you from them but a fourth?"

"Basil, you are not proposing?"

"I scarcely think so," he returned, with slow candor. "I shouldn't care to live in this house; and you——"

"I knew you never liked my furnishings!"

"——and you, I am sure, would never care to live in any other."

"I shall stay where I am," she declared. "Shall you stay where you are?" she asked keenly.

"Perhaps not."

"Confess that housekeeping on your own account is less attractive than it once was."

"I do. Confess that you, with all your outfit and all your goings-on, never quite—never quite—succeeded in . . ."

Medora shrugged. "The young, at best, only tolerate us. We are but the platform they dance on,—the ladder they climb by."

"After all, he was a 'charming' chap. Your own word, you know."

"Yet scarcely worth the to-do we made over him," said Medora, willing to save her face.

Randolph shrugged in turn, and threw out his hands in a gesture which she had never known him to employ before.

"Worth the to-do? Who is?"

# Afterword

THERE have been a spate of gay history books published in the last decade or so which have maintained that homosexuality was not distinguished from heterosexuality until the 19th century, when the notion of sexual identity emerged; that homosexual behaviour was repressed nearly to the point of non-existence during the Victorian era; that it began to emerge from total secrecy only after the Second World War; and that its pleasures began to counterbalance its pain only after Stonewall. The authors of such books hold that the unrealized passions implied in *Brideshead Revisited* inevitably led their victims into a madness as desperate as Sebastian Flyte's. Running parallel to this are other books which suggest that among grand people, homosexuality was always the way of the world, with every member of the upper middle classes keeping a mate from the working ones; with kings keeping male lovers for passion and wives for duty only; with muscular soldiers and effete students living forbidden inclinations behind the choir screens of churches and in ecstatic pissoirs. Indeed, reading much of this material, one is astonished that levels of procreation were sufficient to keep the population growing between the wars. In neither of these lines of discussion, however, is there room for an ordinary life of homosexual men, a life that includes the sexual, the domestic, and the mundane.

Far more revealing than such histories is *Bertram Cope's Year*, a novel written in 1919, which portrays what would now be called normative homosexuality—discreet, occasional, often unfulfilled, neither delirious nor unbearable. The homosexual characters move with moderate ease in a largely straight world. Bertram Cope does not identify himself as "gay"; indeed, the episode of his accidental engagement shows how little he perceives himself to be a particular and singular type of man functioning within that type's established parameters. (Though one cannot help wondering whether the author was aware of the usage that was devolving to the term when he had Bertram write: "Well, I could be pretty gay too with a lot of money behind me; and I think that, for another year or so, I can continue to be gay without it.") The silent duelling between Mr. Randolph and Arthur relies on a moment of recognition, on the part of both men, that they are members of a community within which each can be seen as a threat to the other. Arthur "felt that Randolph . . . was showing himself inclined to 'go' with younger men longer than they would welcome him. Why didn't he consort with people of his own age and kind?" For Arthur, there are certainly rules and systems for men such as he knows himself to be, and the violation of those rules is distasteful to him. And Mr. Randolph felt at once a "physical distaste" for Arthur, the details of which neither he nor the author chose to examine too closely.

The novel treads gently around the edge of the erotic. We seldom get a full sense of these characters as bodily—though Bertram does make quite a good showing when he strips down on the beach near Mrs. Phillips's dune house. We never see them in sexual embrace. The author once wrote that good novels must be "free" of the "botheration" of "repellent sex-discussions . . . indelicate 'close-ups' which explore and exploit poor humanity beyond the just bonds of decorum." He does, however, give constant description of the intimacy between men, of, for example, the way Arthur's hand sits on Bertram's shoulder. The displayed physical intimacy between the two is sufficient to call to Joe Foster's mind "a young married couple . . . [who] had made their partiality too public, and an elderly lady not far away . . . had audibly complained that they brought the manners of the bedchamber into the drawing-room." Mr. Randolph goes to extraordinary lengths in his continuing efforts to seduce Bertram into a long-term companionship, and it is impossible to understand this ambition, focused as it is on the handsomeness of its object, as anything short of a romantic courtship, especially when Mr. Randolph is given to saying that " 'a young man married is a man that's marred.' " Arthur, who has fingers that "displayed certain graceful, slightly affected movements of the kind which may cause a person to be credited—or taxed—with possessing the 'artistic temperament,'" after considering various patterns of silk stockings and impersonating a woman only-too-convincingly, finally makes a pass at a "straight" boy. The physicality of his affections cannot be in much doubt, and one is inclined to suspect that his demanding nature would not accept coy reserve from Bertram.

Even though there is no sex as such in this book, there is a great deal of homely affection. Pre-pride, the proud tell us, homosexuality was either shameful and practiced by men who lived out their public lives in loveless grim marriages, or theatrical and absurd in the Wildean vein. Though Arthur has a Wildean streak, and Bertram goes in for cautious restraint, the author depicts, in a most natural way, the minor and comic troubles of essentially rather pleasurable and straightforward male domesticity, the very ease of life which has been saccharined up by radicals like David Leavitt. Before we have even met Arthur, we have found that Bertram, in addition to writing to him about everything he does, keeps many photos of him to hand, and eagerly awaits his arrival in town so that they may cohabitate. "'We shall look after each other,'" Bertram explains to Mrs. Phillips. "'We are going to live together.'" It is annoying to Mrs. Phillips and to others that it is not possible to invite one man without the other, but Bertram and Arthur insist (albeit passively) on being treated as a unit, and are as inevitably joined in the world as a married couple. Though Arthur and Bertram ultimately separate, the life they lead before things go awry is cheerful, easy, and entirely mutual; "occasionally sharp tones and quivering nostrils, but commonly amity and peace." Bertram often rearranges his plans to suit Arthur's jealousy: he cancels several engagements with poor Mr. Randolph, leaving the older gentleman to worry on his own. He alludes to this compromise in the name of affection: "But remember that I gave up Indian Rock for you, even if you didn't give up Green Bay for me. I hope the fellow who took you hasn't got anything further to propose. If he has, I ask for a tip in turn." These are the negotiations that take place between fond lovers. Bertram is annoyed by Arthur's effeminate extravagances, but ultimately rejects his folly only when it becomes a public embarrassment. When Arthur has helped him recover from the Amy Leffingwell affair, he "impulsively threw an arm across his shoulder. 'Everything is all right, now,' he said, in a tone of high gratification; and Urania, through the whole width of her starry firmament, looked down kindly upon a happier household." Movingly, Arthur and Bertram do not seem to find any aspect of their own relationship peculiar; they never ponder on it as exclusionary, illegal, or morally suspect.

Bertram is something of an anti-hero: what is most striking about him is his failure to be extraordinary in any area. He is a fine-looking fellow, but in a way that doesn't sound very interesting. He is quite intelligent but not remarkable here either; he is charming, but says nothing truly memorable or quotable. He is, despite his appearance of cool self-possession, always a bit anxious about something. He is weak, both physically (witness the collapse at Mrs. Phillips's house after not so much wine, the inability to swim as strongly as Amy, etc.) and emotionally (How unable he is to negotiate the situations with Amy and Hortense, even with Mr. Randolph and Mrs. Phillips!). He is remote, unable to notice or process the effect he has on others and curiously immune to their attentions. It is not that he is above it all so much as that it all goes over his head.

He has no idea what women really want, and therefore doesn't manage to avoid falling into what are for him their snares and webs. "'Wit in a woman,'" he writes, "'or even humor, always makes me uncomfortable. The feminine idea of either is a little different from ours.'" Women are the alien. Relating to them requires "'a knack . . . a technique—that I don't seem to possess. Nor do I seem greatly prompted to learn it.'" There is something poignant about the Amy Leffingwell affair, as Bertram worries about how to sustain married life without ever alluding to the matter of whether it will be possible for him either to give or to receive that erotic satisfaction traditionally a part of life partnerships. "How furnish a house, how clothe and feed a wife?" he wonders, as though the full challenge lay in that. "How, even, buy an engagement ring—that costly superfluity? How even contrive to pay for all the small gifts and attentions which an engagement involved? Yet why ask himself such questions? For he was conscious of a fundamental repugnance to any such scheme of life and was aware that . . . he wanted to live in quite a different mode." And a few pages later, "Most of all he saw—and felt to the depths of his being—his own essential repugnance to the life toward which he now seemed headed." He must have Arthur at hand to head off others at the pass, to give himself a shield against the world whose norms are so alien to him.

The most articulate voice in the novel belongs to Joe Foster, who quite sees through Bertram, recognizes the nature of the relationship between Bertram and Arthur, watches Mr. Randolph making a fool of himself, understands the sheer idiocy of all the women who throw themselves in Bertram's way, but who cannot shake from himself the very fascination he abhors in everyone else. It's as though he could make sense of matters only because he's half-blind and constrained to a wheelchair: only the impotent can see the truth. This is the frequent response of age to youth, once that age is too far gone for even the hopes that Mr. Randolph cherishes. If Foster were not too ill and too deformed to imagine he might attract Bertram, could he be so strong? But his impotence and his knowledge are inextricable. The book was written in the author's maturity, and the awful voice that belongs to Joe Foster seems very much the author's own.

Henry B. Fuller (1857–1929) was described by Hamlin Garland as "the ablest, most distinctive, most intellectual of all our Western writers." A volume of tributes written during Fuller's life includes panegyrics from Thorton Wilder, Booth Tarkington, Jane Addams, Hamlin Garland, and others of some celebrity. Edmund Wilson observes in a 1970 *New Yorker* article, "The Art of Making It Flat," that these writers "seem to feel that, less successful than some of them, [Fuller] was somehow a little above them." He mourns Fuller's fall into obscurity, describing him as one of the few good writers of American fiction in the period from the beginning of the century to the First World War; he is held up as emblematic of a school of "real social critics and conscientious artists" who redeem this otherwise trivial period in American letters. Very little has been written about Fuller. Wilson describes the one biography, by Constance M. Griffin, as "inadequate . . . evidently one of those theses which the estimable Arthur H. Quinn of Pennsylvania . . . induced his students to write on neglected American authors." It is striking that no one has taken up Wilson's call to a topic, and it is to be hoped that some other graduate student in desperate search for fresh material will revise Ms. Griffin's by now rather dated consideration of Fuller.

Like Bertram Cope, however, Fuller is always somewhat less than one would like him to be. He preserved throughout his own lifetime a great mystique, but no pulsing literary genius ever emerged from behind the mask. Carl Van Vechten wrote in an appreciation of 1922, "He lingers, indeed, in a kind of literary purgatory. . . . His contribution to American fiction is a certain calm, a repose of manner, a decorative irony, exquisite in its not too completely hidden implications, a humor which is informed with abundant subtlety, a study of human nature at home and abroad as searching as it is careful, and above all, a delicate, abiding charm. . . . His sweep is never grand. His genre is the miniature." Harriet Monroe conceded that "Fuller found it impossible to tell his whole story. He could not give himself away, and therefore it may be that the greatest book of which his genius was capable was never written, the book which would have brought the world to his feet in complete accord and delight." Edmund Wilson takes Fuller's depiction of a character in a novel and applies it back to the author. "The book of life had been opened wide before him, but he had declined to make the usual advance that leads straight on from chapter to chapter; rather had he fluttered the leaves carelessly, glanced at the end before reaching the middle, and thoroughly thwarted the aims and intentions of the great Author," and then employs another such passage to similar effect, suggesting that Fuller's "participation in life has been, after all, but partial. I have always felt a slight reluctance about committing myself—a touch of dread about letting myself go. I have lived, in fact, by the seashore without ever venturing into the water. Others have gone in before my eyes, and I have recorded, to the best of my endeavor, the exhilarations they appear to feel, the dangers they appear to brave. But as soon as the waves have stolen up to my own toes, I have always stepped back upon the dry sands."

But it is the very flatness of Fuller's enterprise that sets him free. There was no public outcry against (nor, it must be said, public acclaim for) *Bertram Cope's Year* at the time of its publication, and Carl Van Vechten proposes that this was something only Fuller's exquisite understatement could have contrived: "If Theodore Dreiser had written this book, it would certainly have been suppressed. If Ben Hecht had written it, he would probably be languishing in jail. I cannot, indeed, name another American writer who could have surveyed the ambiguous depths of the problem presented so thoroughly and at the same time so discreetly. . . . The story, apparently slow moving, really thrusts forward its emphatic movements on almost every page, but it would probably prove unreadable to one who had no key to its meaning. Once its intention is grasped, however, it becomes one of the most brilliant and glowingly successful of this author's brief series of works." John Farrar characterized it as "a story, delicately done with the most exquisite taste, of sublimated irregular affection." Irregular affection, sublimated or not, was not easy to describe with exquisite taste at that time, and Fuller's beautifully balanced irony on the subject closest to his heart is a triumph. Fuller wrote to the Indiana novelist Henry Kitchell Webster about the book, "Lots of people must have read you in unperturbed innocency, and I hope a good many will read me that way too."

But those who did did so in folly. Edmund Wilson insists that the book, which he calls "Fuller's best," was a broad social satire. "*Bertram Cope's Year*, though it involves homosexual situations, is not really a book about homosexuality. It has a kind of philosophic theme . . . Fuller has merely, in writing of the power exerted by a 'charismatic' personality, extended what was then the conventional range." Wilson was quite unable to penetrate the delicate layers of Fuller's armor, and his reading of this novel is perhaps a prime specimen of unperturbed innocency. Fuller himself was homosexual, and the aura of mystery for which he was so much known was of course a mask for the socially complicated realities of his life. The man who could not tell his whole story, who was constrained not to give himself away, was longing to allude at least to what he could not reveal, and this temptation became his guiding principle in his best book. *Bertram Cope's Year* is in fact a sterling study in the kind of deep ambivalence that must have characterized Fuller's own life. Fuller has created a character who is overrated by everyone around him, and who is worthy of a book simply because he has the valuable commodity of being generally adored. Wilson accurately observed that, "Fuller's rather difficult problem here has been to make Bertram intrinsically uninteresting and even rather comic, but at the same time to dramatize convincingly the spell of enchantment he is supposed to cast. This is seen in his effect on the other characters, but the reader is not made to feel it; Bertram is represented as behaving in an agreeable enough way, but, in his self-centeredness, he never does anything that is made to seem really attractive. And the result . . . is a kind of deliberate flatness."

This flatness is not only the technique, but also the subject of *Bertram Cope's Year*. Bertram Cope is a man without real qualities, and feelings themselves are quite alien to him. He never has a flash of admirable passion. Unintentionally, he disappoints or injures everyone, and he leaves in his flat wake a trail of flat destruction. Light, ironic, delicate as this book is, it is also very bitter; the raging fury of Joe Foster is the most explicit statement of the author's prevailing mood. This is not a book about politics, about social problems caused from outside; it indicates early on that male companionship is technically not too complicated, and no one here seems to be worried about changing the external rules of the game. No: it is about the impossibility of achieving intimacy when one is drawn to chilliness (Fuller compares Bertram more than once to an icicle). What may appear to be understatement and a cautious stepping back from the frightening cold water may in fact be simple selfishness. Fuller himself sought love and real affection, and through his later life was always holding out for a younger man to live and travel with him. He seems to have been unsuccessful in his search. How scaring it is to fail simply because what one has wanted was never available where one sought it. The tragedy here (because the book is in its gentle way a tragedy) is that despite the entirely adequate external circumstances of all of these characters, they all make fools of themselves. No one has much dignity at the end of this book: not Arthur, shunned and excluded; not Mrs. Phillips, languishing and absurd; not the young ladies who have consoled themselves elsewhere; not Mr. Randolph, who has moved fruitlessly to a whole new house at great expense; and not Bertram Cope either, who has lived in the compass of all this love and affection and has got absolutely nothing from it. In the face of the solipsistic reticence of young men, we all fail dismally, and we get by with minor distractions and a modicum of wit—we make ourselves flat as pancakes so that we can live with the flatness all around us. Like Joe Foster, Fuller has a knowledge that is the mingy compensation for his too-late-in-life impotence. Amy Leffingwell, after the episode of the capsized boat, smiled at the tablecloth so that she "seemed to be intimating that there was a special folly which transcended mere general folly and approximated wisdom." It is a nasty lesson for her, for Fuller, and for the reader that such folly is so far short of wisdom as to be still its opposite.

ANDREW SOLOMON